POCKETFUL
OF
B NES

By
JULIE FRAYN

For Deborah Arbic

Blest be the man that spares thes stones, And curst be he that moves my bones.
~ William Shakespeare

1979

I know a bank where the wild thyme blows

Purple dead nettle spewed its musty scent into the late afternoon air. Finnegan pinched one square stem and snapped it off, brought it to his nose and inhaled. The earthy aroma filled his nostrils. Peace settled in his bones.

Dorothy had it all wrong. To heck with home. There's no place like the garden.

His upper lip twitched at the tickle of the fuzzy leaves. He stuck out his tongue and licked one of the weed's pink flowers, put it between his teeth and bruised the petals. His mouth filled with saliva at the hit of sweet nectar that bled from the bloom.

Hinges squealed. "Finnegan?"

Begin again.

He squished the nettle in his fist and glanced at his wristwatch. Shortest date in history. "Here, Mom," he called out.

"Where? I can hear you but I can't see you. Are you in the garden again?"

Her voice was velvet. But when she yelled, it had a gravelly edge.

He pushed off the trunk of the walnut tree, the craggy bark pitting his palm, brushed aside the Mulberry limbs, and sidestepped the yellow rose bush. His legs bore the proof of those roses' hatred, of the punishment they'd inflicted for his time in the garden. Dozens of tiny scratches crisscrossed his calves just above where the protection of his sweat socks ended.

He tiptoed through the creeping thyme, his favourite part of the backyard forest. When he crushed the leaves between his thumb and forefinger and sniffed his hand, summer turned to Christmas.

She stood on the stoop, arms crossed, eyebrows crosser. Smoke curled from the tip of the cigarillo pinched between her slender fingers. Water dripped from her freshly washed hair and dampened her thin cotton robe at the shoulders. "Finny Mac, my love, damn it all to hell. Every day I tell you to keep out of that garden. You're going to make mincemeat out of it. I spend a lot of time making it look nice, you know?"

"Yeah. I know."

"You didn't disturb the new shrub, did you? I just planted it. I don't want you ruining it, stomping all over it before the roots take hold."

He shook his head. "I didn't go near it. It kind of stinks."

She picked a bit of tobacco from her tongue and flicked it into the air, tapped her foot, and eyed the neighbour's house. "Yeah, well, it's that fertilizer. That salmon skin stuff. Just steer clear."

He tucked the nettle into his back pocket. It would go in his collection, alongside the thyme and the walnuts, next to the yellow rose petals that he'd dismembered from the violent bush. "If you'd let me watch TV, I'd stay out of the garden. Nothing to do out here for a whole hour." Or in the case of tonight, under thirty minutes.

"I had a date. You know that."

Finnegan dragged the toes of his thrift store tennis shoes along the manicured lawn until the white rubber tips turned green. "Can I meet him?"

She slid the cigarillo's plastic filter between her pursed lips and inhaled. The tip of the brown stick glowed red, and then turned to ash. She lifted her face to the sky and blew smoke into the air. "No. None of them. Because they aren't good enough to meet you. When I find the right one, then, and only then, will he have the privilege of meeting my sweet little Finny Mac."

Finnegan ran to his mother and threw his arms around her waist. He inhaled the strawberry of her shampoo and the musty odour that clung to her for hours after her dates, like the smell of mushrooms in the garden. "I love you," he mumbled into the soft and cavernous space between her breasts.

She scratched his back and kissed the top of his head, ran her fingers through his ginger hair until they caught in the matted lump at the base of his neck.

"I love you too, Finny."

1969

Heard it Through the Grapevine ~ Gladys Knight and the Pips

"Where've ya been, Tibba, my love?"

Tibba balanced the phone receiver between her cheek and her shoulder and sucked on her cigarette, blowing smoke into the stale air of her tiny apartment. "I'm not your love."

"Come on, you know I'm your favourite." Adam paused for an answer that she wasn't about to give him. He heaved a sigh into the mouthpiece. "I need to see you. To kiss you. Hell, I just need you."

She put her feet onto the chesterfield and rubbed her pregnant belly. "Look, I'm taking a vacation, all right? Even hookers need a break now and then."

"I'll make it worth your while."

"Yeah? In actual cash this time?" She closed her eyes. His breath, heavy with his need for her sex, always smelled of peppermint and unfiltered cigarettes. His tongue tasted sweet, like Christmas candy.

"You know I'm good for it."

She gritted her teeth. "You're good for shit, Adam. You owe me for the last four dates. Send me a cheque in the mail and I'll consider seeing you again. And even then, cash up front. Damn, why did I ever let you skate?"

"Because we have something beyond business. Because you want me as much as I want you and you knew that cash wasn't part of the deal."

Damn him for being right. "You're so full of crap. Don't call me again." She beat the receiver against the cradle once, twice, three times. To hell with him and his handsome, weathered face. His muscles and bronze hair, like a real-life Doc Savage or a ginger G.I. Joe, made her wet between her legs.

Why'd he need sex from a prostitute anyway? He could get any woman with just a sideways glance out of those shamrock eyes that deepened to the darkest pine forest just before he climaxed.

Perhaps it was because he was permanently broke. His gambling addiction always left him short on cash. Never enough for a real date, where women expected a nice meal, perhaps a show, and maybe even a second date before stripping off his clothes to find the gift of him underneath.

She hugged a pillow to her chest. He wasn't short on charm or wiles. Or anything else, taking money out of the equation. Yes, size really does matter. And that's why she kept letting him in, letting him fuck her on credit. Because everyone else was just a paycheque. But with Adam, well damn. She enjoyed the sex. Had real orgasms that rocked her entire body. She never once had to fake an "Oh, God," or pretend he was manlier and studlier than humanly possible. Because he was. Holy hell, was he studly.

But it was no excuse. There was never any excuse for stupid. What decent prostitute doesn't get cash up front?

The baby slammed a foot into her bladder. Or maybe a hand. Kid was going to be a black belt in no time. She swung her legs off the chesterfield and planted her swollen feet on the shag area rug. Only one more month. Then no more grunting when she stood. No more peeing twice an hour. If humans were designed intelligently, then what idiot put a woman's bladder below her uterus?

When the baby arrived, she was going to have to be smarter. More selective in her clientele. No more barebacking it with studly clients. No more thinking she might be in love with a john, no matter how green his eyes. She shook her head. Pregnant. And the father was probably a flame-haired gambler with no assets or moral compass. Or any number of butt-ugly middle-aged lonely men who weren't getting it at home.

Broken condoms. Just one more risk of a risky business.

Happy Together ~ The Turtles

"Push, Tibba!"

She grasped the chrome bed rails and put her chin to her chest. Her groan and scream almost drowned out the tinny upbeat Jesus music coming from the transistor radio on the windowsill. "Shut. That. Shit. Off," she yelled between pushes.

"Tibba, dear. Language." Her mother crossed her arms and sent that judgy right eyebrow skyward.

"The head is out," the doctor pronounced from between Tibba's legs.

She flopped back onto the pillow, wiped her sweat-soaked brow, and turned to face the greying woman sitting beside the bed. "I'll fucking swear if I want to, Mother. I don't want the first thing this baby hears to be your damned Christian pop music. Jesus did a shit job of saving me. He ain't getting anywhere near my kid."

"Really, Tibba. I don't know where I went wrong." Her mother turned the radio dial to a news channel.

Tibba held up her middle finger and wagged it at her mother's back. "I do. Got a year?" Pain shot across her abdomen. Another contraction forced a scream from her throat.

"One more push and you'll be a mother." The doctor patted Tibba's shin. "Come on, then, you can do it."

Tibba mentally flipped the doctor the bird, too. She pulled herself up and grunted like she was taking the biggest crap of her life. Pain seared through her anus. The baby squiggled out, all arms and legs and slime and umbilical cord wrapped around its skinny neck.

"It's a boy! You've got yourself a son!" The doctor slid the cord away and suctioned out the baby's nose. "Come on, son. Give me a breath." The doctor smacked the newborn's little ass and the room filled with his scream.

Well, shit. A boy. If that didn't just hit the irony nail on the head. Tibba wiped a trickle of perspiration from her brow.

A nurse snipped the umbilical cord in two, whipped the baby out of the doctor's arms and wiped the goo from his tiny body.

His coltish legs kicked at the air, his long fingers grasped at nothing. The radio crackled through her fog.

"One small step for man …."

"Okay, Tibba. We need a couple of really hard pushes to get the afterbirth out."

"Yeah, great. Way to ruin the moment, Doc." Tibba propped herself on her elbows, grunted and strained, all the while stealing glances toward the bassinet.

Minutes later, the nurse placed a swaddled newborn in Tibba's arms.

"Well, hello there, young man." She stroked his forehead and liberated his arms and legs from the blanket. All his parts were where they belonged, eyes, ears, fingers, toes, and the sweetest little penis she'd ever seen. The wisp of fine ginger fuzz on his head made her heart skip.

That solved the puzzle of who the father was.

She poked at her son's cheek and sniffed his head. "Now what on earth am I going to name you?"

Her mother stood and smirked. "Why don't you name him after the father?" She crossed her arms and narrowed her eyes. "Oh, that's right, you don't know his name."

Tibba glared up at the woman who'd given birth to her twenty-four years earlier. She wanted to reach up and smack that "I told you so" look right off the smug bitch's face. Would mother get the irony that the father was Adam? "Can the shit, Mother."

Her mother huffed. "If you hadn't slept with any boy who walked past you, maybe this baby would have a man in his life."

"You mean like the man I had in my life? That winner you married? Yeah, I'll pass, thanks."

"Well," her mother sniffled and wiped her nose on her hand. "How about David Luke?"

Tibba snorted. "You'd love that, wouldn't you? A proper biblical name. No way. No how."

Her mother sniffled again. "It could be the last nice thing you do for me before I die. The only decent thing you've ever done."

Tibba turned to her mother, stared at her sunken eyes, the sallow skin, the bones of her skull more pronounced each day that cancer ate away at her. It wouldn't be long now. And finally, there would be peace.

"Go to hell, Mother." She looked into her son's tiny face, marvelled at his mewling cries. The copper fluff on his head brought Mr. Dressup's little puppet's face to mind, but she hated the name Casey. No, she'd name him after Casey's little puppet dog. "Welcome to the world, Finnegan MacGillivray." She smiled. It had a nice ring to it. She bared her breast and cradled her son. He took his first drink of her milk, his cries ceasing. She stroked his head with one finger and repeated his name in her head.

Finnegan.

Begin again.

The devil can cite scripture for his purpose

"Is that legal? Do I have to do that?"

"Sorry, Tibba. It's a condition of her will. Baptize Finnegan, or I sell the house and give the money to the church."

Tibba tapped her foot against the floor and reached for her purse. She rummaged in the bottom until her fingers found the square cardboard pack, heavy with the lighter tucked inside.

Finnegan spit out his soother. It rolled down his romper and landed on the floor.

Tibba lit her cigarette, retrieved the soother, wiped it on her jeans, and stuck it back in her son's mouth.

"She knows I don't believe. Shit, if there really is a God, I'll probably burst into flames on entry to his … lair."

A snort of air blew from the lawyer's nose. Agreement? Amusement? Did he enjoy the visual of her burning in hellfire and damnation? Derisive prick.

"Look, it's just a ceremony. You don't ever have to go back. Put away your pride and just do it, then you get the house." He nodded toward Finnegan. "It's a better place to raise a child than that puny apartment you have, isn't it? Isn't he worth it?"

Tibba softened and melted back into her chair. She looked at the ceiling and blinked away tears. Damn, she hated a kind lawyer.

"Fine. I'll do it." Not that she'd ever planned to live out her days in the hell house she grew up in. But it was a decent neighbourhood. Three levels of schools within walking distance. And that yard. She'd loved that massive yard with the huge garden, a forest she used to hide out in for hours. Had her mother kept it up? Or did it die and fester like her marriage? More likely, she controlled it with an iron fist until it broke free and ran wild. No matter. The garden could be reborn. The house renovated.

Hell, maybe she'd have an exorcism.

She butted her cigarette, lifted her son from his stroller, and plopped him in her lap. She brushed coppery curls from his forehead.

One time only. Appease the bitch who controlled her from the grave. Get the house. Raise her child right.

She kissed his pasty cheek and looked up at the man who held her future in his hands.

"You know a good church?"

Out of this nettle - danger - we pluck this flower - safety.

Tibba yanked off her gardening gloves and tossed them onto a pile of upturned earth. Sweat dripped into her eye, turning her mascara to black tar on her cheek. Her fingers dug under her bra and scratched where rivulets of perspiration made her breasts itchy with heat and moisture.

If Mr. Greer weren't sitting on his fat ass on his porch drinking whisky and leering at her through the wire fence, she'd have just whipped her clothes off and gardened in the nude. But there he sat, like every other damn day, his gut hanging over his skimpy Adidas running shorts. As if he'd ever run a day in his life. Hell, if he shifted his chair just right, she would probably see his balls hanging out.

She shuddered. Shrivelled up, old-man testicles. She'd seen enough of those to last a lifetime.

Time to plant some ivy. Something fast-growing and invasive. Maybe something that would give him a nasty rash if he tried peering through it. She smiled at the mental image of his massive belly, its button pushed out more than hers the day she gave birth, covered in lesions, Mr. Greer frantically scratching at every part of his disgusting body.

He waved and smiled that crooked half-smile. He may as well have screamed, "I'm a dirty old man and I dream of fucking you."

She clamped her lips shut and turned away. He'd thought she was smiling at him. Not laughing at him on the inside. Maybe a trip to the garden centre was in order, to fast-track that poisonous ivy.

The familiar smack of skin on skin split the air. Mr. Greer's missus was swatting at the side of his head, her booming voice and comfortable violence belying her mousy appearance. He raised his hands against the onslaught of knuckles and open palms and ran into the house. Mrs. Greer turned to glare at Tibba. She shook her fist in the air before retreating through the patio door and sliding the glass shut.

The inside of that house probably stank of old man and whiskey. In Tibba's line of work, it wasn't an unfamiliar odour.

She stood and surveyed her progress. Not bad for one summer. The near-acre of garden her mother had left to nature was taking shape. Most of the trees had survived the neglect. Good bloody thing. Cutting them down would have broken her heart. Like hacking off one of her own limbs. The mulberry and walnut were icons of her childhood. They anchored the forest garden where she'd hidden from her battling parents and dreamed of worlds far away. Worlds where fathers didn't touch their daughters. Where mothers didn't turn a blind eye, or blame the abuse on the child. Because in her mother's world, eight-year-old girls seduce their daddies on purpose.

Finnegan's cries drifted from his open second-floor bedroom window. Every time he mewled his hunger, her milk came in and filled her breasts, leaking into the breast pads inside her bra.

Time for a break anyway. Her back was killing her. She made her way out of the garden and wet her hands under the faucet at the back of the house. She wiped dirt from her fingers and splashed cool water on her face, drying her hands on her aqua Capri gardening pants. "Coming, Finny Mac." She pressed her palms to the sides of her breasts. "Mama's got your lunch right here."

When I saw you I fell in love, and you smiled because you knew

The porch light illuminated Adam's bronze hair through the lace curtain and smudged glass, surrounding him with a godlike aura.

Tibba hesitated, her hand on the doorknob. Her heart bounced about inside her ribcage, her legs flooded with warmth. Yes, she was horny as hell and he would be just the thing she needed. But how did he find her? And exactly what did he want?

Sex of course. He always wanted sex.

She glanced back at Finny snoozing in his bassinet in the living room, his fluffy hair growing redder with each passing week.

She couldn't let Adam know. It would change everything. Ruin everything.

"I can see you, Tibba." He rattled the knob. "Let me in. I miss you." He cupped his hands around his face and pressed his nose to the glass. "I've got cash."

She sighed. She could use the money. Her mother's insurance payout was almost gone, after furniture and new appliances. And all the plants for the garden. Tibba only had enough to cover a few months' expenses. Why not let Adam be her first foray back into business? At least she knew what to expect. And she could always lie about Finny's parentage. She rocked at lying.

She unlatched the chain, slid the bolt and swung the door open. There he was, same as he'd always been. The little silver hoop earring piercing his left lobe glinted in the light. That goofy grin animated his comic-book-hero good looks. The persistent bulge in his pants drew her to him like a magnet.

He stepped inside her home, a fan of ten-dollar bills held in front of him. He stuffed them into her cleavage and hoisted her off the ground.

She wrapped her legs around him and kissed him. His lips were as soft as ever, his peppermint breath sweetened by a hint of rum. The taste of his tongue in her mouth brought a moan to her lips and her breasts filled with milk.

He set her down and eyed her from bangs to toenails. "Damn, girl. You put on some weight."

Would he ever learn to keep his stupid mouth shut?

He put one hand on her breast and squeezed. "But at least it's in all the right places."

She slapped his hand away. "What are you doing here? And how did you find me?"

His cheeks pinked. "I know a guy."

"What the hell does that mean? You're having me followed?"

"Shit, Tib, what does it matter? I'm here." He gestured at the money poking out from her bra. "I brought cash. So, let's do a little business." He bounced his eyebrows up and down.

She gave him the side-eye and dug the cash out of her shirt. Fifty bucks. "That'll almost cover your debt. How about you pony up the rest plus another twenty and I'll think about it." She sashayed into the kitchen, confident that his gaze would follow her ass and not veer into the living room where Finny slept. She tucked the money in the cookie jar on the counter. "You want a drink?"

"So, that's a yes to business? Because I miss the hell out of you."

She popped the cork off the open bottle of merlot and filled her glass. "That's a yes to having a drink. I'm being smarter now. Cash up front, no more credit." She raised the bottle and her eyebrows.

"You got any rum and Coke?"

She shook her head. "Wine or nothing."

Adam shrugged. "Wine it is."

She got another glass from the cupboard over the fridge and emptied the rest of the bottle into it. She handed him the wine glass and squirmed. Her underpants stuck to her wet pussy. Best to avoid eye contact, or she may do something she'd regret. "You want to do business? Twenty dollars for straight sex."

"Twenty bucks?" He rolled his eyes. "I know you're the best, but that's double the street rate."

"Yeah? And in my absence, you've been keeping current with the price on the street?" A shot of jealousy surprised her.

"Hey, Tib. You know me. I need what I need when I need it."

"Well my prices went up." She looked around her house. "Working from home now. Not street meat anymore. I believe it's called an escort. Nice digs, clean and discreet. In fact, let's make that fifty dollars. That's only fair for the best fuck, right?"

He stared at her.

"Seriously, Adam. How did you find me?"

"Wasn't that hard, Tibba baby. Looked you up in the phone book."

She squinted. She'd never told Adam her real name, only her street name. And there was no way Tibba LaRue was in the book.

He looked at his feet. "Your old landlord, he told me your real last name. I didn't figure LaRue was for real. The rest was easy." His eyes met hers and he donned that crooked grin that made her pulse race. "'Cause darlin', there ain't no other Tibba MacGillivrays in town." He rounded the kitchen island and slid behind her. His crotch pressed into her ass and his hands circled her waist. "Now come on, love," he whispered in her ear, his chin resting on her shoulder. "I know you missed me too." He kissed her neck.

Tibba swallowed and closed her eyes. "Is that a rocket in your pants," she said in her best Mae West voice, "or are you just happy to see me?"

He chuckled and nibbled on her ear.

Finny mewled.

Adam froze and his hands stopped moving up her shirt. "What the—" He let her go and stepped away.

She gripped the edge of the counter. "Adam, wait."

He walked into the living room and straight to the bassinet. He swung around and glowered at her. "You had a kid? That's why you disappeared? Why you moved without a word?"

"Yeah, I had a kid. Occupational hazard. So what?"

Finny had pulled his blanket over his head and was grappling with the flannel. His flailing arms and legs signalled his adorable mewls were about to become full-on screams.

Adam kneeled next to the bassinet and pushed the blanket from Finny's head. "Aw shit, Tib." He looked up at her, his eyes brimmed with tears. "Is he mine?"

She looked at the ceiling. "Damn it, Adam, how would I know?" She propped her fists on her hips. "You do remember what I do for a living, right? Fuck random men for money? It could be any of them."

His cheeks glistened in the incandescent light. "Don't you use protection? I mean, besides with me sometimes?"

"Yes, of course. But it's not foolproof. It says so right on the box."

"But Tib, the hair. The eyes. Those are me. The scrawny limbs and pale skin, well that's all you, baby." His eyes pleaded with her. He pointed at the bassinet. "But the hair."

"Damn it. Fine. I think you're the father. I'm almost certain of it. Is that what you want to hear? You want to play daddy? Marry me and move in so I can keep fucking other men to feed your gambling habit? Now that sounds like the life, don't it?" She ran her hand through her hair. "Shit."

He caressed the baby's cheek with one thumb. "What's his name?"

She crossed her arms. "Finnegan."

Adam nodded and stared at his son. "Would that be so bad?"

Tibba huffed. "What?"

He stood and neared. "Marrying me."

She held her arm out, palm toward him. "Stop. Just stop." She dropped her arm. "Are you nuts?"

"Tib, you know I love you. Have from the first time I saw you."

She spun around, stomped to the kitchen and snatched her wine glass from the counter. "This is insane." She gunned the rest of the wine. "What loser falls in love with the hooker he pays for sex?"

He approached, pointed his thumbs at his chest. "This loser." He took her by both arms and pulled her toward him, his eyes wide and vulnerable. "Marry me, Tib. I love you. I know you love me too. I can hear it when we make love. You just can't fake it that good."

She pushed him away. "That's not love, you idiot. That's an orgasm. An involuntary muscle spasm. A bodily function. Just because I love the way you fuck me, doesn't mean I love you."

He dropped his hands, his eyebrows knit. "You don't mean that."

She filled her wine glass and brought it to her mouth, shrugged her shoulders.

He shook his head. "You don't mean it." He bit his bottom lip and balled his fists. "Tell me you don't mean it."

She eyed his hands. The hairs on her neck stood on end and she inched backwards. The stance was all too familiar. The tension in his shoulders, the red cheeks and bulging vein on his forehead. He looked like her father just before her mother got a beating.

"Look, Adam," she set her glass on the counter. "You don't have to pay me this time. One more on credit, for old time's sake. Okay?"

"I'm not some random john. I'm the father of your child." He pointed one finger at her. "You do love me. And if you don't, you will." He stepped toward her. "And if you won't," his voice lowered to a growl, "I'll sue you for custody. He's my flesh and blood," he seized one of her arms and jerked her forward, his fingers digging into her skin. "You can't keep him from me."

Her knees weakened and her eyes narrowed.

Finny let out a hungry wail.

Adam let go of her arm turned. "What's wrong with him?"

Tibba reached behind her, groped around until she found the cast iron frying pan on the stove.

Finny's cries turned to screams.

Adam held his forehead and rubbed his temples, his eyes squeezed shut. "Make that kid shut the fuck up." He opened his eyes and glared at her. "Make him stop!"

Tibba took the frying pan handle in both hands and swung the pan at Adam's head. It connected with a sickening crunch and he went down. The pan skidded across the linoleum, pinged off the metal table leg, and came to rest under her mother's antique sideboard. Bits of charred steak dotted the floor.

She sidled up to him. His open eyes stared at her. She'd crushed his temple and jaw on the left side. Blood oozed from his mouth, and several teeth were missing. She poked his ribs with one foot. "Adam?"

She poked him harder but he didn't flinch. Her pulse raced, her heartbeat heavy. The whoosh of rushing blood echoed in her ears. She couldn't peel her gaze from his eyes. Open, vacant, the brilliant green drained from them until they were almost khaki, dull and plain. Not Adam's eyes at all.

Finny's cries cut through the fog. Tibba stepped over Adam's body and hurried to her son's side. She lifted him from the bassinet and cradled him in her arms, rocking and cooing while she returned to the kitchen. "Look what I did, Finny. I had to do it, you know that, right? He was going to take you away. I couldn't let him, now could I? No one is going to come between me and my Finny Mac." She kissed his cheek, popped open the buttons of her shirt, and unhitched her bra with one hand — a trick she'd learned at an early age that finally had a useful purpose beyond seducing boys at school.

Finny latched on and suckled, his cries waning except for the occasional shudder of residual sobbing.

Tibba paced the kitchen, circled Adam's body, and fed her son. "Now what do I do? What the hell do I do?" She bounced the baby in rhythm with his sucks.

Outside the window, dusk deepened and the yard all but disappeared in the darkness. A sliver of orange light reflected off low clouds on the horizon. Tibba cocked her head. An entire grave-worthy trench of freshly turned soil ready to accept the new bushes and trees awaited her in the garden.

She smiled. Perfect. Then her brows furrowed. "Shit, you damn fool. Where the hell did you park your car?"

A pang shot through her breast. She poked her finger between Finny's lips and her flesh and released her nipple from his mouth with a pop. She shifted him to the other side and he latched on, grasping the soft skin of her other breast in his tiny fist. She winced and pulled the cup of her bra over the empty side.

She paced the house, around the body, past the kitchen window, into the living room. At the front door, she peered through the glass. There it was, his damn Sixty-five Mercury Rideau, its tapioca paint job like a beacon under the street light. She eyed the empty street, thankful, for once, that they lived at the end of a quiet one. She made a beeline for Adam's body and kneeled beside him, balancing Finnegan on her thigh. She looted Adam's jacket pockets. His keys were in the left side, along with a used Kleenex, four ten-dollar bills, and three empty condom wrappers. "Yeah, you missed me big time, you bastard." She tucked the cash in her jeans and stood, giving his ribs a hard poke with her foot.

Finny let her nipple fall from his slack mouth. Tibba brought her sleeping baby to her shoulder and patted his back until he let out a man-worthy burp. "Come on, baby boy. We're taking a ride."

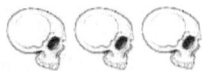

The lake shone with reflected moonlight, like a black mirror nestled between banks of shadowy maple trees.

Tibba sucked on a cigarette and blew the smoke out of the driver's side window she'd rolled down a crack. Finny squirmed on the seat beside her and kicked at her jeans.

"I know, little man." She tickled him under the chin and pulled his blanket up. "It's getting chilly at night." She pointed out the window. "Those leaves are going to turn beautiful shades of red and orange in a couple of weeks." She stabbed her cigarette out in the overflowing ashtray and let the butt fall to the floor. The wind picked up and delivered a shot of autumn chill into Adam's car. A shame she couldn't just keep it. She ran one hand over the maroon vinyl seats and eyed the matching dashboard and steering wheel. It was a reliable vehicle. Even the radio worked. No car she'd ever owned had even had a radio, let alone a cigarette lighter. She pushed the chrome knob and tugged her last smoke out of the pack. The lighter popped out. She put the red coil to the tip and inhaled.

Yup. A damn shame to waste the car. The only decent thing that ever came out of Adam's gambling habit.

She stared into the middle of the black lake and let nicotine fill her lungs and warm her veins. How many boys had she let slip their fingers into her pants on this beach those many summers before? Was she always destined for prostitution? She definitely started having sex early, looking to erase the feel of her father's hands on her skin and in her body. Every boy she chose to fuck brought her closer to independence. One day nearer to walking away from her parents' home forever.

She was damn good at it, too. Boys fell all over her, wanting to go steady, buying her gifts and flowers. The girls hated her. But it never mattered. Girls sucked. So when it came time to make some money, she turned to what she did best. It was the perfect job. For a little while. Unlike boyfriends, you don't get to pick your customers. And the thrill of anonymous hookups wears off after a beating or two at the hands of a drunken john.

But it was better than the alternative. A whole lifetime of abuse at the hands of a drunken husband. Would Adam have ever hit her? Until that night, he'd never had a mean bone in his body. Damn him all to hell, why did he have to say he'd take Finny away? He could've visited, been part of his life. She'd have given him that. Wouldn't she?

She stubbed out the cigarette, turned off the engine, and took a deep breath. "Okay, Finny Mac. Time to get on with it."

He didn't fuss when she gathered him in the blanket and crawled from the car. A bed of moss nestled against an elm made for a perfect baby bed. Tibba set him under the tree and tucked his blanket tighter around his body. She stood and stretched and stared at the massive car parked atop the steep embankment, thirty feet above the still, deep waters of Lake Bridewell.

She climbed behind the wheel, cracked her knuckles one by one, unrolled all of the car's windows, popped off the emergency brake, and shifted the transmission into drive. She inched the car forward until, by her best guess, it was kissing the edge of the hill, then she braked and slid the gearshift into park. She stepped out and held the open door under her left armpit, slipped the gearshift to neutral. With one hand gripping the steering wheel and the other pushing against the frame, her tennis shoes dug into the dirt and brush. She grunted and pushed but the car didn't budge. "Damn it!"

She had to get this car in the lake. She couldn't just abandon it by the side of the road, for someone to find it and report it to the cops. If his car wasn't found, anyone who knew him would think he'd gone off on one of his benders. He'd be gone for weeks, maybe a few months. Or so they'd assume. If anyone even gave a shit where he was.

She hitched up her jeans, flicked on a flashlight, and scanned the ground. Two decent sized rocks would do the trick. They were easy to roll into place behind the rear wheels, just in case the car wanted to shift backwards and crush her. She flattened her palms against the trunk, squatted, and heaved from her legs. The car rolled forward a half a foot. She shifted the rocks against the wheels' new location and pushed again. A scream built up from her gut and spewed from her mouth. The Mercury lurched forward. Tibba ground her feet into the earth and shoved. The car advanced with each step. The front wheels found the edge of the embankment and the car pulled away from her. She lurched forward and landed on her hands and knees. The rear end lifted and moonlight glinted off the chrome bumper. And then, the car disappeared. All that remained was the crunching of dead leaves under tires, and a splash as the car hit the lake.

Tibba scrambled to the top of the embankment. Pockets of air glugged from the open windows and burst on the lake's surface. The car's beige body, glowing blue under the moonlight, sank beneath the water and vanished.

She wiped her hands on her jeans. The water where Adam's Mercury took its last breath rippled, tiny waves broke against the shore. If only she could have lifted him, he'd have been buried with his precious car and her work would be done. But no, his six-foot-two frame had to weigh two-twenty. She had a long night ahead.

She gathered Finny in her arms and covered his face with the blanket to protect his tender cheeks from the cold night air. He didn't sleep this well in his crib. Maybe she'd find some moss in the garden and make a bed out of it.

She looked up and down the deserted road. Shame that damn old pram her mother gave her wouldn't fit into the trunk. How heavy does an eighteen-pound infant feel after a three-mile hike? At least this way she could duck behind the bushes in case of passing motorists. That pram would have ratted her out. The last thing she needed was for someone to see her out here at this time of night.

"Okay, baby boy. Let's try to get home without you screaming and waking the neighbourhood."

R-E-S-P-E-C-T ~ Aretha Franklin

A dam's body had slid easily enough across the linoleum. His head bounced against each riser when she dragged him, feet first, down the concrete back steps and out into the yard. She winced at the sight of his pretty face, all black and blue, the shape of a half-moon from the frying pan forever tattooed on his flesh.

In Adam's case, forever was going to be fleeting.

She'd had to wait out Mr. Greer, sitting on his damn porch in the cool of the evening, upending a bottle of whiskey every minute. She went through half a pack of smokes before he finally hauled his ass inside and left her in peace.

Getting Adam across the dewy lawn and over the little fence she'd built of upright bricks had been a chore. And took far longer than she'd hoped. Once he was next to the trench she'd dug earlier, he rolled in with ease. But damn it, that hole was shorter and shallower than she thought.

The spade leaned against the trunk of the ash tree. She poked the tip of it into the dirt but couldn't dig deeper with him lying there, in the way. Rolling him in was one thing. She had gravity on her side. How the hell would she haul him out? Time to chop him up a bit to make all the parts fit.

The shovel sliced neatly through his neck after five or six blows. An old handsaw she found in the shed ripped the forearms and shins apart. The result wasn't pretty, but no surgical precision was required, no finesse needed. No one would be judging her handiwork. The various bits and pieces of Adam, his cold skin blue under the moonlight, fit into the earth like a puzzle.

Tibba kept her ears trained on the open upstairs window, attentive for any hint that Finny needed her. Not that she had to listen too closely. When he screamed, you could hear him all the way to New York City. What was that, a mere three-thousand miles east and one country down? Tonight, she guaranteed he'd sleep soundly. Half an ounce of brandy in a bottle of warm milk did the trick. Always worked for her mother, so she'd said, though Tibba had balked at the idea of giving alcohol to a baby. Desperate times.

She stabbed the sharp point of her spade into the earth and lifted a shovelful of dirt. Her neck cracked with the effort of hoisting clods over Adam's torso. Lumps of dirt bounced off his severed head, nestled in next to his ribs, and filled his open mouth. An hour later, he was covered. But the mound over his body looked just like what it was.

Tibba eyed the wheelbarrow full of purple dead nettle and creeping thyme. Her work for the morning, ground cover for the bare spots in the garden. She stretched her arms above her head and bent her neck back. The moon glowed bright, surrounded by shining stars. The Big Dipper dangled overhead, the only constellation she could name. Maybe she should've paid more attention in science class. Or in every class. Then she'd be making a decent and honest living, sitting on some boss's lap taking dictation. Or perhaps that was just another form of prostitution.

The roots of the dead nettle came apart with a gentle tug of her fingertips. She kneeled next to the grave and sprinkled the dry earth with a watering can full of rainwater, then nestled the roots into the ground. Would they grow around Adam's bones? Snake through his ribs and wrap around his pelvis? She sat back on her heels and closed her eyes, summoned a vision of his naked form, muscled and lean, tight and well hung. She sighed. Most gingers were pale and freckled. Adam was ruddy and tanned. More Robert Redford-cum-Norse god than Archie Andrews. And in winter, when he grew out his beard, a perfect match to the copper patch on his most special, most wonderful, most huge man part? Damn. Hot, hot damn.

Why the hell did she hit him with that pan? She could have spent her life with him, couldn't she? Except the drinking. And the gambling. The weeks-on-end binges and disappearing acts. She dropped a clump of creeping thyme about where his head was. Nope. She was better off without him. And so was Finny.

A magical bit of mother-son ESP awoke him from his brandy-fuelled stupor and brought his cries to her ears. She bounded to her feet, slapped her hands on the seat of her jeans, and headed to the house. She shot a glance over her shoulder at the mess her garden was in. She'd have her work cut out for her tomorrow.

1974

To beguile many, and be beguil'd by one

"Hush now, you're going to wake my son." Tibba slapped at Officer O'Connor's hand and twisted in his grip.

The man laughed and grabbed at her waistline, pulled her to him. "Come on, Tib. I gotta go. Just one more quickie."

"That'll cost you double."

"Or I could just arrest your sweet ass. What's it called? Common bawdy house?"

"Yeah, right. Then who'd fuck you, you ugly bastard?"

They stared each other down until his face cracked, and they both laughed.

She sat in his lap. "Ah, what the hell. One more. On the bawdy house."

Ten minutes later, he zipped the fly of his uniform pants and shifted his belt. His hands gravitated to the parts he always made sure were in place before leaving. Handcuffs, baton, gun. Two of those made fun sex toys. The third scared the crap out of her.

"Hey, you ever hear from Finny's father?" He leaned into the mirror hanging inside her front door, licked one thumb, and ran the spit over his eyebrows.

Three years later, her heartbeat still hastened at the memory of Adam. His muscles and his square jaw. His severed head and dismembered arms. "Nope. Not a word."

"What an ass hat, leaving you like that. Not supporting his kid." He held her hips in both hands and shimmied her body against him. "Maybe I oughta make an honest woman of you, huh?"

She raised one eyebrow. Just what she wanted, an overweight cop living in her house just steps from Adam's grave. "I'm sure your wife would be on board with that plan."

He snickered. "Shit, I'd trade up in a heartbeat. Except for the whole Catholic no-divorce shit. And, you know, the whole cop-hooker thing. That don't look so good."

There it was. Good enough to fuck. Not good enough to marry. Story of her life.

Except for Adam.

She opened the door and gestured to the outside world with one hand. "Same time next week, officer?"

He stuffed two tens in her bra and winked before turning and galumphing down the steps.

He pulled away from the curb and turned left at the corner. When his taillights disappeared, she pulled the cash from her bra and tossed it on the coffee table, grabbed her cigarettes and lit one up. She sucked on the smoke and tried to picture O'Connor's wife. A twinge of jealousy surprised her. Not that she wanted him, in particular. But a man in her life that wasn't paying for services would be swell. One good man.

Where the hell were all the good men?

1980

I am slain by a fair cruel maid

Tibba lounged against the pillows and eyeballed the hairy back turned to her. His abundant reflection in her grandmother's old dresser mirror made her throw up a little in her mouth.

That's what happens when a hooker ages. Her clientele ages along with her. More beer guts and jowls and wrinkles, more jaded views on life and a sense of having given up long ago. The knowledge that this was the best it was ever going to be. These men who darkened her door week after week either couldn't get fucked without paying for it, or their wives wouldn't fuck them at all — for money or not. And they didn't have the funds to entice a young mistress into the fold of their sad and desperate lives.

"Why you staring at me?"

Tibba sucked her cigarette down to the filter. "Sorry. Just lost in thought."

"Yeah, well, I don't pay you to think." He rolled his socks together and placed them on the pile of folded clothes. His wife must be a hard-ass clean freak, and he was a well-trained dog. "Let's get to this. I gotta catch the last bus."

Tibba cocked her head. "Bus? Your car in the shop?"

"No. I got a ticket last time. Had to take an afternoon off work to pay the damn thing at the courthouse. Just what I need. Evidence of our little .... dates."

She snorted at the term she used to explain her gentleman callers to Finny.

"What's so funny?"

"Nothing." Not a goddamn thing.

"Agnes may not let me touch her no more. But damned if I'm gonna lose out on her pop's money when he croaks. I put in way too many years to give that up now."

"Yeah? He sick or something?"

"Not yet. But he's pushing seventy-five. Just a matter of time." He turned sideways and slapped her thigh. "Now turn over. 'Cause time's a-wastin'."

"Don't hit me."

One of his furry eyebrows shot up. "Or what?" He slapped her thigh again.

Her cheeks burned. "Or I'll kick your ass out of here and you'll never be coming back." She bent her leg and kicked his flabby butt. He slid off the mattress and landed on the floor.

She covered her mouth with one hand and snickered. "Oh, shit. I'm sorry."

He stood, his face crimson, his hands balled into fists. "Damn right, you're sorry." His normally deadpan voice came out with a snarl.

Tibba swallowed and pushed back against the headboard, held one hand out toward him. "Seriously, I'm sorry, Claude. I just don't do it rough, you know that. That's part of the deal."

He grabbed her feet and yanked her forward. "The deal is, I pay, you do what I say."

His open palm hit her cheek. Her head snapped to the side.

He flipped her over and dragged her hips to the edge of the bed. He forced his poor excuse for a dick into her, slammed his hips against her ass, one hand entangled in her hair at the base of her neck. "You'll. Do. What. I. Say." Each word punctuated a thrust inside her and one bounce of her face against the mattress. He held her face down while his body convulsed and shuddered. He growled when he came and collapsed onto her back, his cheek against her shoulder blade, his slimy drool wetting her skin.

Tibba flailed her arms and pushed against the mattress to force her head up so she could catch a breath. Her cheek ached, she scratched at his hand and arm.

He disengaged his hand from her hair and pulled out. His semen dripped onto her leg.

Bastard hadn't even put on a condom.

Tibba clamoured over the bed. She ran to the kitchen, grabbed the cast iron frying pan and stormed back into the guest room.

Claude stood in the middle of the room, standing on one leg, in the process of putting on his pants like nothing had even happened.

Tibba swung the pan. Just before it made contact with the side of his face, he looked at her, his mouth wide open, his eyes huge. She didn't give him a chance to scream.

She stared down at his lump of a body sprawled on the floor, at the blood oozing from his head and mouth and staining her mother's old woollen area rug. The pan slipped from her fingers and bounced on the carpet.

She tipped her head back and screamed. She stepped over the dead man at her feet. "Why'd you do it? Why'd you have to fucking go there?" She kicked him in the groin once, twice, half a dozen times. "Now I've got to haul your lard ass out to the garden." She wiped his cum from her leg and flicked it at his face. "You think I want to spend my whole night doing that again?" She covered her face with both hands, winced at the pain in her cheek. She touched her tongue to her swollen lip. Metallic blood filled her mouth. She propped her fists on her naked hips. "Well, at least I don't have to get rid of your goddamn car."

She glanced at the clock radio on the nightstand. "Shit." Finny would be home from Birdie's house in less than an hour. She ran to the kitchen, lifted the avocado-coloured handset from the phone that hung on the wall next to the fridge. She ran her finger down the list of school contacts tacked to the wall and dialed the Schultzes' number. Her foot tapped against the linoleum through five rings until Birdie's mother finally picked up.

"Hey, Liz, it's Tibba. Can I be a real pain and ask if Finny can spend the night? Sorry for this, but tomorrow isn't a school day, and I'm just not feeling well. I can return the favour sometime, maybe if you and Dusty want a date night?"

Liz called to her husband and asked if it was okay for Finny to stay. Tibba could hear muffled arguments from him. Liz must have had her hand over the receiver.

"Tib, he says it's fine."

"You sure? He didn't sound too pleased."

"You know Dusty. He's worried about a boy/girl sleepover. I

assured him that it was fine. For heaven's sake, they're only eleven!"

"Right." Her father's face loomed in Tibba's memory, his fingers inside her eleven-year-old body. She shook her head and banished him once again. "Thanks so much, Liz. Tell Finny I'll see him tomorrow and that I love him."

She set the receiver back in the cradle and glanced back into the guest room. "Here we go again."

Tibba circled Claude and assessed the possibilities. The carpet was already ruined. May as well hack him up right there, make it easier to haul him outside. She snatched his wallet from the dresser and peered inside. Seventy-two bucks in cash and a coupon to Ponderosa for half off a steak dinner for two.

Perfect. She hadn't taken Finny out in months.

1981

Temptation: the fiend at my elbow

A pencil lead jabbed into Finnegan's thigh. He slipped his hand across the aisle, his eyes riveted on the teacher's back. A slip of paper tickled his palm. He drew his hand into his lap and unfolded the page. He smirked, scrawled a hasty reply, scrunched the paper into a ball and tossed it back to Birdie. The unfolding of paper filled the room, as did her throaty snicker.

Mr. Anderson whipped around and glared at the class. "Quiet." He eyed the clock above the door. "Five more minutes to finish the test. I suggest you use it wisely. Some of you are this close," he held his thumb and forefinger half an inch apart, "to joining me again next year. Who wants to repeat grade six with me, eh? Start junior high a year behind your friends?" He squinted at the clock. "Four minutes."

Not much of a threat. Repeating grade six would beat the hell out of junior high. Being the youngest crop of kids, prime meat for froshing. Life already sucked enough here, stuck with bullies his own age. Older bullies? No thanks. Not that Finnegan had a choice. His grades were always too high to be held back. Even when he tried to fail, he just couldn't bring himself to write down the wrong answer.

The balled up paper flew through the air and landed in the middle of his desk. He snatched it and tucked it into the front pocket of his jeans as Mr. Anderson spun around, his eyes slits under his prominent brow line. Mr. Anderson's forehead was proof that Neanderthals once roamed the earth. When he turned his attention to the papers on his desk — probably another pop quiz he'd spring on them on the last day of school — Finnegan peered across at Birdie.

She stuck her tongue out at him.

Finnegan tapped his pencil against his completed test paper. He always finished first. Had to sit there for the rest of the hour while the dumb kids scratched out their answers, flipped their pencils, and erased half of them, managing a few C-minus-worthy words. All around him, halos of pink eraser debris littered the linoleum. No eraser bits near Finnegan's desk. He rarely got the answer wrong, always got the highest grade. Always gold stars and happy report card days.

No wonder he had no friends.

"Finnegan!"

"Yes, sir?"

"Stop with that incessant tapping."

"Yes, sir."

Birdie snorted.

Finnegan gave her the stink eye. Not that she needed it. Hers were already pretty stinky. They didn't smell or anything, just that they were weird. One of them pointed out a bit, the other pointed in. They were different shapes, and her eyebrows were too hairy. All of her was too hairy.

No wonder *she* didn't have any friends.

But they had each other. And that would have to do.

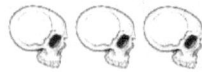

The Alley Cat was bad enough. The Hustle, humiliating. But the waltz was just plain evil.

Day three of dance class during gym. It was even worse than the torture of the Canada Fitness Tests. What could be more embarrassing than the fact most of the girls could beat him at the bent arm hang? That he collapsed in a ball of wheezing snot during the three-hundred-yard run? Or, worst of all, speed sit-ups. When his crush since grade two, Deborah Arbic, was tasked with holding down his feet while he grunted and moaned through sixty seconds of belly-twisting agony only to end his last sit-up with a fart. He'd hoped the teacher's whistle had drowned out his toot, but the smell, and the look on Deborah's face, had dashed that dream.

The bullies were right. He was a total loser.

He stood straight, his left hand holding Birdie's right, his right hand on the small of her back. An intimate gesture. One he wasn't prepared for. His hand hovered, rather than held. His palm floated above the soft cotton of her *Star Wars* T-shirt. The one her mother bought her when the first movie came out four years earlier. It was too small now, too tight. But she wore it all the time anyway, even if it did expose an inch of her flat, bare belly.

He rocked back and forth, to and fro, like C-3PO trying to tango, his limbs stiff, counting steps in his head. He looked over Birdie's shoulder, down at their feet, glanced at the wall. Anywhere but her face. When he did chance a peek at her, she stared at him like he was Prince Fucking Charming, and she was some poor man's Cinderella from the wrong side of the tracks.

It was like dancing with a guy. Because that's what she was to him. Best bud. A dude in a girl's body. Or a girl in a dude's body. Either way worked. Birdie was stick thin and had not one curve. Not like Deborah.

He scanned the room and found her swaying to the music twenty feet away. Her budding breasts made his legs weak. That long, black hair that she used to wear in symmetrical braids, was tamed into a French plait trailing down her spine. It was an arrow pointing straight at her round ass, begging him to look at it, all apple-shaped and stuffed into tight, dark blue, Jordache jeans.

Deborah giggled and smiled at her dance partner, some tall-for-his-age D-student with wavy blonde hair that hung past his shoulders. The teacher approached and put a hand between their bodies, admonished them for dancing too closely.

Finnegan twitched, ready to rush over and cut in. Shove the tall kid to the ground and take what was his.

In real life, he'd get his ass beat and Deborah would laugh at him. If she even knew his name at all. In five years of sharing the same classes, the only time she'd ever paid attention to him was to parrot calls of "carrot-top" or "freckle face" or "teacher's pet." Had she ever spoken to him, said his real name, even just once?

Birdie put her hand on his cheek and turned his head to face her. "You're dancing with me, not with pigtail, slut-face over there."

Finnegan prepared to rebut his best friend's distasteful view of the girl of his dreams, but the look on Birdie's face gave him pause. He'd hurt her feelings.

"Besides," Birdie whispered in a low, hoarse growl. "She's all show and no go. She'll flirt and tease and string you along but she will never love you. She only loves herself. Just you wait and see."

Lay her i' the earth: And from her fair and unpolluted flesh May violets spring!

A butterfly flitted around Birdie's head and landed on her shoulder. "Holy shit," she whispered. "You see this? Isn't it good luck or something?"

Finnegan got closer and eyed the orange-winged insect, its black lines and white spots. "It's a monarch. That's got to be lucky."

"Catch it!"

He cupped his hands around the butterfly and scooped it from her shirt. Its wings and feet tickled his palms. He shuddered and shifted his hands, pressed the wings until the tickling ended. He swallowed hard and glanced at Birdie.

Birdie leaned in and peeled his hands apart. "You killed it. Way to go, shit-for-brains."

He dropped his head. "Sorry."

She took the dead butterfly and placed it on a fern frond, positioned its wings as if it had just landed. As if it were still alive. Her face scrunched up like she was going to cry.

He had to cheer her up. Or at least make her forget that he was the one who made her sad. He snapped a pod off a branch above his head. "Hey, catch." He tossed the pod at Birdie.

She snatched it out of the air. "Ow, shit!" The green, spiky capsule fell to the ground. Birdie fished it out of the creeping thyme, sniffed the shell, stabbed at its spiny bits with one finger. "What the hell is this?"

"It's a horse chestnut."

Her eyebrows shot up. "Not like any nut I've ever seen." She cracked it against a rock and peeled away the shell, exposing the brown lump of buckeye inside. "Oh, lovely."

Finnegan grinned at the conflicting sides of his best friend. One minute she's a foul-mouthed tomboy who'd rather wade into the muck to catch frogs than wear a dress. The next she's a prissy lady who pulls out a fake British accent when she likes something cool.

She lifted the nut to her mouth.

He smacked it out of her hand. "No, don't!"

"What the shit is wrong with you?"

"It's poisonous. You'll be puking all over Mom's garden. She'd kill me."

Birdie crossed her arms. "As if."

He crushed the nut under his sneaker.

"Why'd you give it to me if it's poison? You tryin' to get rid of me or something? Kill me like you did that butterfly?"

"Nah." If he did that, he'd be alone all the time. "Just that it's cool and I thought you'd like it." He scuffed the toe of his sneaker into the thyme and inhaled. His mouth watered at the scent of Christmas the thyme spewed, at the thought of a turkey dinner complete with stuffing and gravy. He'd only ever had that when Birdie's mother invited him to join them two Christmases back. Best dinner ever.

"Well, good." She uncrossed her arms.

"You want to stay for dinner? We got Salisbury steak." The imagined plate of turkey was replaced with reality. "The Swanson kind."

She shook her head. "I can't. Dad would kill me if he knew I was here. Like, for real, he'd ring my neck."

"Does he hate me?"

"You? Nah, he feels sorry for you. I mean, he doesn't like you or anything. It's your mother. He calls her a slut bag."

"Hey, take it back." Finnegan pushed her shoulder with one hand, his other balled into a fist.

"I didn't say it. He did. I like your Mom. Where is she?" Birdie peered through the walnut tree toward the house.

He sighed and looked at the ground. "She has a date."

Birdie reached out and took his hand. "You ever want to take me on a date?"

He huffed. She was losing her mind. "No way. You're my best friend."

"Well, can't we be more than friends?"

He shook his head. "Nope. No fire. Not even a spark." Not like with Deborah. Her raven hair, and that space between her front teeth. Those velour, zippered jackets, and just a hint of makeup. No other girl in grade six wore mascara. She was always polished and perfect. Whenever he looked at her, his stomach ached and his legs burned. That wasn't spark either. It was fireworks.

Birdie took a step forward. "Well shit, Romeo. Ain't you never heard of spontaneous combusting?" She clutched his shirt with one hand, yanked him toward her and grabbed him around the waist.

Her lips, dry and scratchy, smashed into his. He squirmed in her grip and brought his arms up to push her away, but she rubbed one hand over the zipper of his jeans, then squeezed between his legs.

He froze, his fingers pressed into her collarbone. Pressure built in his boxers. He closed his eyes and groaned. Blood pounded in his ears, nausea rolled across his stomach.

Birdie stuck her tongue in his mouth.

His eyes sprung open. Her ugly face was right there, an inch from his. Her dumb, boyish, short hair hung in front of her eyes, which were pinched shut.

He loved her in a weird way. But not *that* way. He put his hands on her shoulders and shoved.

She stumbled backwards and tripped on a big rock, her hands grasped at branches.

Finnegan lunged forward and grabbed for her arm, but the sleeve of her plaid shirt slipped through his fingers. She landed flat on her back, one fist full of leaves.

He laughed and pointed at her. "Nice job, klutz."

Birdie's face contorted, her eyes wide and frantic. Her wall-eyed stare searched his face and she opened and closed her mouth like a drowning guppy. Pink spit gurgled from her lips. Between her legs, the wooden handle of his mother's pitchfork peered through the creeping thyme.

"No," Finnegan whispered. He flung himself to the ground, his knees crushing the plants beside her. "Birdie, talk to me." One pointed metal tine poked out of her arm. The other two protruded from her chest. Crimson stains blossomed on her shirt and spread across the beige and aqua stripes. "Birdie. Birdie, say something." He tugged on one tine, ran his hand over her bloody shirt.

She dug her fingernails into his arm. "Help." Her voice was a hoarse whisper.

He glanced around, his fingers twitched. They were deep into the garden, he couldn't see the house through the leaves. But he just knew his mother was watching. "I— I can't. She'll kill me!"

She smacked at his arm. "Please."

He swiped at his wet cheeks with fingers stained with his best friend's blood. He stroked her forehead. "Birdie, don't die. Please don't die."

She coughed and squeezed his hand.

"I'll kiss you if you want me too. I'll do anything." A spasm choked his throat and tears gushed down his cheeks. "Anything!" Finnegan sobbed. "I'll go get help. I promise. Don't leave me, Birdie. Just don't leave."

She stared at him, unblinking.

"Birdie?" He poked her cheek, took one of her hands and shook it. "Birdie, answer me!"

She didn't.

He pulled his hand from hers and turned away. "God damn you, Birdie." The moist ground wet the seat of his Levi's. He rested his arms on his knees and stared at the thyme leaves. "I love you, Birdie," he murmured under his laboured breath. His body quaked, his lungs aching. He stole a glance at her. Her mouth was frozen open, her skin ashen. Her face blurred behind his tears.

What would he do without her?

Time passed. It must have. It always did. The walnut tree's shadow lengthened across Birdie's still form. The neighbourhood settled into the same early evening lull it did every night, when all the children with normal mothers were inside, washing up for dinner.

Finnegan couldn't tear his gaze from Birdie's blank stare. Her lazy eye seemed lazier. The brown of her irises seemed duller. Flatter.

Like drops of dried mud. He reached out and touched his fingertip to her eyeball.

Here's mud in yer eye, Birdie.

The screech of rusty hinges pierced the silence. Finnegan jolted back to reality.

"Finny Mac? You're in the garden again, aren't you?"

He scooted through the bushes, split the branches with his hand, and peered between the leaves. His mother stood as she always did after her dates, hair dripping wet, arms crossed, cigarillo perched between two fingers.

His throat burned from crying and his ribs hurt from the pounding of his heart. He held his hands in front of his face. Birdie's blood had dried and browned on his skin. He wiped his hands on his shirt, already streaked with her death, but the stains remained. He'd been branded. A killer. Heartless and evil.

"Finny? Dinner is getting cold. Where are you?" She shifted her bare feet onto the first step of the cement stoop. "Damn it, Finny, I'm going to eat without you."

He held his breath and wished her to go away. He was safe for now, unless she put on her shoes. Despite the hours she spent kneeling in the dirt, she hated the feel of grass under her feet. Some dog might have pissed on it. Or worse.

She shook her head and stubbed her cigarette out on the brick of the house, mumbled something he couldn't hear. The wooden screen door slapped shut behind her.

His chest ached. His body trembled. He fell back onto the ground, landing in a patch of purple dead nettle. How would he tell his mother?

Her old Buick rattled to life. He caught a glimpse of the taillights through the open gate as she pulled out of the driveway.

Searing flames of adrenaline shot down his legs. He pounced to his feet, turned Birdie over and tugged on the pitchfork. It stuck in her tight, her body jostling with every pull. His fingers slid along the handle, the wood slippery with her blood. He swatted at flies that were buzzing around her, planted his foot on the seat of her pants and heaved. The tines gave way and the fork slipped from her flesh.

He lurched backward, flung the pitchfork aside, and flailed his arms for support, grasping at branches. "Ow, shit." He ripped his hand away from the yellow roses and cradled it against his chest. Where thorns stabbed his palm, droplets of his fresh blood mixed with Birdie's. He rubbed his hands together, forced her into his wounds. Accepted her into his body. He would keep her with him. Forever.

He disentangled the tines of the pitchfork from the hops vines that climbed the fence and kept the prying eyes of Mr. Greer from watching Finnegan's mother while she gardened. The seedpods scraped against his skin. He was used to the rash they caused, but the red welts always tattled on him. His mother knew where he'd been by the lesions on his arms. She loved her hops. Used them as an excuse not to get him a dog. Poisonous to canines, she told him. Was that even true? Who would rather have a plant that you can't touch than a soft, furry dog to love?

A spade leaned against the trunk of the chestnut tree. Finnegan grabbed the handle and pushed through to the older part of the garden where his mother never bothered with the weeds. He plunged the sharp tip of the shovel into the overgrowth. It barely sliced the ground. Sweat trickled from under his hair, traversed his forehead, and dripped from his brow. He wiped his face with one sleeve, the denim crusty with dried blood. The spade did little to loosen the hard soil. At this rate, he'd never get a grave dug for Birdie. His mother would find her. Smell her. Then his mother would kill him and bury him right alongside his best friend.

At least they would be together.

He chipped away at the dirt, jabbed the shovel into the earth, stabbed and plunged, each thrust coming faster and harder. Tears joined perspiration and landed in muddy droplets in the upturned soil. The edge of the spade glanced off something with a ping.

Finnegan dropped to one knee and tossed aside an oblong rock. It landed in the dirt with barely a sound. He eyed its off-white shade, the pitting along the narrow end. He plucked it from the ground, rolled it in his hand, ran his fingers along the length of it.

It was no rock. It was a bone. The ends were like wads of

chewed gum pressed on with a thumb. Not a steak bone. Maybe chicken. A wing, or a tiny drumstick. Only … different.

A chill ran through him and gooseflesh bloomed on his arms. The sun dipped low on the horizon, the air cooling fast. Dusk. When the mosquitos came out to play. Would they suck the last bits of life from Birdie's drying veins? He smacked at his neck and eyed the dead bug on his palm, squished into a tiny crimson splotch. Nope. The little pricks preferred his flowing blood. Maybe life just tasted better.

He dropped the bone into his pocket, jumped up and kept digging until the shallow hole looked deep enough to cover most of Birdie. Two more tiny bones were disinterred from the soil. He snatched them up and dropped them into his pocket. They'd make the start of a new collection. Bones and rocks and all things hard.

He gazed into the grave, hung his head and let the handle of the spade slip from his fingers. If he knew a prayer, he'd say one for her. But he didn't. There was no God or heaven anyway, so what did it matter?

He trudged back to Birdie, grabbed her feet, and dragged her to her final resting place. He rolled her over, then one more push and she landed on her back in the indented earth. Her open eyes stared at him. No matter where he moved, they followed him, implored him, bore into him. He kneeled next to her and, with a thumb and forefinger, closed her eyelids.. He touched his lips to hers, dry and cold and no different than when she was alive. "I'm sorry, Birdie."

He used his hands like a Tonka bulldozer and shovelled dirt into the grave. Clods plopped in beside Birdie's body, loose soil sprayed over her frozen face. Why was there not enough dirt to cover her? He felled some stinkweeds and spread them on top. He never understood why his mother allowed those smelly things to thrive in her otherwise pristine garden. This one section was derelict, untended. Weeds ran amok, wild and unpulled. Not that it mattered. At that moment, those weeds were his silent accomplice. And perfect camoflage.

He got to his feet, slapped the ass of his jeans and sent a cloud of dusty dirt into the air. He lifted his watch and pressed the button on the side. An eerie green glow lit his face. Seven-fifteen. Where the hell had his mother gone?

Finny picked up the bloodstained pitchfork and squeezed the tail of his crusty shirt. How would he explain this? How would he cover it up?

He pushed through the brush to the back of the garden, where the bougainvillea bloomed year after year despite being abandoned. And behind the vines, a hole in the fence that bordered the alley, one he'd used often to sneak back into the yard without his mother's knowledge when he'd spent her date time out exploring with Birdie.

He pushed aside the woody vine and shoved his head through the hole. Nothing but silence and the lump of Mrs. Atwater's five-hundred-pound cat lounging atop her garbage can. "How did you get your fat ass up there?" he mumbled at the animal.

He tossed the pitchfork into the alley and climbed through the hole. The bougainvillea clawed at his shirt. Pain stabbed at his calf. A nail poking through the fence's splintered wood caught on his pants, tearing into the denim and his skin. He stuck his finger in the rip and touched his warm blood. "Shit. She's gonna kill me." Fresh tears stung his eyes. He grabbed the pitchfork.

Grow up and stop bawling, crybaby.

Birdie was right. He had work to do. He peered around, hunkered over, and ran toward the river, to her favourite frog-catching spot. The boggiest part of the bank, overgrown with all manner of vines and moss. Deliciously mucky, she used to say. The ground oozed between their toes and stained their jeans and fingernails. It's what he loved about her most. She wasn't afraid of a little dirt. Hell, she thrived in it. She'd always been more boy than girl, much to the dismay of her mother. No number of pink dresses and shiny, patent leather shoes would sway Birdie. She only dressed up on Sundays and only for as long as church lasted. The one time Finnegan had seen her like that, a bow in her hair, her dress all flouncy and frilly, he wouldn't let her live it down. His relentless teasing pissed her off, and once it made her cry.

He was an ass. A bully. Just like the rest of them.

He held the pitchfork like a spear and aimed for the river. He drew his arm back and flung it as hard and straight as he could. It sailed through the night in a flawless arc and sliced the water's surface with barely a splash.

The water would be icy now. In the heat of summertime, they would jump in with all their clothes on just to find some respite from the swelter. In the fall, the river temperature dropped fast. Or maybe it was an illusion, because the night air had such a nip in it.

Finnegan unclasped his watch and laid it on a rock, then waded in. When the water hit his waist, he sucked in a gasp of air and a shiver rocketed along his spine. He pushed against the water to the sweet spot, before the soft silt underfoot gave way to slick rocks. Where, two feet ahead, the gentle current, broken up by logs of fallen trees and the uneven bank, turned rapid and swirling and dangerous.

He scooped silt and slime from the bed, smooshing it into his clothes. The dirt stained, and no amount of Tide or bleach ever got it out. His clothes came out of the dryer all brown and rusty.

His mother was going to kill him.

"Damn it, Finny, it's getting too cold out for your river romps." His mother handed him a cup of hot chocolate.

He held it under his nose, the steam warming the tip of it, the smell filling his mouth with saliva. "Sorry." He sipped at the sweet drink, slurped a few melted mini-marshmallows into his mouth. A shudder passed over him. *Someone is walking over your grave*, Birdie whispered in his ear.

"Yeah, yeah. You're always sorry."

His mother took the mug and set it on the coffee table. She pulled the quilt up around his shoulders and rubbed his wet hair, sweet with her strawberry shampoo, with a bath towel. "Those stains are never coming out of your clothes. And the rips? Your favourite jeans, ruined."

He stared at the blank television, wishing for it to turn on, for *Mork and Mindy* to fill the screen, to drown out his mother's voice and block the image of Birdie's dead eyes.

Nanu, nanu.

She rested one arm across the back of the chesterfield. "I'm not throwing them out, you know. Next time you feel the need to dive in that bog — and you will, won't you? Well, you'll have to wear those. So I can quit wasting all my hard-earned bucks on you." Her half-grin always gave her away. Her anger was short-lived, and she soon became amused by him. He was all she had. Nothing she did for him was a waste and he knew it. She'd told him as much on many nights such as this. "I bet Birdie's mom is having herself another bloody bird if her jeans look like yours. Imagine if she came home in one of those ridiculous dresses all stained and soaked?" She smirked and shook her head.

Finnegan pinched the underside of his arm to keep tears at bay. "She wasn't with me."

At least it wasn't a lie.

He rested his head on his mother's shoulder. The sweet cherry and almond lotion she slathered all over her soft body soothed him, the feel of her warm skin brought him a sense of peace that belied the pain in his chest. He slid his hand into his mother's palm, sighed, and stared at the blank television. "Can I watch *Mork and Mindy*?"

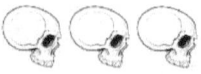

Sleep didn't come. The phone rang, breaking the silence of the night. Finnegan sat up and strained to hear the conversation his mother was having with whoever was bold enough to call after midnight.

The timbre of her voice seeped through the walls and up the stairs, slipping under the crack at the bottom of his door, riding the sliver of hall light that had kept his childhood monsters at bay. But the sonorous tones of her normally mellow voice had an edge. She was talking faster, the volume louder. Then her footsteps ran up the stairs and his room filled with light.

"Finny, wake up."

"I wasn't sleeping."

The bed frame creaked at the slight weight of his mother perched on the edge. "Did you see Birdie today?"

Birdie.

Her name, spoken aloud, made the dull ache in his heart explode into pain. Sparkles of light teased at the edge of his vision.

"At school." He could barely muster a whisper.

"Not since school? She didn't go to the river with you, right?"

He swallowed. "Nah. Her dad won't let her hang out with me anymore."

She squinted and cocked her head. "Since when?"

"Since a long time. We were sneaking around without telling him, but she didn't want to anymore. He hits her."

"He does what? Are you sure?"

"She told me. She has bruises all the time."

"And why won't he let you play with her? What did you do, Finny?"

His mouth opened and closed, but nothing came out.

"You didn't try to kiss her or anything, did you?"

"No way!" He scooted backwards. "She said it's because —" He glanced away.

"Oh. I see. Because of me."

He nodded.

"Well, that's his problem. And Birdie's loss." She cupped her hand over his. "And you didn't see her since school?"

He shook his head. "Why?" he whispered.

"Because, baby. She's missing."

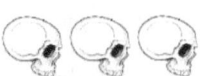

Cigarettes and aftershave. The smell of his mother's evening dates lingered for hours after they left. But this was no date.

One officer stood by the dining room door, blocking the entrance. And the only exit. As if Finnegan, all ninety pounds of him, could get past the mountain of uniformed cop and make a break for it. Finnegan eyed the man's legs, the muscles evident through his uniform. He must have thighbones like a gorilla.

The other officer sat across the table. Finnegan couldn't look him in the eye for more than a couple of seconds. He stared at the faded daisies on the worn tablecloth, glanced up at the cop, at the broad face and prominent cheekbones, like they'd been carved from stone, and had the urge to shit in his boxers.

"Where did Birdie go after last bell?" The man gave the good buddy thing his best try, but no buddy of Finnegan's had arms that big, or fists the size of pomelos.

"I don't know, sir. Home, I guess."

"Son, look. We know you walked off the grounds with her. At least a dozen of your friends saw you."

He didn't have that many friends. Only one. And now zero. He sucked in as much air as his lungs would hold without them bursting and spewing spit all over the cop. "I guess we did," he said on the exhale. "But I went home. Birdie kept walking."

"And she didn't say where she was going?"

"Nope. Only that she couldn't come to my house because her father thinks my mother is a slut bag." His cheeks warmed and he looked over his shoulder. "Sorry, Mom."

"It's okay, baby."

The cop scratched some words in a notepad. "How long you and Birdie been friends?"

Nice grammar. "Since first grade."

The cop put his pen down. "And you just let her father end your friendship like that?"

"She said he'd kill her if she came over here."

The cop's forehead accordioned when his eyebrows arched. "He said that?"

"I don't know. But that's what she told me."

"I see."

"Aren't you going to write that down?"

The cop smirked and picked up his pen. "What else did she tell you?"

Finnegan tugged at the collar of his pyjamas. "That he hit her. And her little brother. I saw the bruises."

The pen grated against the pad. "Have you seen him hit her?"

"No, sir. But I heard him yell at her a lot." Sweat dampened his armpits. His own fear filled his nostrils. Could they smell it? They were trained to sniff out the bad guys. Did criminals and murderers have a particular scent? The odour of pure evil? "That was before he told me not to come over anymore."

The cop wrote in his notepad and smiled at Finnegan's mother. Maybe strawberry shampoo and sex musk masked the smell of death. She exchanged twisted smiles with Pomelo Fists. The strap of her tank top slipped down her shoulder to reveal the lace of a scarlet bra.

"Right," the cop said, his eyes never leaving her face. "Well, kid, I guess that's all we need for now." He stood, reached out a big paw and tousled Finnegan's hair. "Now don't go fleeing the country or anything. You know, just in case we need to arrest you or something."

A loud gurgle erupted from Finnegan's intestines. He grabbed his stomach with one hand and swallowed. "N-n-no sir."

The cop chortled and the officer standing guard in front of the door snorted. Pomelo slid a business card across the table at Finnegan's mother. "Just give me a call. You know, if you or the boy think of anything else."

His mother touched one long, lacquered nail to the card and dragged it toward her. "I'm sure we will," she eyed the card, "Officer ..." The left side of her mouth curled up and she raised her eyes to the cop. "Everhard?"

Officer Everhard hooked his thumbs into his belt loops. "Yes ma'am." He grinned. "We'll let ourselves out."

The door cracked shut and the air returned to the room. Finnegan's mother brushed his hair to one side. "You okay, baby? You look a little green."

"I don't feel so good."

"Go lie down on the chesterfield. I'll bring you some cinnamon toast fingers and warm milk."

He was too old for warm milk. But he didn't protest.

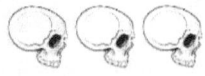

The cool of the soft bedsheets succumbed to his body heat. Coppery blood and pungent river silt overwhelmed the fresh-laundered smell. Finnegan rubbed his hands on the cotton in a frenzy, then sniffed his fingers.

Pennies.

It was never going away. He would smell of Birdie's death until his own crept up on him. He'd probably live to be a hundred, forever tortured by this one mistake. Or at least this mistake over all others. The effing motherlode of all mistakes.

Murder. He was an evil, murdering bastard.

He slid a scrunched-up piece of foolscap from under his pillow and unfurled it. The button on the flashlight stuck and he poked it hard until a beam of yellow illuminated Birdie's awkward penmanship. Chicken scratch, he'd always teased her. Birdie writes like a chicken scratching in the dirt.

A tear rolled down his cheek. It was the last note she'd lobbed across the classroom at him. He ran one fingertip along the curve of an oversized S, made the sign of the cross over one tiny T. A vision of the silver crucifix that hung around her neck tugged at him. It was a gift from her parents upon her confirmation last summer. Why hadn't he taken it off her? Her mother would love to have that necklace back.

They'd have to stop looking for her eventually. And when they did, Finnegan would dig her up and take her crucifix. He closed his eyes and apologized to Mrs. Schultz. She should have it. It was only right. But damn it, he was going to keep that cross. A permanent reminder of his crime. Of his friend. Of the only real love he'd ever felt, other than for his mother.

But love for Birdie was different. It was comfortable and awkward. It made him prickly and tight, but loose and free. It made him feel like he could fly, but made his stomach lurch with repulsion. It was hot and cold, light and dark, up and down, morning and night. Safe. And dangerous.

It was everything.

He blinked away tears. Until he killed her, he'd never even realized he loved her at all. And now, it was all he could think about. He sniffed the paper, hoping to find her in the pencil lead, in the lines on the page. It just reeked of school, and of his guilty sweat. One torn corner of the paper dangled and caught in the flashlight's beam. A shadow danced on the bedsheets. He ripped the corner from the page and touched his tongue to it. The tiny piece of Birdie stuck to him. He sucked on it, rolled it around in his mouth until it formed a tiny spitball. He squished it between his teeth, closed his eyes, and tasted her. Then swallowed the only bit of her he had left.

How camest thou in this pickle?

An icy breeze nipped at Finnegan's freckled cheeks. He stood on the back porch and stared into the shadows of the garden. Snow would come soon. Winter would whitewash the kill zone. Until spring arrived and turned it into a gooey, oozing pot of Birdie stew.

He'd avoided the back yard the whole month since it happened. The police had been back to interrogate him again. The longer Birdie was missing, the more agitated and aggressive they became. And the more flirtatious Pomelo Fists got with his mother. Maybe missing kids turned him on. Sick bastard.

Another reason to avoid the backyard was the ridiculous amount of time Finnegan's mother spent in the garden. Her fall clean up, she said. Best time to plant Dutch irises and Darwin tulips.

Whatever.

She'd been out there for hours. Was she digging around Birdie? Desecrating her grave? He'd watched from his bedroom window, peered out between the curtains, lest his mother catch him spying and wonder why he cared about gardening all of a sudden. But with all those damn trees and bushes, he could never figure out where she was.

It was their favourite day of the year. The one day when he and Birdie could be whoever they wanted to be, hide behind masks and costumes, summon their inner heroes and rule the world. Or at least their tiny corner of it.

There'd be no dressing up. No trick-or-treating, no pillowcase full of candy. It wouldn't be right without her. Instead, he would pay her a visit. An All Hallows Eve nocturnal viewing of her gravesite. He might even partially unearth her if he could remember which end he'd buried her head. A way creepier way to spend Halloween. Worse than any vampire mask or toilet paper mummy he'd run into on the cul-de-sac. Besides, he needed to talk to her. To tell her how they'd shut school down for two days, the police looking through her desk and interviewing students. How the school brought in counsellors and social workers.

He had no choice but to get out of the house anyway. His mother had a date. The first in a month. It was as if she'd been mourning Birdie. Even though only he knew she was dead.

He stood straight and set his shoulders back, took the stairs of the cement porch one at a time, slow, like when a glacier slips down the mountain crushing everything in its path. But he crushed nothing. He could barely even breathe.

Would Birdie be all decomposed? Nothing left but bones and teeth? Or mummified? Maybe she would awaken and set off the zombie apocalypse — and the first brains she'd eat would be his.

He'd be a Finny snack. *Rooby rooby roo!*

He stole glances over his shoulder. Was his mother watching him? Did the kitchen curtain just move? No, no, no. She had a date. Some random man was doing disgusting things to her behind closed and locked doors in the guest room. Just be cool, Finnegan. Just be cool.

He trudged across the yard. The lawn widened with each step, the garden slipping further into the distance. It was all in his demented head. Like being waist-deep in quicksand in some Freudian nightmare. Trying to go up the down escalator, running but getting nowhere. Crawling through the desert toward an oasis that disappeared as you neared.

At the garden's edge, where lawn met dirt, he took three deep breaths, snuck one last peek at the kitchen window, serene and silent as it always was on date night, then ventured into the graveyard.

He wended his way past the angry roses, sidled along the bare fence, the hops chopped down to stubs in preparation for winter. Damn, there was Mr. Greer, sitting on his porch, wrapped in a red plaid quilt, drinking whiskey straight from the bottle and smoking up a storm.

Finnegan dashed past the walnut tree, ducked behind the chestnuts and peered out. Greer upended the bottle and let out a belch. Just a few yards ahead, the untended section of the garden, Birdie's final resting place, awaited him. He rubbed his sweaty palms against the nap of his thrift store pants, the swish of corduroy on corduroy announcing his presence with every step.

He pushed branches aside and froze. Birdie's grave was all neat and tidy, not the mess of disinterred earth and savaged weeds he'd left behind. His mother's fall clean up. She'd done it right here, right on top of Birdie, planted fresh bulbs that would arise in spring. Irises and tulips, no doubt.

His heart thumped against his ribs. His knees hit the ground and he ripped through the freshly planted bulbs, digging both hands into the earth. He swiped at tears that dripped from his dirty cheeks.

Gone. Birdie was gone.

Saliva filled his mouth and he swallowed against a rising tide of vomit. He plunged his fingers deeper into the ground, clawed at the dirt until his nails ached with embedded soil. A foot down, his fingers found something smooth and hard. He pulled out a tiny bone. One little bone with a tendril of muscle attached. It was all that remained of his best friend. He rubbed it between his fingers until the flesh fell away, squeezed it in his fist and held it to his wet cheek. Then he tucked it into his back pocket.

Flower bulbs lay strewn about. His mother would kill him for desecrating her sacred garden. He shovelled earth into the holes he'd made, poked bulbs back into the ground, and brushed the dirt with his hands to smooth it, to erase the evidence of his attack on her precious plants.

The squeak of the screen door echoed through the garden.

"Finny? Where you at, baby? Dinner is in five minutes. I'm eating with or without you." She had become rather apathetic about the possibility of him being in the garden.

The hinges creaked and the door spanked the jamb as it closed.

Finnegan wended his way through the bushes and trees, his gaze on his dirt-covered sneakers. He grasped the iron railing and pulled himself up each step to the back door. The smell of macaroni and cheese, or, as his mother called it, Finny Mac and cheese, wafted out to greet him. The only dish she could cook right, other than scrambled eggs and fried steak. Every other meal came frozen in an aluminum tray. Any other day, he'd race to the table and load a plate with too much of his favourite food, eat every bite and then lay on the chesterfield until the pain in his stomach eased.

Totally worth it.

But not this day. His stomach lurched at the thought of oozy ketchup dripping between the elbow-shaped bits of pasta. Like blood on pebbles in the dirt.

He washed his hands in the sink, didn't even glance up at his mother, couldn't bear to look into her eyes. The smell of her strawberry shampoo and the musk of men and sex swirled around her and taunted him with every move she made. She had to know he'd murdered Birdie. How could she not know?

He sat in his usual seat and threw up a little in his mouth. He swallowed it and rubbed his aching gut.

His mother placed a plate in front of him and set a fork next to it. She sat with her meal and a glass of wine, ate a few bites in total silence, except for the wet sound of tender pasta being crushed between her teeth.

"So." She placed her fork on the side of her plate and took a sip of wine. "Any word on Birdie?"

He shoved a huge forkful of macaroni in his mouth, kept his eyes on the tablecloth, and shook his head.

"I see. Aidan — I mean, Officer Everhard — said they've not found any sign of her. Must have been abducted by some child-molesting stranger, don't you think?"

She was on a first name basis with him now? Finnegan looked at his lap. No matter how hard he tried to stop them, tears dripped from his eyes. "Maybe," he whispered.

They sat in silence while his mother finished her meal and Finnegan stared at his plate.

She squeezed his hand. "Come on, baby. Eat something."

He pulled away. "Not hungry."

She sighed. "I'll wrap it up then. I can heat it up for you later if you like." He jumped at the clank of her plate hitting the stainless sink. She sidled up to him, placed one hand on his shoulder and slipped the other hand into the pocket of her robe. She pulled her hand out of her pocket and slid her closed fist along the tabletop. When she spread her fingers, something rustled against the vinyl tablecloth. She squeezed his shoulder and lifted her hand from the table.

Birdie's cross and chain. The kitchen light glinted off its silver edges, scrubbed clean of her death.

Finny stared at it and held his breath. Could his mother hear his heart pounding? And did he just piss in his pants a little?

She kissed the top of his head and took his plate.

The grief that does not speak

If life imitated cartoons, Finnegan's knees would be knocking together to the sound of clapping coconut shells. His entire body shook, the trembles infiltrating the small muscle fibres in his fingers. He closed his eyes and fingered the bone in his pocket. A memory of the desiccated flesh he'd discarded from it made his chest ache. Birdie's phalange. He'd looked it up in the anatomy text in the school library.

He held his fingertip a millimetre from the lighted doorbell and took a deep breath. At the sound of the old-fashioned chime that echoed inside the house, Birdie's British accent filled his head. That doorbell wasn't the regular ding-dong like every other house in the neighbourhood. Nope, it was a royalty-friendly, aristocratic eight-chimer that fed his imagination with images of tea with the Queen of England. Maybe Birdie had actual royal blood after all.

Footsteps stomped toward the door and Mr. Schultz yanked it open, already demanding to know "Whaddya want?" before he even knew who was standing on his stoop. He glared down at Finnegan, the look of permanent disgust on his face morphing into vile hatred. "You."

His undershirt had mustard stains on the crest of his belly. Pregnant with beer and pretzels, Birdie used to say. He was rough around the edges, to say the least. The "white is right" type, with no patience nor love for all the new people of colour infiltrating the block, coming from all these foreign places and bringing down the value of his crappy-ass house. He was Archie Bunker. A goddamn cliché. Definitely not an ounce of royalty running through his veins.

"Hello, sir." Finnegan couldn't meet his gaze. He focused on the man's hands. Rough and cracked from manual labour, grease stains permanently embedded in the swirls of his fingerprints and under his never-manicured nails. When he smacked Birdie around, did he smell like gasoline? "Just wanted to see how you and Mrs. Schultz were." He dared a glance at the man's face. "If you'd heard anything about Birdie?"

Why did he ask that? He knew exactly where she was. At least, he used to. This charade was going to kill him as much as it had killed what little joy Mr. Schultz had ever known. But Finnegan was desperate to see Mrs. Schultz.

Mr. Schultz opened his mouth and Finnegan braced for verbal impact.

"Finny, is that you?" Mrs. Schultz peered from behind her husband. Her question-mark eyes softened when she saw him. "Oh, Finnegan." She brushed past Mr. Schultz and stepped outside, enveloped Finnegan in one of her cocoon-style hugs that Birdie always complained about. But Finnegan knew better. Those hugs were like air, like water. Like baseball and catching frogs. Those hugs were the stuff of life.

He rested his ear against her breastbone. Her heart still beat, even if the light in her eyes had gone out. Why couldn't she have been his mother? She was safe. When he was near her, he was calm. When his own mother hugged him, his feelings were jumbled and confused.

"Mummy," Birdie had called her mother, always with that accent, the emphasis on the first syllable. Not even the whole syllable, just the "Mu" part. The "mmy" sounded less like "me" and more like "may." *Muhmay.*" He repeated it over and over in his head.

He melted into Mrs. Schutz's embrace, inhaled the scent of her. Vanilla and garlic, Lysol and disappointment. The first time he got one of those hugs, he was hooked. It didn't happen often, and this was the first time it'd happened in front of Mr. Schultz. When she finally let Finnegan go, Mr. Schultz stood stalk-straight, arms crossed, eyes squinting at the intruder on his porch.

"How are you doing? You keeping up your grades?" She cupped his chin with the fingertips of one hand and lifted his face.

Mrs. Schultz was the kindest person he'd ever met. But behind those eyes? Misery. Desolation. A bottomless chasm where all of her dreams and expectations had gone to die. She'd shared her hopes with Birdie once, when Birdie was upset by all the bullying. Mrs. Schultz told her daughter that she'd wanted to travel the world. Be a photographer. Capture the beauty of distant lands and different people, the colours and culture, the historical and the contemporary. But she couldn't afford it. The equipment, the travel. In reality, she wasn't brave enough. Then she met Mr. Schultz and fell in love.

How had that ever happened?

Birdie told Finnegan that when her mother told that story, her voice trailed off and her gaze became detached and sorrowful. She encouraged Birdie to be strong. To go after what she wanted even if it scared the shit out of her. Because reality was a harsh mistress.

"School's okay." Grades were the least of his worries. Even with the crushing weight of murdering his best friend, he aced every test, was top of his class in every assignment. His brain just didn't know how to fail. Like some kind of mental autopilot. An easy genius, his mother called him.

Still, no one picked him for group projects, and they avoided his gaze when it was time to partner up in science lab. The damnable offense of being close to the school's redheaded pariah whose best friend's fate was the subject of whispered gossip outweighed the desire to bring up their grades by virtue of being on any team he was on. The only place their complete and total alienation of him made sense was in gym class. He understood why no one picked him for sports. He sucked at everything.

He had so many questions for Mrs. Schultz. But with the looming spectre of her husband growling down at him all he could spit out was, "How are you?"

She ran her fingers through his hair and mussed it up. "Best as can be expected." She managed a pained smile. "I made cookies. Do you want to come in?"

Mr. Schultz raised an eyebrow, pursed his lips, and shook his head at Finnegan behind his wife's back.

Finnegan looked at his feet. "Thank you, but I have to get home. Homework, you know?"

She held up one finger. "Wait here. I'll get you some to go." She ducked back into the house.

Mr. Schulz and Finnegan waited in an awkward and silent standoff, mortal enemies from the get-go. He could never figure out why until Birdie told him it wasn't about him. It was about his mother. The man hated his mother because of all her dates. That they weren't actual dates was the worst kept secret in the neighbourhood. Why it mattered to anyone else, Finnegan could never understand.

"Here you go. Snickerdoodles and oatmeal raisin."

Birdie's favourites.

He hesitated. Mrs. Schultz gave the paper bag full of cookies a gentle shake. "Go on, Finny." She placed a hand on his shoulder and smiled a joyless smile. Tears welled in her eyes. "It's okay."

No. It was not. It never would be.

He took the bag and thanked her, cut his eyes to Mr. Schultz's face, his lips drawn together in a thin, tight line. Finnegan backed off the steps, turned, and hurried down their front walk, propelled by the laser gaze of Mr. Shultz boring into his spine.

Half way down the block, he turned back. The door was shut tight and Mrs. Schultz was out of view. Probably forever. He hung his head and dragged the soles of his sneakers along the concrete, avoiding every line in the sidewalk. Birdie sang in his head.

Step on a crack, break your mother's back.

He hadn't broken Mrs. Schultz's back. He'd broken her whole self. Extinguished her light. Right alongside Birdie's.

He opened the paper bag and sniffed the cookies. Cinnamon. Birdie's face, her chin covered in cookie crumbs and sporting a milk moustache, jumped in front of his eyes. His stomach flipped. He ripped off a piece of the bag where greasy butter had turned it translucent, and tucked the brown paper inside his cheek. He sucked on it, tasted the essence of snickerdoodles, of Elizabeth Schultz. And Birdie. He swiped tears from his cheeks, shredded the paper with his teeth, and swallowed his feelings.

1983

...there is nothing either good or bad, but thinking
makes it so. To me it is a prison

Finnegan's mother glided into the living room, the sway of her hips sweeping her skirt side-to-side. She poked at her pierced earlobe with a massive fake gold hoop until she found the hole. "Dinner's in the oven. Should be ready in fifteen minutes. The timer will go off."

He turned his attention back to *The Beachcombers* end credits. "So?" He picked up the remote and pressed the mute button.

"So, I have a date."

Finnegan sighed and tossed the remote onto the seat beside him. "Fine. I'll be outside."

"No, silly. You stay and watch your shows. I have a real date. An outside-the-house date."

He tried not to raise his right eyebrow, but the damn thing had a mind of its own.

"Very funny, mister skeptical." She leaned over him to use the glass of his baby picture hanging behind the chesterfield as a mirror. Her breasts grazed the top of his head.

He leaned into them until they pressed against his hair. His groin prickled and he squirmed in his seat. She smelled of good perfume. The Chanel stuff that she couldn't afford to wear every day.

She stood back and smacked her lips together, pressed the dark red lipstick into her skin.

He hated that lipstick. When she kissed him, it tasted like oil and perfume. Back when he was young and innocent, the colour reminded him of cherries. For the last two years, it looked like she'd dipped her lips in Birdie's blood.

"Bed by ten, it's a school night."

"You won't be home by ten?"

"I guess it depends on how things go. So hopefully not." She opened the clasp of her handbag and pitched the lipstick in. "I really like this guy."

The doorbell rang. Finnegan waited for his mother to shoo him upstairs or scoot him into the kitchen. Anywhere he couldn't see, hear, or worst of all, meet whatever perverted schlep was standing on the front porch. But she didn't scoot. Never shooed.

She ran her hands down the front of her skirt and performed an awkward twirl. "How do I look?"

She looked amazing. Glossy and joyful and — backlit. Like a Lite-Brite version of herself with coifed hair and more makeup than he'd ever seen on her face. He shrugged. "You're okay."

A little of the light drained from her eyes. "Gee, thanks. High praise."

"Kind of weird to tell my own mother she looks pretty."

"Aw, pretty? Thanks, Finny Mac." The glint returned to her eyes. She took an audible deep breath, turned the doorknob, and swung the door open wide. "Good evening, Officer."

A shot of adrenaline tingled through Finnegan's body.

His mother turned and cocked her head. "Baby, you remember Officer Everhard?" She squinted. "Close your mouth," she said through gritted teeth. "And sit up straight."

Finnegan shifted on the chesterfield and straightened his spine.

"How you doing, son?" Everhard stepped forward and held his hand out.

Finnegan scratched at his arm, his eyes darted about the room.

"Finny, darling," his mother's voice had that pissed-off edge. "Say hello and shake his hand."

He did as he was told. The officer's skin was hot and dry against Finnegan's clammy palm. Everhard's pomelo fist surrounded Finnegan's entire hand, could have crushed his bones to dust if the cop felt like it. But his grip was surprisingly gentle. "Hello, officer." Once the cop released his hand, he rubbed it on his pants and crossed his arms. He couldn't make eye contact lest the man see right through him. Was this creep really interested in dating his mother? Or had he figured out Birdie's fate and was biding his time, waiting for Finnegan to slip up and spill his guts?

No way was that truth going to pass over his lips. That was a secret he'd keep to his grave. One only his mother knew. It bound them, more than flesh and blood did. Connected them in lies and deceit, like partners in crime. Or star-crossed lovers.

The officer helped her on with her winter coat. He crooked his arm and smiled at her. He looked genuine enough. Or he was a pro at deception. At getting the perps to trust him before they spilled the beans and confessed to their crimes. "Shall we? Reservation is at seven-thirty."

She threaded her arm through his and put her other hand on his biceps. "Reservations? Fancy."

"Nothing but the best for you, m'lady."

Finnegan rolled his eyes. Did she just blush? He'd never seen her cheeks pink like that. She turned back, blew him a kiss and wiggled her fingers at him then pulled the door shut. She really did like that guy. And a date that didn't require a shower after? Maybe things were looking up.

For his mother.

He split the curtains with his fingertips. Under the yellow glow of the streetlamp, Officer Everhard opened the passenger door, placed his hand on Finnegan's mother's lower back, and helped her into the car. Finnegan squinted and clenched his teeth. "Take your damn hands off her." He wiped his breath from the icy window with a closed fist.

Just what he needed. A man around the house. Finnegan's house. The same man on a regular basis. And not just any random guy. A cop. The bloody police hanging around the scene of the crime. How could he derail this … romance? Was that what it was? Relationship? No matter. He had to end it before it went too far.

The oven timer buzzed. Finnegan rubbed his aching stomach. If he didn't eat whatever barely edible meal she'd prepared, she'd be annoyed. Disappointed even. He hated it when she got that look on her face, like she should have popped out a better kid or something.

He put on the oversized oven mitt, eyed the reddish stains — raw steak, perhaps — and the semi-circles of char where it had met the stovetop burners. He sniffed it, searching for his mother's almond and cherry Jergen's lotion, but found only grease and a hint of sour meat. He slid the aluminum tray onto the stovetop and shook the mitt off, peeled the foil away. Steam curled up from the Salisbury steak and Tater Tots, and what might be kernels of corn. At least he could eat in front of the television. As long as Pomelo Fists didn't poke around in the garden, find any evidence of Birdie's demise, maybe this arrangement could work out all right. His mother might be happier. Her dates would be outside the house. And Finnegan could be inside for a change.

Fuck that. If Pomelo Fists got too handsy with his mother, Finnegan would knock the guy's block off.

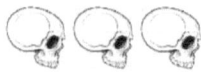

The glow of the living room lamps was punctuated by intermittent white strobes from the television. It was eerie in the evening fog, like that awful horror movie Finnegan and Birdie had watched in her basement that one time her father let him sleep over. The priest standing in that fog was far more terrifying than pea soup vomit or cheesy special effects. Anything could be hiding in the fog.

Finnegan maneuvered between the bushes of the tiny garden plot at the front of Schultzes' house. Only three shrubs and a bunch of dead pansies. Maybe there were bones amid the roots of those plants too. Perhaps the entire neighbourhood sat on some ancient burial ground and the bodies were starting to float to the top. A zombie uprising. An apocalypse in the making. He grinned, crouched low, rested one knee in the dirt, and peered in the front window.

The Love Boat? Mr. Schultz must be passed out on the chesterfield. He hated that crap. He only ever watched sports and news.

All Finnegan could see through the sliver of open curtain and the condensation dripping on the inside of the window was half of the television and the entry to the kitchen beyond, bathed in darkness after dinner was eaten and dishes were done. He could smell the garlic from his stakeout spot. His mouth watered. Maybe it was Mrs.

Shultz's baked spaghetti with the tiny meatballs she made from scratch. Or the breaded chicken with actual chunks of garlic and fresh parsley, so moist and tender and delicious.

He rubbed his hands together and blew on them, his breath turning to mist when he exhaled. He pulled his jacket tighter around him. It had to be minus ten. He should have worn his parka, the fake down-filled one with the puffy sleeves that he hated so much. It made him look like the Michelin Man. An electric blue Michelin Man with orange stripes down its sleeves. It was warm, but not terribly subtle. Hell, it might even glow neon under the streetlights. And then, his cover would be blown.

His nocturnal spying had become less frequent in the past few months. He couldn't bear to face Mrs. Schultz, to hear her voice and see her misery. And like hell was he going to ring the doorbell and raise the ire of her husband. Finnegan would have to be content with the knowledge that she was in there somewhere. Alive. Breathing. Mourning. Grieving.

Backing out between the shrubs, his foot caught on a garden gnome and he tumbled to the ground. The gnome fell over and broke in half against the concrete walkway. The front porch light came on, bathing the yard in a yellow glow that bounced off the ice crystals in the air.

Finnegan scurried backwards, crab-walked under and around the pine tree fifteen feet from the house, dried needles poked into his bare palms. He sat with his back against the trunk, the top of his head crushed into the lowest limbs, and peered around. She was there, on the porch, squinting into the dark, her breath coming quickly.

"Who is it?" Mr. Schultz's voice boomed into the yard. His silhouette, backlit by the porch light, was just as intimidating as the daylight version of him.

"Oh, no." Mrs. Schultz scampered down the stairs and kneeled by her decapitated gnome. "He's broken."

"It's that damn cat." Mr. Schultz opened the door. "Your own fault. I told you he was trouble. But no, you just had to have a pet." He tromped back into the house and left his wife alone to mourn the passing of the gnome.

Mrs. Schultz gathered up the ceramic body parts and set them in the garden. She stood, her shoulders slouched, and grabbed the railing. She exhaled a cloud of foggy breath and dragged herself up the stairs as if she were facing the gallows.

When the door clicked shut and the light extinguished, Finnegan let his lungs deflate. All he wanted was for Birdie's mother to be happy. Breaking her favourite gnome was hardly the way to go about it. Nothing would ever fix what he had done. Unless he could make Birdie rise from the dead and bring her home.

He fingered Birdie's silver cross that he'd tucked into his jacket pocket, and banged his head against the trunk of the tree. He should drop it in their mailbox. Or hang it from a gnome. Mrs. Schultz should have that crucifix. It was only right. So why couldn't he part with it?

"She can't have it, Birdie." An icy breeze stung his cheeks where tears wet them. He squeezed the cross until it broke the skin of his palm. He hugged his knees to his chest and rocked against the tree. "It's mine."

Waiting for a girl like you ~ Foreigner

Silver cutlery clinked against china plates. Actual china. And real silver, the kind that tarnishes if you don't polish it all the damn time. The ping of crystal glasses raised in toasts sent musical notes bouncing about the restaurant. Tibba squirmed in her seat and glanced around at the clientele.

Fancy indeed. Too fancy. She didn't deserve this kind of treatment.

She rescued the last shrimp that dangled from the side of what looked like a margarita glass and dunked it in the tangy dip. "Aidan, I just gotta ask." She put the shrimp up to her lips. "All this?" She waved her other hand over the table. "On a cop's salary? Are you — I don't know. You on the take or something?" She sucked the dip off the shrimp before biting it off at the tail.

He grinned at her. "Would that be so bad? Dirty cop equals great benefits."

She pursed her lips and shook her head. "You're not dirty. I don't think it's your style."

"You're right. It's not. Honestly? This is my first time here." He blushed. "And probably my last. I just wanted our first date to be really special. Because I hope there'll be more than one." He reached across the table and wiped dip from her chin. "But from here on out, it's pizza and beer." His laugh startled the hushed-toned, low-key diners around them.

"Works for me. As lovely as this is, you and me?" She leaned in and lowered her voice. "We're not cut from the same silk cloth as most of these folks." She leaned back. "And that is one of the things I like about you. You're real and down to earth. Fried chicken and mashed potatoes, just like me."

The waiter swooped in and placed her dinner in front of her.

"For Madame, filet mignon medium rare, potatoes Boulangéres with rosemary, and glazed carrots."

Potatoes what? It looked like a miniature mountain of her mother's scallops, with a tiny tree planted in its peak. The carrots still had the tops attached. Who cooks the tops? That's the garbage part.

She plucked the plant from her potatoes and flicked it onto the tabelcloth. The waiter gave her the side-eye while he recited the snooty-sounding contents of Aidan's plate. The waiter topped up their champagne glasses and upended the bottle in the ice bucket before sticking his nose in the air and traipsing away.

"Yum, you got gravy." She dipped one finger in the small pool on his plate and licked the sauce from it.

"I think they call it a demi-glace. Whatever that is." He tucked his napkin into his collar. "Let's eat!"

She smirked at the sight of him, his knife and fork held in his fists, his lopsided grin. An excited child in a man's body. She smiled and her eyelashes fluttered. "Yes. Let's."

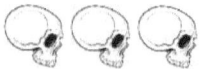

It was a frosty January night after a warm December. What little snow had fallen hadn't stuck to the ground. Tibba drew the collar of her fake fur coat closer around her neck and pulled on her vanilla cigarillo. Damn stuck-up place that wouldn't let its patrons light up in the cozy warmth of the restaurant.

An icy wind picked up and waved the hem of her dress, sending a shiver up her legs. She stamped her patent red pumps to keep her feet warm and peered in the restaurant window. How long did it take to pay a tab and take a leak?

"Wow, Tib. You're looking hot tonight." Officer O'Connor stood a few feet away in civilian clothes.

Stealthy bastard. "John. Nice night." Just what she needed. A damn client asking for services when Aidan came out. She held her smoke aloft and pressed her lips together.

An elderly couple exited the restaurant. Tibba nodded at them and glanced up and down the street. When the couple got in a cab and drove off, she turned to John. "What are you doing out here? You undercover or something?" He looked almost handsome in his suit. It slimmed his frame. But she knew what fat lay beneath.

"I could ask you the same."

She ignored the question he didn't voice and raised an eyebrow.

He sighed. "Sorry I ain't been around in a while."

She shrugged. Their weekly dates had grown farther apart over the years. He only came around every other month or so now. Maybe it was because she'd raised her rates. Or perhaps it's no different than any long-term relationship. Eventually, they all become tedious. But she did miss the guaranteed income.

He scuffed his shoes on the pavement like a shy teenager. "I sure do miss you, though. Things just been a bit rough between me and the missus. Actually, we're gettin' a divorce."

"Oh, sorry to hear that. Not because of me, I hope."

"No. And yes." He scratched his balding head, emptied his lungs through pursed lips sending a wave of frosty fog into the air. "She doesn't know about you. But you made me realize how unhappy I was. In the marriage, I mean. She caught me havin' an affair. A neighbour of mine." He stared at the sidewalk and shifted his weight. "Look, I'm real sorry."

Tibba snorted a small laugh through her nose. "Why are you apologizing to me? It's not like we're married. Or even dating. Hell, John, we're barely friends." She blew smoke out one side of her mouth, tossed the cigarillo on the sidewalk and stubbed it out beneath the pointed toe of her shoe.

His brows furrowed and he shoved his hands deep into the pockets of his wool overcoat. "Geeze, don't say that. You know I care about you."

"You pay me to fuck you. It's a business transaction. Always has been."

He grabbed her arm and turned her to face him. "It's more than that." He jutted out his chin and straightened his shoulders. "Always has been."

"Let go, John," she said through gritted teeth. "You're hurting me."

He dropped her arm, held up his hands, and took one step back. "O'Connor?"

Aidan slipped his arm around Tibba's waist.

John's face tightened, and her heart missed a beat. In this big city, these two cops just happen to know each other? Just her damn luck.

"Everhard. You're with her?"

"I'm with Tibba, yes. You know each other?"

She leaned her body into Aidan's. "John and I are old friends. He helped me out once, so many years ago. Remember, John? When those kids vandalized my house."

John gave her a blank stare. Then he nodded. "Right. Yeah. Years ago."

She glanced from one cop to the other and back. "Are you in the same, what is it called, unit?"

"District." Aidan squeezed her waist. "Years ago. A group of us get together once in a while. Play some cards."

Her eyes narrowed. "Cards? You gamble?"

"Just a bit of poker. A little OTB at the track once in a while to blow off steam."

O'Connor cleared his throat. "So, you two a couple or something?"

Aidan beamed. "Sure hope so." He squeezed her closer. "First date. I think it went well, hey, Tib?"

She smiled up at him, placed her palm on the chest of his jacket, and swallowed hard. "It went great."

"I'll go get the car." He extended his meaty hand. "O'Connor, good to see you, man."

John shook Aidan's hand with all the enthusiasm of child getting vaccinated. "Yeah. See you around." He watched Aidan stride down the block and around the corner before turning back to Tibba. "He doesn't know, does he?"

She shook her head. "And I'd like to keep it that way. You know what I mean?"

He nodded. "It'll be our little secret." He leaned in closer. "I'll be around to see you, real soon."

Her eyes narrowed. "Just so you know, my prices have gone up again."

He huffed. "I don't think so. In fact, my price just went to zero." He winked, brushed past her, and disappeared into the bar two doors down from the restaurant.

Tibba's eyes fluttered shut and she clenched her jaw. "Fuck."

To be or not to be

Finnegan lingered at the threshold of his mother's room, his temple resting on the door jamb. Her bed and floor were littered with clothes. Jeans sat in a lump on the floor, hardwood visible through the leg holes, like she'd disappeared into thin air and her pants collapsed where she'd stood. A flowery blouse was draped across the end of her bed next to a lacy, scarlet bra.

Dangling from the doorknob of her closet was a pair of red underwear. Shiny. Silky. Not much more than string. His breath caught in his throat. He glanced at the stairs, listened to the sounds she made in the kitchen: the click of a lighter, the pop of a cork, the crinkle of tinfoil. He tiptoed in and snatched the thong, tucked it in his pocket.

The steps creaked and his heart jumped.

"Finny, dinner in half an hour!"

He froze. When she retreated back to the kitchen, he sighed, put her underwear back on the knob, and trod into his room.

He laid on his stomach on the hardwood of his bedroom floor and stretched his arm as far under the bed as he could reach. His index fingertip found the box his old winter boots came in and he dragged it out, leaving a path through the dust. One thing he could always rely on — his mother would never look under his bed. She loved a tidy house, but drew the line at anything the eye couldn't see without crawling around on her hands and knees. She saved that effort for the garden.

He sat up and rested his back against the bed, blew fine powder off the lid, lifted it, and peered inside.

His collection. What started so many years ago as just weeds and plants and flowers, bits and pieces of the garden that he loved, whose odours filled his head with memories of springtime and dreams of

Christmas dinner. To that, he'd added dismembered rose stems, the ones with evil thorns that cut his flesh, along with roses he'd beheaded from the malevolent stalks.

He shimmied the box side to side. The bones always fell to the bottom. Their rattle calmed him. Birdie's cross and chain shushed against the cardboard and kept her memory fresh. Kept his guilt front and centre in his life, where it belonged. He didn't deserve to be calm. Hadn't earned the right to be happy. Shouldn't be allowed to live at all. A sharp knife drawn across his wrists at just the right spot would be all it would take. He'd do it in the garden, next to where he'd buried her. But his goal was to join her. And if she wasn't there, what was the point?

All he'd had to do was let Birdie kiss him. How terrible could that have been?

Grade nine finals started the next week. Then he faced another summer without her. The last summer before high school. He needed her now more than ever, what with his mother sending him off to be a camp counsellor for half of August. And with all the changes in his body, his voice. The inconvenient erections. But would he have told Birdie those private things? Could he tell anyone about his growing obsession with his mother's body?

He fished out Birdie's cross and stared at it, traced the pattern carved into the silver with one fingertip. Her crucifix connected them. Ensured he never forgot what he'd done — not that he could if he wanted to. It was more than a memento of their friendship. Not just a souvenir of the worst day of his life. It was a talisman, but without the good luck. A manifestation of Birdie herself. And it needed a better resting place. Somewhere less dusty and not surrounded by the bones of strangers. Somewhere soft and warm.

He opened the top drawer of his nightstand, kissed the cross, rubbed it on his jeans to wipe his nasty spit off, and shoved the necklace way in the back amid his socks and underwear.

He plucked each dried and dead bit of flora from their makeshift casket. Purple dead nettle. Fuchsia bougainvillea. Blooms of impatiens and his mother's prized hellebore. Expensive, so there weren't many, but poisonous to animals while being okay for birds to eat. She called them the Cerberus of her garden domain, protecting it from devilish rodents and pissing cats. When he was a kid, he liked to repeat the plant's name because he didn't get in trouble for saying the hell part.

With a cemetery of floral corpses laid out on the floor, he upturned the box and dumped out the rest. Bones clattered against the wood like a macabre game of Yahtzee. He picked up each piece, his collection now numbering in the dozens, and laid them in a group alongside the plants.

He slipped his hand deep between the mattress and box spring and retrieved the pages he'd hidden there. Ripped from the anatomy text at the library, the illustrations of the human skeletal system helped him identify each bone. Folded between the bone drawings was an inventory list of human remains. He'd figured out long ago that they weren't chicken bones. Not birds or mice or small animals. There were actual human bones buried in his mother's garden. Fifteen partial phalanges, two clavicles, six metatarsals — which might have been more phalanges, it was hard to tell — five vertebrae, a fragment of a mandible, one sacrum, and seventeen teeth including two with gold fillings.

And then there was the jewelry ....

He tore a corner from the paper his list was written on and tucked it into the hollow of his cheek. He speared the hole of a gold band with one finger, raised it to the light and examined it as he had done so many times before. Would this be the night the ring exposed its origins? Whose hand had worn it? It appeared to be a man's wedding band, thick and sturdy and wide. At least seven millimeters, maybe even a whole centimeter.

He slipped it off his finger and peered at the engraving on the inside. It was worn down, but he could make out "18k," which more library research told him meant eighteen karats, seventy-five percent pure gold.

He turned the ring so the light would catch the rest of the engraving. "Olive Juice." Whatever the hell that meant. Maybe it was an antique. He used to imagine the garden was an old burial ground, an ancient cemetery and the whole house was resting atop a mass grave from some prehistoric war. But that wouldn't explain the portion of nylon strap attached to a broken wristwatch. It was unlikely that Timex existed in cave man days. He'd toyed with the notion that his grandfather had been a serial killer. But the nickel from 1975 proved that wrong. His grandfather had been dead for years by then. His grandmother too.

Finnegan sighed and tossed the watch back in the box. It landed next to a tiny silver hoop earring. He pressed his palms to his face, rubbed the metacarpal of his thumb against his supraorbital process. No, there was only one suspect. Only one killer in the family.

A tear dripped down his cheek.

Correction. Two killers.

... thy mother's bleeding heart

Static and white noise spit from the speakers. Finnegan squinted against the bright August sun and twisted the tuner knob until it finally landed on something resembling music. Some oldies station with shitty reception and some dude singing about how wonderful the world was.

Bullshit.

He squirmed against the passenger seat, his bare legs sticking to the hot vinyl. The fuzz of puberty-fueled hair that had blossomed on his lower legs had darkened and thickened over the summer. His budding manhood barely fit inside his old jean's that his mother had cut into shorts. The denim squeezed in all the wrong places and pulled his pubes out by the roots.

An edge of peeling skin on his forearm from one of the many blisters brought on by his biggest nemesis, the sun, taunted him. He tugged at it until a two-inch long piece of dermis came free from his body. He held it aloft and let it wave in the hot summer breeze coming in through the open window before flicking it out into the big, wide world.

His mother tossed her cigarette butt out the driver's side window and lit another. She stared at the road, but he wasn't convinced her mind was on her driving.

"Do you want to know how camp went?"

She didn't respond.

"Do you even give a damn?"

She blinked. "Don't swear."

"At least I know you're in there."

She blew smoke out the window. "How was camp?"

He rolled his eyes. "It sucked. I'm not going back. I make a shitty camp counsellor."

"I doubt that."

"I do. The little brats don't listen to me at all. And the last night? They put a snake in my bed. A snake!"

"You love snakes."

"Not in my fucking bed."

She turned and glared at him. "You picked up some choice new vocabulary out there in the wilderness."

He nodded. "Yes I did. Along with a sunburn, a million mosquito bites, poison oak, and blood loss from a thousand leeches."

She snickered. "Exaggerate much?"

"It was awful, Mom. I'm never going again. You can't make me." He picked at a scab on his elbow. "How was your holiday from your burdensome child? Couldn't have been too restful. You look like shit."

"Gee, thanks."

Dark half-moons below her puffy eyes betrayed her exhaustion. Her fingernails were all broken, dirt beneath them. She used to take such good care of her hands. He closed his eyes, welcomed the memory of her nails scraping against his skin. When was the last time she'd scratched his bare back? He shivered, opened his eyes and cleared his throat. "Work in the garden much?"

She pulled into the driveway and jammed the sticky gearshift into park. "You could say that."

What the hell did that mean?

"Keep out of the northwest corner. Fresh bulbs."

He squinted. "Fresh bulbs. Right." He eyeballed her as she swung her tanned legs out of the car. The stitching on the car's seat left red lines on the backs of her legs, starting at the tender skin behind her knees and ending at the hem of her short shorts. He peeled his gaze from her toned legs and pinched his thigh hard.

The ashtray overflowed with lipstick-stained cigarette butts. He plucked one from the heap, sniffed it, and licked the paper.

"You gonna sit in there all day and bake?" His mother stood behind the car, hands on hips.

He tucked the butt into his back pocket and climbed out of the sweatbox the car had become, hauled his duffel bag from the trunk and slung it over his shoulder. "So am I coming in? Or do you have a date?" He made air quotes. "In which case, maybe I'll take my dinner outside, eat under the bougainvillea, and kill some time."

She unlocked the back door and swung it open, following him into the kitchen. "Cut the tone, mister. You wouldn't have anything to eat if I didn't have all those dates." Her eyes rimmed red and tears welled up.

He gave her a blank stare and yawned.

He was so sick of this life. Of the lies and the hiding. Of sitting outside knowing full well what was going on just inside the door. Now it all just made her sad? Whatever. It was so much better when he was little and stupid. There was a glimmer of hope that maybe, one day, in some fairy tale that would never come true, one of her "dates" would magically turn into a father. And now there was more than a glimmer. Now she had Aidan. One man, the same man, in her real bed, not the one in the guest room. Reality made Finnegan sick to his stomach.

"Aren't you getting a little old for this? Hell, you're pushing forty. Maybe it's time you got a real job. One I didn't have to be embarrassed by."

The slap of her open palm against his cheek stunned him.

"You're fourteen. Maybe you ought to get a job. You can support me for a change. How does that sound?"

He touched his fingertips to his face. "You hit me."

She dropped to her knees, covered her face with both hands, and sobbed. "Oh, God. I'm so sorry, Finny. I'm so sorry."

He patted the back of her head and sat beside her, encircled her shoulders with both arms. "I deserved it, Mom. I was an ass." He wiped her tears with his shirt. "You've always taken care of me. Protected me. When I need you most, you're always there." Tears wet his cheeks. "I'm sorry, Mom. You know I love you, right?"

She melted against him and continued to sob. He'd never seen her like this. She'd never been anything but strong and confident. This was new.

He touched his lips to her forehead and stroked her hair until she calmed, breathed in strawberries and musk.

She pulled away and sat with her back against the kitchen cupboards, motioned at a box of Kleenex on the counter.

He reached for it and handed her one. "Did something ... happen?"

She blew her nose and wiped mascara from her cheeks. She stared at the linoleum, wouldn't look him in the eye.

"Officer Everhard didn't break up with you, did he?" Please, please, please let it be true.

She shook her head. "No. We're good. He's coming for dinner tonight."

Finnegan's shoulders slumped.

"I guess," she tilted her head back and banged it gently against the oak, "I'm just tired." She tugged another Kleenex from the box and blew her nose again. "You're right, you know. I need to get out. Get a real job. Stop hooking."

That was the first time she called it anything other than dating. He blinked. "You do?"

She nodded. "If I don't, Aidan will find out one day. I don't want to lose him."

Finnegan patted her bare knee, stared at the contrast of his burned skin against her natural, easy tan. He swallowed. "You really love him, don't you?"

She smiled and fresh tears filled her eyes. "I really do."

Finnegan forced a smile and squeezed her knee. "Then we'd better get dinner started." He helped her up off the floor and sent her upstairs to shower. If that cop's presence meant she'd stop selling her body, Finnegan had to find a way to be okay with that. Okay that they might get married one day. Okay with her having sex with another man in the room right next to where Finnegan slept.

He closed his eyes and envisioned his mother's head bobbing in Pomelo Fist's lap.

No. This was not okay. It never would be.

Thou art thy mother's glass

Another week, another date. But no shooing him out of the house tonight. His mother didn't demand he march outside and bide his time wandering the neighbourhood, or listening to his Walkman, or mastering the skateboard. Like that would ever happen.

She and Officer Everhard, or Aidan as he now insisted on being called, had spent the evening watching videos on their new Betamax, drinking wine, and necking on the chesterfield not five feet from Finnegan. He'd stormed from the room, ran up the stairs, and slammed his bedroom door shut. But did they get the message? Hell, no. Less than an hour later and bang, bang, bang, her headboard bounced against the wall right next to his bed.

He turned up his radio to drown out the sounds of his mother fucking. He'd never heard it before, being that he was always in the garden. Reading, thinking, killing his best friend. Never right in the next room where his mother's every moan and gasp whispered in his ear.

Bang, bang, bang.

Had they been doing this the whole time he was at camp? Was this his new normal?

He put his headphones on, but it barely muffled the noise. He tried to concentrate on his collection, sorting the bones by body type, or at least body region. Arms in one box. Hands in another. Feet, legs, spines each got their own container. He rubbed his palm down the biggest find yet, a femur. A long, solid bone, the shaft smooth like ivory except for three hairline cracks. He stroked the bone in time with the banging headboard to the sound of his mother's sex and Romeo Void's *Never Say Never.*

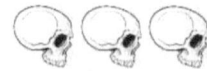

The blanket rose and fell with her breath. In the moonlight, the repeating circular pattern of thread nubbins on the bedspread threw tiny shadows, like a thousand miniature Stonehenges. On every exhale, a tiny whistle sang through her nostrils. Finnegan smiled. He gazed at her skin that glowed an eerie blue in the dark, like a breathing corpse.

She stirred and shifted position. Musk wafted from the covers. Finnegan closed his eyes and breathed it in.

"Jesus, Finny!" His mother sat up, clutched the bedspread to her chest and scooted away until her back was against the headboard. It banged against the wall. "You scared the shit out of me." She ran her hand through her hair and peered at the clock. "It's four-thirty. What are you doing?"

"I don't want him in our house."

She squinted. "Who?"

"Officer Everhard. You need to stop seeing him."

"Aidan?" She yawned. "Don't be ridiculous."

"I'm not being ridiculous. You want to sleep with him? Do it somewhere else. His place. Hotel. Back alley. I don't really care."

"He's not that kind of date."

"Well you screw that kind of date here. So it stands to reason you'd do your boyfriend somewhere else." He slid along the bed and leaned his elbow on her bent knee. "Or just don't have sex with him at all. This is my house too, and I don't like him."

"If you want to go hang out in the garden while he's here, feel free." She tossed the bedspread aside and swung her legs over the mattress, knocking his elbow off its perch. "Who I have sex with and where we do it is none of your business. This is my house," she tapped her clavicle with her fingertips. "I pay the bills. I'm the adult. You're just a kid." She stood and shifted her satin nightgown. It fell around her torso, the lacy hem caressing her thighs. "Go back to bed." She touched his forehead with the back of her hand. "You're delirious or something."

She shut the bathroom door behind her and flicked on the light.

The shadow of her feet shuffling around the tile crept under the door and stretched across the bedroom floor. Finnegan squeezed his eyes closed and imagined the sound of her metatarsals rattling at the bottom of a shoebox.

It is the green-ey'd monster, which doth mock the meat it feeds on

Finnegan peered over his book and stared across the lunchroom. His noontime routine: spying on Deborah Arbic while pretending to devour whatever out-of-date novel was required reading. This semester? *The Great Gatsby*. A tedious book filled with unlikeable characters he just couldn't relate to.

High school was proving to be no different than junior high. The cool kids were still cool. The jocks still jocks. The fact he'd grown three inches over the summer, that his body was filling out and his muscles were developing didn't change a damn thing. He was still a ginger-haired outcast.

Hi-ho the derry-o. The cheese stands alone.

Deborah glanced in his direction, a half-smile on her face. He lowered the book and gave her a slight wave, his own grin impossible to hide.

She raised one eyebrow, grimaced, and rolled her eyes.

Finnegan slid down in his chair and stared at the printed pages without seeing the words. He peered around the book. Deborah ignored him anew. She sat at her regular table, the queen surrounded by her court. In grade two he would dream of her raven pigtails, each plait shining, reflecting any tiny bit of light in sparkles of blue. She gave up pigtails years ago and now opted for teased hair and sky-high bangs glued in place with helmet-like hairspray. He loved that her bangs were off her forehead. It showed off her prominent supraorbital foramen.

Every popular girl followed her fashion lead. Leg warmers, slouchy tops with one shoulder bared, and so many crosses. Symbols of a god she worshipped on Sundays, but conveniently set aside

Monday to Saturday to pursue more earthly pleasures. Like fucking Jason, jock and airhead with perfect blonde hair and a leather Members Only jacket.

Finnegan would steal Deborah away. Swoop in and rescue her from the cliché she had become. Separate her from her tribe, that group of so-called friends that made his life miserable for not fitting in. Not one of them could express their own identities. They just followed the trends, followed Deborah and Jason. Followed, followed, followed.

Was that what Finnegan hated? That they were followers? Or was it that they wouldn't let him follow too? He hadn't made another real friend since Birdie died. No one wanted him. Or maybe he just couldn't bear to let anyone else in. Not anyone he had a real chance of being friends with anyway. But he'd let Deborah in. In a heartbeat. Despite the fact that she was a bitch and barely acknowledged his existence. But that ass. And those lips.

Would Birdie have fallen prey to teased hair and Madonnaesque fashion choices? Not a chance in hell. She'd still be a cross-eyed tomboy, wearing T-shirts emblazoned with images from the latest sci-fi movie she'd be obsessing over. He'd still be helping her with her homework, making sure she didn't fail grade ten, like he'd helped her through every year since they'd found each other in Mrs. Findlay's grade one class. The shunned and the bullied and the friendless, they do stick together.

More than two years later and the world still thought Birdie was missing. Kidnapped maybe, even though no one ever called her parents for ransom in exchange for her safe return. Some whispered how she'd been killed by a lunatic after being molested. That there was a serial killer on the loose. But no other girls had disappeared and no one had found a body. So many rumours. So many lies.

The cool kid table erupted in laughter. Finnegan brought his gaze into focus on the group, all of them pointing at him and making faces.

"What's the matter, Finny baby? You on another planet like usual?" Jason high-fived the guy to his right.

"Don't call me baby." It's all he could think of to say. Lamest comeback on earth.

Deborah backhanded Jason's coat. "Don't be such an ass." She gathered her schoolwork, freed her legs from the picnic table seat, and sashayed toward Finnegan, headed straight for his table.

He laid his book down, his eyes riveted to her face. Could she hear his heart beating? He swallowed. This was it. She was going to make a move. Maybe ask him to join her crew at lunch. Slip him her number.

She dropped her schoolwork on the table and propped one foot on the seat of a chair.

He ogled her knee while she slouched her leg warmer down to her ankle, baring most of her calf. He got an erection and his cheeks burned. He sat up straighter and pinched his thigh.

She'd sit down with him. He could offer her some of his lunch. Maybe the apple he hadn't touched yet. He'd let her have a bite, then he'd take one, taste where her lips had been, mingle her saliva with his. He swallowed. "H-hey, Deborah."

She glanced at him sideways, rolled her eyes and shook her head, retrieved her books, and walked away without one word.

His chest tightened as he watched her perfect ass retreat.

What did he expect, that after eight years of ignoring him, she'd suddenly throw herself in his lap and stick her tongue down his throat?

A slip of paper had floated from her notebook and alighted on the table next to his hand. He snatched it and drew it into his lap. It was a part of an assignment, torn from the lined pages of her math workbook, filled with numbers written by her soft, porcelain hand. The exaggerated curves of her twos and that funny way she had of crossing her sevens made his groin ache. He sniffed the paper, touched his tongue to it. Then ripped a little piece off with his teeth and sucked on the essence of Deborah.

"Hey, loser. What the fuck are you doing?"

A shadow crossed his book. He looked up, the paper still in his mouth.

Jason laughed. "You're eating paper? What are you, two? Hey, Deb, check it out. Loser here is chomping on your math homework."

Deborah stormed over and took what was left of the paper from Finnegan's hand. "How did you get this?"

He dropped his head. "It fell from your book."

"And you ate it?" Her squeal pierced his ears. "You freak! Never speak to me again." She spun around and stormed off.

When had he ever spoken to her before?

Jason laughed and pointed at him, then held his thumb and forefinger up to his forehead in the shape of the letter L. "Loser, Finnegan. Big, fat, red-haired loser."

Finnegan closed his eyes and fought back tears. No way would he let Jason see him cry. If he ever got the chance, he'd beat the jock's face in with a shovel. Bury him in the garden right next to Deborah. She'd make a lovely corpse.

1984

Keep thy foot out of brothels

One thing about having a straight job — it was boring as hell. The pay was shit, the work tedious. Without any prior experience, the best Tibba could get was stocking shelves at Food City and spending endless hours pricing cereal and coffee, Stove Top stuffing and Hamburger Helper. Another month of the daily *shick-shick-thud* of the pricing gun and she may just go back to prostitution.

No. She wouldn't. The stakes were too high. Aidan's love. Finny's too. And her self-respect, that had to count for something. Besides, she got discounts on food here, so really, the steaks were lower than ever.

Her son's face darted through her mind and morphed into a vision of Adam. It wasn't just her imagination anymore. Finny was maturing. Every day that passed, the soft edge of adolescence mutated into chiselled cheeks and a square jaw. Into biceps and hairy calves. Did he inherit his father's ….? She blinked and dropped her chin, fumbled with the pricing gun.

The way Finny looked at her had changed. His gazes lingered, a hint of a smile in his eyes. And he hugged her more often than he had in years. No more frustration at being banished to the backyard. She'd lied to herself all those years that he didn't know what her brand of dating included. Of course he did. How could he not? Now he looked, what? Pleased? Dare she consider that he might be proud of her?

She tugged on the hideous blue polyester vest that kept shifting around her breasts and cutting off the circulation under her armpits. A year later and her manager still claimed her special-order-sized vest hadn't arrived. He just liked how it squeezed her boobs together. And he spent most of the day staring at her cleavage.

Sexual harassment. That wasn't new. Not being able to throw him out and deny him services in the future? That was hard to swallow.

She finished pricing the canned pork and beans and moved on to the bakery section where loaves of fresh bread were waiting for her in the chrome rack. She wheeled it out in front of the shelves and checked her sheet. "Sixty-six cents for a loaf of bread? That's too much." She peered around. No manager in sight. She set the pricing gun to fifty-six cents. "Much better." *Shick shick rustle.* She kind of liked the sound of the price stickers on plastic bags of soft bread. More satisfying than the dull thud of cardboard boxes, or the hollow clink of tin cans.

"There's my working girl."

Two big arms circled her waist from behind. Aidan's nightstick pushed against the ass of her brown nylon pants and he ran his hands up to her chest.

She closed her eyes and leaned back to rest her head against his shoulder. "Pardon me, mister, but please don't squeeze the melons."

He snickered in her ear and nibbled on the lobe.

If he wasn't careful, she was going to drop to the polished floor and fuck his brains out right there in the bakery aisle.

"So," he spun her around, "dinner tonight?"

"Sure, what's your fancy? I can put a roast in when I get home." Please say no. Cooking was a chore and, though she was really trying for Aidan's sake, she sucked at it. His partner stood behind him. "Hey, Dan."

Dan nodded and tipped his hat. He had a weird grin on his face like he knew a secret.

"No cooking required. I'm taking you out. How about Mexican?"

She clasped hands together and placed them under her chin. "Chi-Chi's?"

"Yes ma'am."

He always looked so pleased with himself when he made her happy, so she over-acted her appreciation. She clapped and threw her arms around his neck. "Yay! Con queso and fried ice cream!"

For the rest of her shift, she hummed a little tune in her head. Not only because she loved nights out with Aidan, but because she'd do anything to drown out the Muzak version of top-forty hits that played incessantly from the tinny speakers in the ceiling. What was that? An organ and accordion version of *Little Red Corvette*?

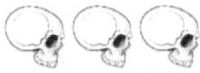

"You want more?" Tibba pushed the remains of the chili con queso closer to Aidan.

He held both his hands up and leaned back in his chair. "I'm stuffed."

She ran her index finger inside the bowl like a spatula and sucked the spicy cheese dip off. If her eyes could roll any farther back in her head, she'd be looking behind her. Best foodgasm ever.

"Can I get you dessert?" The waitress in the long, brightly coloured dress with puffy off-the-shoulder sleeves grinned down at them. "How about some fried ice cream?"

"God, yes," Tibba said.

"And you, sir?"

Tibba squinted. Did that little tart just wink at her man?

He patted his stomach. "Just the one please. And two spoons. And two more margaritas."

She pranced off to fetch the deep-fried yumminess. Tibba eyed her tiny waist and imagined a perfectly pert ass under that festive, striped dress. Pert like she used to have. Before pregnancy, motherhood, and almost twenty years of hooking. In a little over a year, she'd be forty years old. Forty! How in the hell did that happen?

The tart returned and deposited their drinks. She gathered up the empty glasses and — winked! That little bitch winked at Aidan again. The heat rose in her cheeks. She might have to kick some pert little ass.

Aidan held up his glass. "To you. Woman of my dreams. Love of my life." He blushed and shook his head. "Wow. That sounded way less lame in my head."

She reached out and took his hand. "It was perfect." She lifted her glass with her other hand. "To me!" She licked salt from the rim and took a big slurp. Something clinked against her teeth. Something that was not ice. She peered into the glass. "Ew, there's something in the bottom."

"What is it?" Aidan was awfully eager to discover what grody shit the bartender had dropped into her booze.

She hooked the nasty thing with the tines of her fork. She blinked. Lime juice and tequila dripped from a diamond and gold ring. She looked up at Aidan. "Is this what I think it is?"

He pushed his chair out and dropped to one knee, retrieved the ring from the fork. "Tibba MacGillivray," he took her left hand and held the ring in front of it.

Her heart accelerated.

"Will you marry me?"

Dear, sweet, corny Aidan. His face blurred behind her tears. Words wouldn't come out of her mouth, so she nodded her head with enough vigour that he couldn't mistake her intention.

He slipped the ring on her finger, cupped her face in both his hands and kissed her.

The tables around them exploded in applause and a few hoots and hollers.

He rested his forehead against hers. "I love you, future Mrs. Everhard."

She didn't have the heart to tell him she'd never give up her name. For Finny's sake, MacGillivray was staying. She couldn't start calling him Finny Ev, now could she?

The waitress appeared beside them, patted Tibba on the shoulder and winked at her. "Congratulations."

And oft, my jealousy shapes faults that are not

"He what?" A phantom pomelo fist punched Finnegan in the gut.

"Proposed." She held her left hand up and wiggled her fingers. "Finny, I'm getting married! Can you believe it?" She stretched her arm out and admired the gold band in the sunlight.

He tossed the remote aside and dragged himself off the chesterfield. He held her ring finger, leaned in, and eyeballed the paltry excuse for a diamond engagement ring. "Kind of minuscule."

She pulled her hand away. "Can't you just say small? Besides, he's a cop, not a Rockefeller." She stared at the small stone and smiled. "I love it."

"Gee, Mom. Great observation skills. Yes, he's a cop. Can't wait for you to marry the guy. To have the fucking police move into the house. *This* house." He gestured to the guest room. "*Our* house." He crossed his arms and stuck his chest out. "I wonder if he likes gardening?" He raised his eyebrows.

Something he couldn't pin down skittered across her face. Panic perhaps. Or simply denial. "I — I don't know what you mean."

"Oh, come on, Mom. We don't have to talk about it. I'd rather we never, ever talk about it. But you know exactly what I mean."

"Fine." She chewed her lower lip and stared down at the ring. "We'll just have to set some boundaries. He'll have to understand that the garden is my special place. That he can look, but he can't touch."

Finnegan snorted. "Look but don't touch. Not exactly the axiom you live by."

She slapped him.

He held one hand to his face. "You hit me." His other hand drew into a fist. "Again."

"Well, this time you deserved it. Don't disrespect me like that." She eyed his fist and took a step backwards.

"You mean out loud? I can keep on disrespecting you in silence?" He brushed past her and ran up the stairs, slammed his bedroom door shut behind him. He launched himself onto his bed face first, covered his head with a pillow, and screamed into the mattress until his throat was raw. Spent and sweaty, he tossed the pillow aside and rolled onto his back. He searched the popcorn ceiling for familiar shapes. A dog's head in the corner. A lopsided Bat-Signal by the closet. A coiled snake, which doubled as a pile of shit, near the window. And straight above his head, a cross. When he was younger it was just a plus sign with a long tail, but the past few years it had transformed into Birdie's crucifix. Math was comforting, the known, the calculable. But math didn't bring Birdie back. That ceiling cross kept him off-kilter. Filled him with unrest. Denied him peace. Thanks to him, she'd find no peace, so he didn't deserve any. Didn't deserve to be calm or content. Torment was his jam.

He slid off his bed and dug several boxes out from under it. His collection was getting so big he'd soon be out of floor space. He sifted through the bones and dried plants with one finger.

Boring.

He needed some new body parts. And a new storage space.

He tugged at the closet door. The wood always swelled up in the warmer months. It popped opened, the squeal of wood-on-wood like a cry of pain. A pile of old board games took up most of the top shelf. Time to dump this crap in the garbage. To put away childish things. He tossed the games onto the floor and slid in one box of his collection. There was lots of room for expansion.

He groped around near the back of his underwear drawer until his fingers found the silver chain of Birdie's crucifix. Held in his thumb and forefinger, the chain emerged from its hiding place. The sun glinted off the sharp edge of the pendant. He undid the clasp, took a deep breath, and placed it around his neck. He closed his eyes and fingered the vertical and horizontal bars, the stipes and patibulum. It was heavy, all albatross-like, and it burned his skin.

Or he was losing his shit.

These pretty pleasures might me move, To live with thee and be thy love

"Move in? Before we're married?" She touched her fingertips to her chest and pulled out her best shocked-damsel face.

Aidan looked around the room. "Did I just step into Nineteen-Fifty-three?" He took her hands. "Come on, Tib, it makes sense. My rent can go toward your mortgage. We can split the utilities. And no worries about driving home after some wine and some," he grinded his hips, "bow chicka wow wow."

She laughed. "I know it makes financial sense." Even though she had no mortgage, the cash would come in handy since minimum wage didn't bring in the bucks like hooking did. "I'm not sure Finny is ready for that. It's just been me and him forever, you know?" And he was right. Maybe this whole idea of living with a cop within yards of her burial ground was crazy. How long could she put off marrying him since she'd already said yes?

"I get that. I can tell by the way he looks at me. Boy's got daggers for eyes. But we'll live together after the wedding anyway. Speaking of which," he pulled her close, "let's set a date."

She put her hand to his chest, inhaled his cologne. Why had she been so stupid and fallen in love with him? Why not pick some simple schmuck without a badge and a gun? "Slow down, tiger. We've only been engaged for three weeks." She pulled away and fished a cigarette out of the pack that always sat on the coffee table.

"True. But we've been dating for almost two years. Why wait?"

She blew smoke at the ceiling. Why indeed? "But it's fall. It'll snow soon. And I'd love to be married in the summer. Maybe in the backyard? It's big enough. We'd save some money." Especially since she didn't have parents to foot the bill.

He took her left hand and twisted her ring until the diamond faced up. "I do."

She scrunched her face. "You do what?"

"Just practicing. I do accept your summer wedding? In the meantime, what about living together?"

She took a long drag on her cigarette. "So, how much do you owe?"

He raised one eyebrow. "Owe?"

"Your gambling habit. Wasn't any of my business before, but now that we're getting married, I need to know. How far down the rabbit hole are you?"

"It's just poker with the guys. A couple of bucks on the ponies."

She crossed her arms. "And? How much?"

He mirrored her stance. "Not a red cent."

That was different. And she didn't buy it for a second. "We're going to need some kind of agreement before we marry."

"What, you don't trust me?"

"I trust you with my heart. With my son. Hell, I trust you with my life. But I don't trust anyone with my money."

He set his jaw and put his hands on his hips. "I see. I don't have any debt. None. And, I don't need nor want your money. But if you're worried about it, we can have a pre-nup."

She nodded. "I can live with that. What other skeletons are in your proverbial closet. I need full disclosure."

He looked amused, his smirk both adorable and irritating as hell. "Well. I guess the biggest issue is, I still live with my mother."

She laughed until she realized he was serious. "You're joking right? Shit, you're almost forty." But now it made sense why he never invited her to his place.

"I am. Which is why I'm desperate to get the hell out of there. And I totally relate to the whole whack mother-son dynamic you and Finn have going on."

She squinted. "Fair enough. Before anybody moves anywhere, we need to have a few … ground rules."

"Name it."

"Finny's space is off limits. He needs his privacy. I don't want to have to put a lock on his door, but I will."

"Got it. Keep out of Finn's room."

"And the garden."

He beamed. "I love gardening."

She shook her head. "No." She pointed at him. "You stay out of my garden."

"Stay out of the garden? Why? Is that where you keep all your exes' bodies?"

She let out a stilted cackle. "No, silly." She turned away and wiped a bead of sweat from her upper lip. "It's *my* garden. My sanctuary. Planting and weeding, it keeps me sane. You can have the lawn, do whatever you want to that. Just stay out of the garden."

His brow furrowed and he pursed his lips. "All right."

"I mean, we can take a couple of lawn chairs out, sit in it. Have a drink at sunset." Her words tumbled out. "Just the upkeep, the planting. The digging. That's all for me."

He crossed his arms. "Is that it? For rules?"

"Nope. One more." She butted her cigarette and sauntered toward him, grasped his lapels in both hands and pulled him into her. She pecked at his mouth, stiff with indignant confusion, then darted her tongue past his teeth.

He succumbed, as he always did.

She took his hand and led him upstairs. "Rule number three." She glanced back at him and blinked a long blink. "Fuck me. Every day."

I would challenge you to a battle of wits, but I see you are unarmed

Finnegan turned a page of the worn copy of *Hamlet* his Language Arts teacher had given him. All the other students were still slogging through *Lord of the Flies*. He'd speed-read it, finished the book report, handed in the extra credit work two weeks ahead of schedule, and devoured an anthology of Shakespeare's lesser-known plays. The second he cracked the cover — which wouldn't be part of the actual curriculum until grade eleven — he was hooked. The intricate prose, the twists, the humour, the violence. And the insults. Those barbs were poetic.

His gait slowed at the curb, his route home so oft travelled he could do it blindfolded. Except for the traffic. A quick glance to ensure no oncoming cars would splat him onto the pavement and he scurried to the other side, his attention rapt by the graveyard scene unfolding before his eyes.

"Hey, carrot top!"

Finnegan spun around at the familiar taunt. "Really, Jason? Carrot top? What are you, ten?"

A block away, Jason crossed his arms. "Okay. How about fire crotch?"

"Real original, shit-for-brains."

A rock whizzed past Finnegan's head and sideswiped his ear. He staggered backward. Another rock hit him in the stomach, punching the air out of his gut.

He doubled over, his arms cradling his belly. When he caught his breath, he straightened to his full height. He stood at least an inch taller than Jason. He wasn't buff yet, but not scrawny either. And, for the first time in his life, he wasn't afraid. "That all you got? Come on, chicken. Bring it." Finnegan clenched and unclenched his fists. "I'll beat thee, but I would infect my hands."

"The fuck you say?"

Finnegan smirked. "I would challenge you to a battle of wits, but I see that you are unarmed."

"That's it, nerd. You're dead." Jason's two best friends and reprobate sidekicks appeared from behind a hedge.

Of course he didn't come alone. They always travelled in a pack.

Finnegan's heartbeat quickened. *Come on, feet, time to turn tail and run.* But he was frozen in place. He'd been terrorized for too many years. And he'd had enough. "Come," he yelled, "come, you froward and unable worms!"

The three boys broke into a run and closed distance fast. Finnegan's feet beat out his indignation. He turned and he ran.

Jason tackled him at the waist and brought him down, knees first, against the pavement. Coach would be so proud.

Jason turned Finnegan over and straddled him while the delinquent accomplices held Finnegan's legs and arms.

Punch after punch landed on his face. Pain seared across his cheek and stars danced behind his eyes. All these years, he'd figured that only happened in cartoons, but there they were, flashes of light in the periphery.

Jason scrabbled to his feet and kicked Finnegan in the gut. "That's for Deborah."

Finnegan rolled on his side and spat blood onto the concrete. "For what?"

"Everyone knows you have the hots for her. She's mine."

Finnegan coughed. "I thought you were fucking Alison."

He took a kick to the groin, groaned and blinked back tears.

"Back off, you ginger, paper-eating, nerd freak. Aw, is fire crotch crying? Poor widdle Finny baby. Go on and run home to your mommy."

Finnegan rolled onto his back and swallowed a mouthful of metallic blood-tinged saliva. "Speaking of mommies." His voice cracked and he wagged a finger in the air. "Villain, I have done thy mother."

Jason's face turned crimson. "You sick fuck." Each boy delivered another kick to Finnegan's ribs and then jogged away. "Next time," Jason called over his shoulder, "I'll break something."

Finnegan sat up. His head spun. He wiped his mouth on his T-shirt, the white cotton marred by scarlet streaks. He poked at his ribs and winced. "Villain, I believe thee already has." He laid back on the sidewalk and laughed. The leaves of a maple tree fluttered in the breeze, their shadows danced across his body.

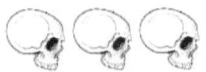

His mother dabbed at his split lip with an alcohol-soaked cotton ball.

He pulled away. "What the hell is that?"

"Bourbon. Now hold still."

Drops of whisky fell from the cotton and stung his tongue. It hurt like hell, but warmed all the way to his belly.

"You might need a couple of stitches. Tell me the bastard's name so I can give him a matching scar." Her face and the freckled skin between her neck and cleavage was pink. It was her tell. He never needed to hear her words to know when she was furious.

Aidan paced behind her. "While I can't officially condone your mother's revenge plot, I agree we need names. Now, Finn."

"Mind your business." Finnegan touched the tip of his tongue to the open wound on his lip.

"They assaulted you. It's a crime and they need to be punished." Aidan crossed his arms and stood in the legs-spread, chest-out, tough-cop stance Finnegan had become all too familiar with.

"You want to go arrest them? That's just great. My mother's boyfriend riding in on his white horse to save the day. They already think I'm a mama's boy. Next time they'll beat me to death. I pass."

Aidan placed a hand on Finnegan's shoulder. "Listen, son."

Finnegan shook his hand away. "I'm not your son. Leave me alone."

"Finnegan Adam MacGillivray! You may not be happy about this arrangement, but you will show Aidan respect. He's been nothing but kind to you. He's just trying to help. Now, apologize."

When he was young, hearing his full name spew from her mouth in that tone sent a chill through him. It didn't mean she was mad. It meant she was disappointed. And that was far worse.

Aidan's face had reddened. But it wasn't anger. He looked embarrassed as hell.

Finnegan turned to his mother. "Screw you." He pushed past her and took the stairs to his room two at a time.

1985

Wedding Bell Blues ~ 5th Dimension

Since the moment Tibba got out of bed — unrested, anxious, joyous — tears had flowed freely down her face. Her breath caught in her throat. She touched her fingertips to her mouth.

Finny gamboled down the stairs fumbling with his tie. It was a gnarled mess of paisley, the tail hanging several inches past the wide blade. His face was a mask of frustration, evidenced by the pink in his cheeks.

He'd grown so tall in the past few months. His scrawny frame was long and lean and muscled. The flaming hair that used to hang in his eyes was a short crop of thick bronze. What did they say? Business in the front, party in the back. She'd asked him to braid it for this occasion, but he'd scrunched up his face, the hint of a moustache atop his full upper lip twitching, and said, "You want me to sport a rat tail to walk you down the aisle? No way."

He stopped a few feet from her and grinned. "Wow, Mom. You look," he gestured at her with both hands. "You're beautiful."

Finny wasn't long on compliments. His understated approval was high praise indeed.

She held the ruffled edges of the flouncy skirt of her bohemian wedding dress and curtsied. "Thank you, kind sir." She eyed his crooked tie. "Here, let me." Her deft fingers undid his mess and in three breaths he had a perfect double Windsor, snug under his burgeoning Adam's apple.

Tibba swallowed hard. Adam's apple. So literal in this case. He was a doppelganger for his father, a poltergeist of her past mistakes. If she could go back, would she change anything?

Hell no. She'd do it all over again, including smashing Adam upside the head, hacking his body into manageable pieces and burying him just metres from where she slept, just to have these moments with her baby boy.

Finny tugged on the tie to loosen its grip on his neck, bent and kissed her cheek. "It's not too late you know."

"For what?"

"To back out. Call it off. Run away."

Her head snapped up. "Stop that right now. Why can't you just be happy for me?"

"Because, mother, this is ridiculous."

"I'm marrying him, Finnegan. End of discussion. Can't you see how good he is for me?"

"Well, he's not good for me." He clenched his lips and glanced at the ceiling. "Ever think that maybe, just maybe, he's suspicious? He's interrogated both of us so many times, you think it's a coincidence he," he made air quotes, "fell in love with you?"

"You're being paranoid. And ridiculous. He does love me. For real." She backed away from him, overtaken by doubt and nausea. "I forgot my shoes upstairs. Get them for me."

He saluted her. "Yes ma'am."

A slow trickle of people shuffled by the front walk and made their way into the back yard. Through the lace curtain that covered the little window in the front door, a procession of cops, cops' wives and kids, and her co-workers and the spouses she'd never met, filed past. A sea of law enforcement stood in her yard, milling about near the entrance to her garden. The irony amused her and made her heart race, in equal measure.

At least you didn't choose white, you little whore. You should be wearing red. Or maybe black. Half whore, half murderer, one hundred percent the devil's bride. God will make sure you rot in hell. Won't be hard, Lucifer already owns your soul.

Tibba wiped a fleck of mascara from under one eye and ignored her dead mother's voice. Fuck her. She wasn't invited anyway.

She caught her reflection in the mirror by the front door. Not too shabby for a forty-year-old broad. Tiny pink flowers of every shade, from the palest pastel to bright hellfire red, adorned the ecru dress, embroidered along the peasant neckline and ruffled edges that dangled off the shoulder. A red sash cleaved the frock at the middle. She'd tied it in a large bow at the base of her back, the bow's tails dangling over her backside and ending near the skirt's edge just below her knees.

"You ready?"

She turned to find Aidan standing behind her, his forage cap cradled in his arm. His dress blues were starched and pressed, the red stripe of his pants and the band of his cap, a perfect match to her sash. The silver buttons that ran from mid-chest to below his waist gleamed almost as brightly as his smile.

"Hey, isn't it bad luck for the groom to see his bride before the ceremony?" Finny dropped her red satin shoes at her feet and held her hand while she stepped into them.

"I don't believe in bad luck." Aidan squeezed Finny's shoulder with one hand. "Only good luck. And today, I'm pretty sure that's all I've got ahead of me." He held out his hand.

Finny hesitated, rolled his eyes, then took it. Aidan teared up, pulled Finny into a hug and slapped Finny's back, macho-man style.

Her son's shoulders inched toward his ears and his whole body stiffened. But he held his tongue. It was more than she could have hoped for.

Tibba blinked back tears. Whose life was this anyway, and when was the hammer going to come down and screw it all up again?

Maybe right now. And maybe by her own words.

"Finny Mac, can you give Aidan and me a minute?" She waited until her son exited the back door. When it clicked shut, she turned to her future husband. Or at least she hoped he still was.

She took both his hands in hers, keenly aware of the size of his. For months after they'd started dating, she waited for one of those hands to clench into a fist and strike her. Waited for his nasty temper to bubble to the surface. But that day never arrived. He'd never so much as raised his voice. Never made her feel small or stupid. He was even gentle in bed.

Right up to that moment, she'd been okay with him not knowing her truth, because this relationship, like any other she'd tried to have over the years, would not last. Hell, she'd figured he'd be buried in the garden by now. She couldn't stand it any longer. He had to know so he could make an informed decision about the rest of his life. It was only fair.

He bounced her hands up and down. "What's up? Folks are waiting." He relinquished one hand, put two fingers under her chin, and lifted her face until she looked him in the eye. "And I'm in a hurry for you to be my wife."

She winced. "Well, maybe you won't be." She led him to the chesterfield and sat. "If we're going to do this—"

His eyebrows shot up. "If?"

"Just let me finish, then you can be all indignant." She patted the seat cushion until he sat beside her, and took a deep breath. "I wasn't exactly up front with you. About me."

"What, you're married already?" He winked.

"Nope. Never married. That was true." Her stomach knotted. Maybe this wasn't a good idea.

"You mean the part about you being a prostitute?"

"What? You know? How? When?" She fought to keep her meagre breakfast of toast and tea down. "Or more importantly," she narrowed her eyes, "who?"

"O'Connor. He mentioned it once. Said he responded to some call here, something about an abusive john."

She blinked. That was a lie. "When did he tell you that?"

"Not long after I met you. I think he wanted to warn me off. But I couldn't stop thinking about you." He brushed a lock of curled hair from her face. "I was thrilled when you got a job. Figured that meant that maybe you weren't hooking anymore."

She stared at him, her cheeks went cold. He knew before they'd started dating. Before they ran into O'Connor outside of that restaurant. She kept fucking that bastard free of charge for nothing. She stared at her hands, at the dirt she could never get out from under her nails, the soil embedded into her flesh. She rubbed them on her skirt and squeezed her eyes shut. Bastard deserved what he got.

Aidan cupped her chin in his paw. "Hey. I don't care."

She searched his eyes and face for the truth. But why would he lie about this? Why would he take the drastic step of marrying her if he gave two shits about her sordid past? Or if he suspected her, or her son, of harming Birdie?

"Just because that's what you did to make a living, that doesn't make you a bad person."

Did murdering people make her that?

"I love you, Tibba. I knew I would from the moment I saw you. The way you are with your son. That's all I need to see to know that you are a wonderful mother. A nurturer. Not to mention, gorgeous."

She looked at her lap and smiled. Finny was so wrong.

"So let's go get hitched. What do you say?"

She nodded and met his gaze. "Yes. Let's go do that."

Signed, Sealed, Delivered, I'm yours ~ Stevie Wonder

Aidan strode to the front of the small crowd and nodded. Another cop pressed the play button on the boom box and turned up the volume.

The first notes of their chosen wedding march, *Crazy Love,* filled the yard. The sound of Van Morrison's voice was Finnegan's cue. This was happening. And nothing he'd done or said had prevented it.

He opened the back door and stepped out onto the porch ahead of his mother. He hooked his arm toward her and she slipped hers through. She smiled up at him and touched his face. Her hand trembled.

He led her down the stairs to the entrance of the makeshift aisle created by rows of rented folding chairs. They paused, Finnegan counted to three, then he was supposed to go. But he just stood there, rooted to the ground.

Aidan jerked his head at Finnegan. He was getting impatient to make an honest woman of her. Like marriage could do that.

Finnegan timed their march to his breath. One step per inhale, one step per exhale. He glanced at the justice of the peace standing thirty feet ahead. That breathing advice worked great during rehearsals when a hundred pairs of eyes weren't boring into him, watching his every move, waiting for him to trip on the aisle runner that kept bunching up and catching on the toes of his shiny new leather shoes. And there was Aidan, all smiles and anxious sweat beading on his brow. This was it. End of the line. There was going to be a cop living under his roof. Not just any cop. This cop. The one who nearly scared ten year's off Finnegan's life the night he killed Birdie. His breath quickened. His heart quickened. His pace quickened.

His mother tugged on his arm. "Be cool," she said, never breaking her smile. "A little slower."

He ignored his breath and listened to the music, delivering his mother to Aidan at just the right moment. Finnegan kissed her cheek and breathed in the smell of her skin. "I think you're crazy and this is the worst idea ever," he whispered in her ear. "But I do love you."

She smiled and patted his arm. "I love you too, baby."

He presented her hand to Aidan and took a seat in the front row.

Finnegan glanced across the aisle. Aidan's mother fanned herself with one white-gloved hand, bored out of her mind while the justice of the peace spoke of love and partnership, understanding and sharing. All the typical blah-blah that most married people quickly forget when the realities of daily life jump up and bite them.

Mrs. Everhard hated his mother. All these years the old bat had her son all to herself. Aidan's father, also a cop, died in the line of duty when Aidan was just a toddler. Mrs. Everhard had tried all manner of guilt-stick beatings to get Aidan to dump Finnegan's mother. But that wasn't about to happen. Aidan was hooked. So to speak. Just like Finnegan's mother was. But why? What was the draw?

Maybe it was his huge hands.

As much as he hated the pomp and bullshit surrounding him, Birdie would have loved it. She'd have pulled out her best prissy British accent. She might have even worn a dress. And since his mother didn't have many female friends, Birdie would have made the perfect maid of honour. Finnegan closed his eyes. Birdie stood before him, all grown up, her scrawny body filled out and curvy, her hair long and falling around her face in gentle waves. She stood next to his mother, gripped a small bouquet of daisies from the garden, and made faces at him in the audience.

His mother delivered her vows. Promised to love Aidan for the rest of their days. A shiver passed over Finnegan.

The justice of the peace announced that Tibba MacGillivray was now Mrs. Aidan Everhard. Finnegan smirked. She had no intention of taking Aidan's name. When was she going to drop that little bomb on him? Unless he'd convinced her to change it. Then Finnegan would share nothing with his mother except DNA. And a graveyard full of secrets.

The justice commanded Aidan to kiss his bride, and kiss her he did. He took off his hat and tossed it at Finnegan, brought Finnegan's mother to his chest, dipped her, and kissed her with an open mouth. Her arms circled his neck and they made out for at least thirty seconds to the cheers and jeers of the crowd. Finnegan couldn't watch any longer and looked away. He caught Mrs. Everhard's eye. The battle-ax couldn't bear to watch it either.

Stevie Wonder started singing from the tape deck. Everyone stood, and the newlyweds turned to face the rows of guests.

Finnegan's mother beamed, the sunshine glinted in her cornflower eyes, her smile dazzling and genuine. The guests cheered as his mother and newly minted stepfather danced back up the aisle.

She was right. Aidan was good for her.

He just couldn't find the will to give a shit.

1986

How many fond fools serve mad jealousy!

Finnegan set the table for dinner, turning to face his mother at every opportunity, flaunting his button-up shirt, open to mid-chest. Was she avoiding him on purpose? When he moved closer, she skittered away. When he reached past her for the salt and pepper shakers, she backed up. He couldn't bear it any longer.

"So, what do you think?" He dropped the shakers on the table near Aidan's place setting. He so loved his salt.

"Of what?" She didn't even turn around. Just kept plunging that masher into the pot of potatoes, adding a touch of milk and a spoon of butter.

One good thing about this marriage. The food got better.

He sidled up to the counter, his butt leaning on the edge, and tugged on one lapel to open the shirt wider. "This."

She glanced at his chest and back at the potatoes, then froze, mid-mash. "Why?" she whispered.

"Looks good, don't you think?"

She dropped the masher and stared at his chest, touched her fingers to the cross around his neck, a tear in one eye. Then her face hardened and she pulled her hand away like it burned. "Are you crazy? Aidan will see that."

"I need to keep it close."

"Why?"

"So I never forget."

His mother buttoned his shirt to the top. "Or you're just acting out because you can't stand that I'm happy." Her words spat out like water in hot oil.

"Hey, folks!" Aidan blustered in the back door, his uniform disheveled after a double shift in the summer heat. "Smells great in here." He kissed her cheek and undid the top button of his uniform. "Do I have time to shower?" He took a gulp out of her wine glass.

Her whole face changed when he walked in the door. She *was* happy. Calm even. Downright content. "Of course. Dinner's in twenty minutes. I'll open another bottle of wine." She watched him leave the kitchen and head for the stairs, a satisfied grin on her face. The second the bedroom door smacked shut, she spun around and took three fast strides toward Finnegan.

She undid his buttons and took hold of the cross. "You put this away. Somewhere well hidden, you hear me? Are you trying to get caught?" She undid the clasp and pressed the pendant into his hand. "I never should have given this to you. I just thought you'd like a memento. A reminder of your friendship. A little piece of Birdie."

He blinked. She'd never talked about it so openly before. It was their unspoken arrangement. That it remain unspoken. He'd never asked. She'd never told. That little outburst amounted to a confession. Or testimony against him.

"Go!" She flicked her fingers at him. "Before Aidan is out of the shower."

He stood his ground, straightened his spine. At his full height, he now towered over her half a foot. "And what if I want to keep wearing it? What are you going to do about it? I mean, it's not like he's going to know it's hers."

She rolled her eyes and tsked at him. She flipped the cross over. "Except for the engraving."

Birdie S. 1980.

He'd forgotten about that.

"That cross is on the top of their list of things to look for. She didn't have much on her when you —" She bit her thumbnail. "when she … disappeared." She crossed her arms. "Now did she?" She stood in front of him, toe-to-toe, staring up at him.

Her breasts grazed his bare chest. Her breath was sweet with merlot; the ever-present scent of strawberry shampoo filled his senses.

He leaned in and placed a tender kiss on her lips, his heart racing.

She kissed him back. A mother's kiss. Sweet and tender and without one shred of passion.

"Now, Finny. Baby. Take off that damned necklace." She patted his chest. "And find a good place to hide it away."

He didn't even glance at Aidan when they passed on the stairs. He stood inside his bedroom door, his forehead resting against the jamb. Their voices echoed up the stairwell, Aidan's baritone recounting his day, and the lilt of hers acting like she cared. Their sickeningly sweet nightly ritual that made Finnegan want to throw up.

He shut his door, sat on the edge of his bed, and held his head in his hands, the edge of Birdie's crucifix poking into his forehead.

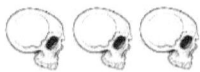

Bells dinged overhead and the door swished shut behind him.

"Can I help you?" The young woman behind the counter was a tapestry of body modifications. Her otherwise pretty face was marred by piercings. Hoops through her eyebrows, her nose, and one through her bottom lip.

Finny approached the counter. "I want a tattoo."

"That's what we do here." She yawned.

The silver of a tongue stud caught the light. Vines and flowers curled up both her arms, swirls of black and lilac danced in and out of the neckline of her top. He had an urge to strip it off her and see where the ink ended. Find out if it was true that tongue piercings enhanced fellatio.

He rolled up his sleeve and pointed to his forearm. "Right here, where I can see it every day."

"We can do that. What do you want?"

He slammed the crucifix down on the counter. "This."

Hours later, he glanced around the half-empty bus, rolled up his sleeve, peeled the tape off, and lifted the gauze. His arm was emblazoned with Birdie's name in cursive, the letters entwined with fern fronds and flowers, a Monarch butterfly and two tiny frogs nestled in the fern. The bottom left of the "B" and the tail of the "e" became a short chain that held her crucifix.

"Love you forever, Birdie." He ran one finger over the letters of her name. "But damn you for leaving me."

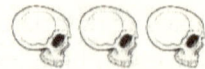

Finnegan pulled a box out of the closet and plucked a butterfly from among a host of other dead insects. Not the one that landed on Birdie in the garden. That one was long gone, probably blown away in the wind or snatched by an opportunistic Blue Jay. No, this was another poor soul that happened by a couple of years later. He'd grabbed it out of the air and snuffed out its life without a second thought, just so he could have it in his collection. Another piece of Birdie.

Sometimes, life-and-death choices were easy.

He held the insect in one palm and tucked his other hand in the front pocket of his jeans, fingering the silver cross. He needed to commune with his best friend. Get her perspective on his fucked up life. He could always count on her to straighten him out, to bring him back down to earth. Since her body was gone, the best place to find her was the river. Hell, maybe they'd even catch a frog or two, for old time's sake.

Finnegan bounded down the back stairs and headed for the garden. He could go out the front, use the sidewalk, take the long route. But what fun was that? He wanted a good old-fashioned twelve-year-old's experience complete with climbing through the hole in the fence and sneaking down the back alley.

Would he still fit through that hole?

Greer sat on his porch, glowering at the world. He only ever smiled at Finnegan's mother, and that smile was nothing more than lustful sneer. Pervy old bastard. Finnegan flipped Greer the bird, and stepped into the garden. He wended his way through the ferns, between the ash and the hops. As he rounded the horse chestnut, the sounds of his mother digging in the garden became louder.

He froze. It couldn't be her, she was at work. He glanced around. A pitchfork, the one his mother bought after her old one went missing, rested against the maple. His chest hollowed at the feel of it in his hands. It was lighter, shorter. Or he was bigger and stronger.

He tiptoed down the path. Not far from the ornamental cherry tree, there was Aidan, weeding near the bougainvillea, right where Finnegan had laid Birdie to rest. For the first time, he was grateful that his mother had moved her.

Aidan stabbed at the ground with a small spade. The hand-held weeder lay on the ground at his feet, and a shovel leaned against a tree.

He knew it. The motherfucker was looking for evidence.

Finnegan sneaked closer until he was just four feet from Aidan's back. There was a pile of debris including a few twigs and rocks and … two halves of a broken bone. Metacarpal perhaps. Or a proximal phalange. He leaned in for a closer look. A twig cracked beneath his feet.

Aidan jumped and spun around. "Oh, hey, Finn." He slapped his dirty hands together, his face red and sweaty. He eyed the pitchfork.

Finnegan dropped the fork. "Shit, man." He crossed his arms. "I thought you were an intruder. She's going to kill you, you know."

"I was just checking out the garden and found some thistles. Thought I'd clear them out for Tib."

"Isn't that breaking the rules?"

Aidan propped his pomelo fists on his hips. "Yeah, well." He wiped his forehead. "It's a dumb rule."

"I'm sure my mother will be interested to know that."

Aidan grimaced. "Now, come on, son."

"Once again, not your son."

Aidan put his hands up. "Sorry. No, you're not." He gestured to the debris. "Somebody's tossing chicken bones in the yard."

Finnegan kept his smirk inward. The broken — metatarsal maybe? — could pass for a wing bone. "That's probably me. Sometimes I bring a bucket of Barney's chicken back here."

"You sneak around with KFC?"

Finnegan shrugged. "I don't want to hurt her feelings. I mean, you've had her cooking."

Aidan gave him a knowing nod. In the snap of finger bone, his amiable and slightly embarrassed demeanor stiffened. He grabbed Finnegan's arm and pushed his sleeve up. "What the hell?" He stared at the tattoo, tapped the cross with one finger. "When did you do this?"

Finnegan wrested free of his grip and shoved his sleeve down. "A few days ago."

"Does your mother know?"

"Not yet."

Aidan wiggled his fingers and gestured for Finnegan to show him. He obliged.

"Birdie." He heaved a deep sigh and patted Finnegan on the back. "You still miss her?"

Finnegan swallowed and blinked. "Every day."

"Is that her cross? The one that's still missing?" He leaned in closer. "It's awfully detailed." One eyebrow crept higher up his forehead.

Finnegan swallowed and looked away. "It's how I remember it. No clue if I got it right." He shrugged. "Just a memorial to her."

Aidan squinted. "Memorial? We don't know that she's dead."

Finnegan tossed his hands in the air. "Kind of likely, don't you think? And if she is alive, she'll love the tat." Sweat beaded on his upper lip. "Look, it's no big deal."

"I'm sure your mother would disagree."

They stared at each other for an uncomfortably long time.

Finnegan flinched first. "So, anyway …."

Aidan rubbed the back of his neck. "Look, your mom won't be off until nine. I was thinking of having a beer. Want to join me? We can order pizza, on me."

Finnegan's stomach growled at the mention of food. "Beer? I just turned sixteen. And you're a cop."

"I'm not on duty, now am I? Sixteen is close enough. Hell, I was buying beer by that age." He stepped closer and put a paw on Finnegan's shoulder. "Look at you. You could pass for eighteen easy. Besides, in the privacy of your own home, you can do almost anything you want."

Ain't that the truth?

Finnegan eyed the bougainvillea, thought of the tiny hole in the fence and that one nail that always caught him in the leg. In that moment, the whole escapade seemed so Nineteen-Eighty-one. And damn, he was hungry. "All right. Why not?"

Aidan turned to head out of the garden. He glanced back at Finnegan over his shoulder. "You're, uh, not going to tell your mother about the weeding, right?"

"If you don't tell her about the ink."

Aidan sighed. "I promise."

Finnegan smirked. He didn't believe a word of it. He snatched the broken bone from the pile and tucked it in his pocket.

... and all the idle weeds that grow

Tibba raced up the stairs and burst into the bedroom. "You were digging in the garden?"

Aidan lounged on her bed, his nose buried in another western. *The Quick and the Dead.*

You're either one or the other.

He held up one finger and kept reading. Made her wait until he finished his paragraph.

She tapped her toes on the floor and crossed her arms. "For God's sake, you can find your place again after I rip you a new asshole."

He glanced up at her over the rim of his reading glasses. "Yes, I was in the garden. Horror of horrors, I pulled a few thistles. Thought you might appreciate that."

"Well I don't appreciate it. I told you no gardening."

"Jesus Christ, Tib."

He'd never snapped at her before.

He dog-eared the page and tossed the book on the mattress, swung his legs over the edge of the bed and glared at her. "It's a ridiculous rule. I live here and I can't even pull an occasional weed? That's messed up." He furrowed his brow. "Just what are you so worried about?"

She took a deep breath and put on a lighter air. "I don't want you screwing up my plants, that's all. I put a lot of sweat into that space. Blood too." She held her hands out. "See? Scars. And I told you, I love to do it. It's my thing." She sighed and looked at her hands. "Don't ruin it for me."

He rolled his eyes. "Fine. But I don't see how me helping is ruining anything. We could do it together."

She blinked a long blink. This was never going to work. He was never going to stay out of the garden.

He shook his head. "Finn obviously told you."

"Yes. We have no secrets."

He snorted. "Right."

"What does that mean?"

"He's a teenage boy. And you're his mother, not his buddy. Not his friend." He stood and booped the tip of her nose. "Trust me. You both have secrets. Lots of bloody secrets. I ought to know. I lived alone with my mother for far too many years. And believe me, I told her nothing. Did he tell you we had a couple of beers tonight?"

"Beer? He's not old enough to drink. You gave it to him?"

He nodded. "He's plenty old. Point being, he kept that a secret, didn't he? Did you know he got a tattoo?"

Her mouth fell open. "He what?"

Aidan took her hands. "Keep your voice down. I promised I wouldn't tell you. It's for Birdie. Her cross and a couple of bugs or something."

Of course it was.

"It's pretty detailed." He pulled a box down from the top shelf of the closet and rummaged through some paperwork. He thrust a picture at her. A photocopy of a blurry close up of Birdie's cross. It was clipped to a copy of the original picture, a family portrait.

Her gut spasmed. "Oh, Birdie."

"I mean," he took the photo and put it back in the box, "it's identical. How did he remember that?"

"What is that box?"

"Just a copy of the file. I go through it now and again." He shoved the box in the closet. "Seriously. How would he remember those details?"

Her chest hollowed. Finny was right. Aidan was looking for evidence. He suspected her son. But why would he marry her just to close a case? "Well," her eyes flitted around the room, "he is a borderline genius. Maybe he's got a photographic memory or something. And she was his only friend."

His brows knitted and his jaw stiffened.

She undid her polyester vest and slipped off her pants. "I'm still pissed at you, you know. For the gardening." Deflect. Distract. She unclasped her bra.

He gazed at her as she undressed, his rigid stance relaxed. "I'm sorry I broke your rule. I can't say I won't do it again."

She pressed her lips together and squinted at him.

"Now let's grab a couple of lawn chairs and have a glass of wine in the garden. Watch the sunset through the trees." He honked her boob. "Make out under the stars."

She grinned and pushed his hand away. Damn him and his disarming smile. "Fine." She slipped a sundress over her head and turned to lead him out of the room.

Finny stood inside his bedroom door, a scowl on his face, his eyes narrow. He stared at her, unblinking, and inched his door shut.

For never was a story of more woe, Than this of Juliet and her Romeo

Tibba flicked the silver bell with one finger and closed her eyes. That little chime was the sound of her new life. A life without dates, without johns. A life with a man who truly loved her. Who never spoke out in anger or raised a hand to harm her.

She opened her eyes and sighed. If only Finny Mac loved him too. He didn't even like him. At one point, he downright hated him. But in the fall, there was a thaw. Some kind of macho détente. Perhaps he just gave in to his new reality and went with the flow. Or he'd gotten good at pretending. It really didn't matter, as long as there was peace.

At sixteen, Finny had grown into a full-blown man. One who looked so much like his father that she found herself wistful for a good Adam fucking. He sneaked into her thoughts often. She'd be having a beer with her baby boy, or cooking Finny Mac and cheese. One look at her child and there was Adam. Hell, his face — and other body parts — even interfered when she was making love to Aidan.

What kind of mother was she? That the sight of her own child brought out such lust and desire?

The bell was a gift from Aidan on their first Christmas the year before. Engraved with "T & A Forever 1985." It was a sweet and loving gesture. And she hadn't meant to snicker. But T & A? Seriously? Like usual, he just laughed along with her. Should have asked for A & T, he'd said, and kissed her like it was their first time.

The tree sparkled with tinsel. Light from the old frosted globes bounced off glass and plastic ornaments. Her father's tacky star jostled precariously atop the tree. It was the only thing of his she hadn't thrown away or burned out of spite. The only decent memory she had of the man. Not even a good memory, more of a mixed bag of shitty and okay. Because no one was allowed to tinsel the tree but him, and don't touch the lights, don't break that, it's an antique. The only positive thing about Christmas tree decorating was at the tail end of the ritual, when he'd lift her up and let her place the star on the crown of that plastic tree, then plug it into the light string. That was the magic. When it all came to life. Then he'd put her down, slap her ass, and demand she fetch him a beer. The joy only lasted five minutes. But it was joy nonetheless.

She stood on her tiptoes and flicked the base of the star. The fringe of stiff tinsel around each bulb danced and shimmied.

She hummed along to *Merry Christmas, Baby* and futzed with the ornaments. The scent of pine filled the house. She'd never had a real tree until Aidan came along. Just kept poking the twisted metal ends of those fake branches into the colour-coded holes in the fake tree trunk, same as her mother before her. Aidan was baffled. All those trees outside in that massive forest garden, but plastic in the house? He wouldn't hear of it. So the plastic tree went to the dump and they took Finny to a place out of town where you cut down your own.

That first tree was seven feet tall and had taken up a quarter of the living room. The star nearly touched the ceiling, and they barely owned enough ornaments to fill it. They went a little less crazy this year and settled for a six-footer with a thinner profile.

In the kitchen, she put the finishing touches on the gift wrapping, using the sharp edge of the scissors to curl ribbon, and wrote out gushy "love from" gift tags for Aidan and Finny. She nestled the gifts under the tree.

The old console stereo dropped another LP onto the turntable, and Bing Crosby sang just for her. She swayed to her favourite Christmas music, sang harmony with Bing, and even did a little twirl, sending the skirt of her kitschy holiday-themed dress up in the air.

Is this what happened when you became content? You turned into a Hallmark card? A made-for-TV movie where every ending was a happy one?

She'd take that all day long. She sipped rum-laced eggnog and glanced at the clock on the back of the stove. Six-fifteen? Aidan should have been home an hour ago. Finny would be home from work soon, and she was anxious to get Christmas Eve underway. The wine was mulling, the house replete with the scent of cinnamon and cloves, nearly burned sugar cookies and re-heated frozen sausage rolls.

Holy shit. She really had become June Cleaver.

Footsteps on the porch made her heart skip a beat. Aidan was home. Or Finny. Either way, life was good.

The doorbell rang.

Tibba stood in the kitchen, frozen. Who the hell? Maybe Finny forgot his key.

She hurried to the front entrance, unlatched the bolt and threw the door open wide. "Merry Chr—"

Dan and the lieutenant stood on her front stoop. Large snowflakes drifted from the sky and perched upon their hats and uniforms, like the world's worst case of dandruff.

Tibba swallowed and grasped the doorknob. Her knees trembled and adrenaline shot through her heart. "Hello, Dan."

Dan nodded and removed his hat. He was pale as the snow and his eyes were rimmed red.

This wasn't happening. It had to be a joke. A Christmas April Fools' joke. And not even remotely fucking funny.

The lieutenant also removed his hat. "May we come in?"

She shook her head. "No. Aidan will be home any minute. And my son." She gestured to the tree, then pointed toward the kitchen. "It's Christmas Eve!" Her voice wailed from deep in her belly.

"Ma'am," the lieutenant held his hat with both hands. "I'm sorry to inform you —"

Tibba fell to her knees, covered her face with both hands and screamed. "No! No, it isn't true." She scrambled to her feet and rushed at him, beat on his chest with both fists. "You're lying." She looked over his shoulder. "It's a joke, right? He's just in the car, right?" She pushed past him and raced down the snow-covered sidewalk in her bare feet. She yanked the door of the cruiser open and stuck her head inside.

She dropped her elbows on the leather seat, slid to the ground, and landed in the slush in the gutter.

Dan pulled her up and crushed her into his body, holding the back of her head while she sobbed. Her feet wouldn't hold her up, so he carried her into the house and sat her on the chesterfield. He held her and rocked her until the sobbing subsided.

She pulled away and wiped her runny nose on the sleeve of her sweater. The lieutenant sat beside her and handed her a Kleenex out of his pocket. She blew her nose and dabbed tears and mascara from her cheeks.

"How?" Her voice was barely a whisper.

"It was a domestic." Dan looked at the ceiling and squeezed his eyes shut. "We got the call at about three. Guy killed his girlfriend. Stabbed her. He was holding their kid at knifepoint." His voice caught in his throat. "The second guy let his guard down, Everha— Aidan. Aidan rushed him and pushed the boy out of the way. Saved the boy's life."

"And lost his? How?"

"The knife caught him in the groin. Femoral artery. He bled out quickly."

She stared at her hands. At the soiled tissue. "Do you think he suffered?" Her stomach knotted.

The lieutenant patted her knee. "Not for long."

She leaned back and rested her head on the chesterfield, stared at the Christmas tree, at the sparkling silver bell. "Killing a cop. That's automatic first degree, right? Automatic life?"

Dan shifted in his seat. "Normally."

She sat up. "What does that mean, normally?" She grabbed him by the lapels of his uniform. "Don't you dare let him get off. No loopholes. No technicalities. Don't you dare!"

Dan took her hands. "I shot him. He's dead."

She stared into his eyes while his words sank in, then stood and made her way to the fireplace on unsteady legs. "Good. I'm glad." She would have happily doled out the death penalty, up close and personal. But it would not have been so quick.

The latch of the storm door clicked and a wave of cold air

rushed into the room. "Mom, sorry I'm late." Finny's voice carried into the house. "Why'd Aidan bring his cruiser home?" The hollow sound of stomping feet on the concrete porch to free the snow from his boots echoed through the room. "Does he have to go back to work?" He stepped into the entry unzipping his parka and stopped short at the sight of the lieutenant.

Dan stood. "Hey, Finn." That's what all the cops called her boy. Finnegan was too Mr. Dressup. Finny was too mama's boy. Finn was a man's name.

Finny looked at her. "Mom, what the hell?" He brushed past Dan and the lieutenant and met her at the mantel.

She fell into his arms and wept.

He squeezed his eyes shut and pressed his lips together. Then he turned to Dan. "You can leave now." His voice cracked.

They mumbled their condolences, Dan through tears, and shut the door behind them.

Tibba looked up at her son. He was playing it tough, all stoic and rigid. "What the hell am I supposed to do now?" she wailed. Her knees buckled.

Finny gathered her in his arms and carried her up the stairs. He laid her on her bed, stroked her hair and kissed her forehead. "Can I bring you anything?"

She fell back against the pillows and nodded. "Bourbon."

He stood and turned away.

She reached for his hand and squeezed his fingers. "Bring the bottle."

1989

Something wicked this way comes

Tibba shifted the rubber kneepad two feet to the right and stabbed her weeder into the ground. The blade end was coming loose, the wooden handle embedded with soil. She poked the end of one finger through a hole in her best gloves. It was time to upgrade her tools. Money might be tight, but this place kept her from completely losing her mind. She could afford to invest a little cash in her mental health. Maybe one of those sweet seats on wheels so she could stop kneeling all the time. Her body parts were starting to feel every bit their age.

She took off her sunhat and wiped sweat from her brow. The blazing late-June sun was hot and blinding, even filtered through the leaves of the chestnut. A large shadow crossed behind her, projecting the globular shape of a rather fat man onto her petunias.

"I know what you are." He poked her shoulder.

She twisted around and peered up at the imposing silhouette.

"Mr. Greer." She let her disdain for him drip from her voice, his feelings be damned. He and his bitch wife never gave a shit about her feelings. Nineteen years this bastard had leered at her, his wife always shaking her damn fist like it was Tibba's fault that she was born with the big boob gene, and Tibba's fault that Mrs. Greer's husband was disgusting pond scum. "Get the fuck out of my garden."

"You're a whore. You think no one sees it? All the men, coming and going."

She lifted the weeder and plunged it into the dirt. "No man has gone." She raised one eyebrow. "Or come for that matter, since my husband died."

He smirked. "No matter. Once a whore, always a whore."

She stared up at the old man. He had to be pushing seventy, his wrinkles deepened by too many hours baking in the sun. His nose bulbous and red from too many two-sixes of whiskey. She pulled off one glove, a finger at a time. "I'm going to say it again, Greer. And this time not so nicely. Get. The fuck. Out. Of. My. Garden." She put one hand on the ground for leverage and started to stand.

He knocked her down with an open-palmed push on her shoulder.

She tumbled to the dirt, landing face first in her petunia bed. Before she could get up, his repulsive, flabby body was on top of her, pinning her to the ground. One of his hairy arms pressed against her shoulders, flowers and earth crushed into her cheekbone. She thrashed her arms, tried to scream, but she could barely get any air.

He yanked her shorts down and rammed himself inside of her. "This is what whores want. This is what whores get." He shifted his weight, laid his entire bulk on her, one hand on the back of her head.

She stopped moving. Stared at a petunia a few inches from her face. In her younger days, she could have focused on it until it was over. But without her reading glasses, the bloom was a blur of green and purple. The handle of her weeder came into clear view two feet behind the flower.

His body shuddered and he grunted like a rutting pig with its snout in a slop bucket. He lay there, his heavy breathing assaulting the back of her neck, his fingers still tangled in her hair. The sweet perfume of crushed flowers mixed with the salt and sour of his slimy sweat, a noxious cocktail that made her stomach lurch. When he finally pushed himself off, he slapped her naked ass on his way to his feet.

She stared at the weeder, nothing in her ears but the throb of her pulse and the zip of his camouflage shorts.

"Thanks, whore. Let's do this again some time." He tapped her foot with his sandal and laughed.

She grabbed the weeder, yanked it free of the earth, spun around onto her knees and lunged at him, aiming for his pitiful excuse for manhood. She only caught fabric, ripping his shorts near where the femoral artery should be.

So close.

He would have bled out in no time. She could have buried him right here under the petunias. He'd make quite a lot of fertilizer.

His face turned purple. He backhanded her with a powerful blow and she landed in the flowers again. A trickle of blood dripped into her mouth.

"Bitch. You ever try that again, I'll just kill ya next time. Don't think I won't. I killed enough Nazis back in dubya dubya two. I think I can handle one little Canadian whore."

Plants crunched under his feet as he stomped through her garden. She lay in the flowers a few minutes and let tears drip onto their petals.

He was too big to fit through the hole in the fence. The bastard had the nerve to walk right through her gate, across her lawn, and enter her sanctuary. He invaded her private spaces. Every damn one of them.

She reached out and used the trunk of the ash tree for balance. Her legs wobbled and her head throbbed. The flowerbed was in shambles, dismembered blooms spread everywhere, blossoms and foliage tamped down by her body and his stinking feet.

Her fingers twitched and her heartbeat pounded in her ears. She dropped to her knees and ripped the petunias out. Purple, pink, red, white. Flowers strew across the path and under the ash and chestnut. The leaves stained her fingers and the hairy stalks irritated the tender skin of her wrists.

It didn't matter. They had to go. She couldn't look at them anymore. She grabbed the weeder and drove the blade into the earth, penetrated the flowerbed and pierced the roots. A roar built up in her gut and gurgled out of her mouth.

Minutes later, she sat back on her heels. She wiped sweat from her brow and surveyed the damage. "Oh, no. No, no." She gathered an armful of the devastation and cradled it, petting the shredded petunias. "I am so sorry." She crushed the plants in her fists, looked up at the sky and wailed.

She stood, still naked from the waist down, Greer's demon seed running down her leg. With any luck, she had HIV and he'd get AIDS and die a slow, painful death. Or maybe she could speed the process up a bit.

She pulled her shorts on and ran to the house, stripped in the kitchen, and took the scissors to her clothes, shredding them into tiny strips. She stuffed them all in the fireplace and lit a fire. The clothes he'd soiled would never touch her skin again.

In the shower, she used her Loofah to scrub herself raw, put her soapy fingers inside herself to cleanse him from her body. When the water ran cold, she sat in the bathtub with her arms around her knees and planned his slow death.

The clock beside the vanity mirror said five forty-five. Finny would be home soon. She had to put something in the oven.

She shut off the water and climbed out of the tub, slipped on a loose-fitting dress and wrapped herself in a blanket. Despite the summer heat, she shivered. Water dripped from her hair onto the blanket and the carpet with each step she took down the stairs. In the kitchen, she poured a tumbler of bourbon. The idea of cooking, of any form of raw meat, made her gut clench. She took her drink to the living room and curled up on the chesterfield.

A car door slammed and Finnegan's footsteps came up the walk.

She touched her swollen lip and tried to straighten her wet hair. She wiped mascara from under her eyes, but there was nothing to wipe. She'd not bothered to style her hair or apply makeup. What would he think? Had he ever seen her with a bare face?

The door swung open. "Home, Mom!"

"I can see that," she said, her voice cracking.

He looked up. "Sorry, thought you'd be out back." He tossed his car keys into the bowl on the ledge and flipped through the mail that sat there. "Kind of early for bourbon, don't you think?"

"I've had a rough day."

He looked at her, his face scrunched. He slipped off his shoes and walked over, sat on the coffee table in front of her, touched her face with one hand and turned it into the light. "What the hell did you do?"

She brushed his hand away. "Just a little gardening accident. Tripped on the pitchfork, landed in the dirt, my face met the trunk of the ash."

"It's a big cut. You want me to take you for stitches?" He eyeballed the rest of her. "You look like shit."

"Well, gee. Thanks. No stitches. I'm fine. It just shook me up a bit."

He shrugged. "All right. What's for dinner?"

She drank the remaining bourbon and shook the glass at him for a refill. "Not up to it tonight. How about Chinese?"

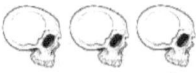

Finnegan had done what he usually did in the evenings — retreated to his room to lift weights or study or do whatever it was he did up there behind closed doors. Maybe whack off into a sock for all she knew. Tibba had finished off half a mickey of bourbon and needed some air. She stepped out onto the back porch, left the light off so she could remain in the dark, sat on the still-warm concrete, and lit a cigarette. Acrid smoke filled her lungs and she held her breath, counted as long as she could stand it. Got all the way to seventeen before she let it all out in one long exhale. The smoke dirtied the night air, glowing in the orange light of the streetlamp on the corner.

The creaking of Greer's damn rocking chair intruded on her calm. From the back stoop, she could just make out his head, light from those lame-ass paper lanterns bouncing off his bald scalp. Any other night she'd have slipped into the garden where the summer growth blocked his leering view. Not that night. She stood, her creamy dress luminescent in the moonlight, and stared at the spectre of his raping form.

He raised his glass at her.

She should vault over that fence and wipe the sneer off his ugly face. Lop off his favourite body part and stuff it down his throat. Her pulse quickened and her vision clouded as if a fog had rolled in.

At that moment, Mrs. Greer stepped out of the house, smacked him upside the head. She peered into the darkness and found Tibba, shook her fist at her, as if Tibba was out there begging for that bastard's attention.

Tibba huffed. Some of her attention was exactly what he was going to get.

O, swear not by the moon, the fickle moon, the

inconstant moon ...

Finnegan jolted awake to a scream and a gunshot. Sometimes his dreams were so lifelike, so damn vivid, he couldn't tell if it was in his head or in the real world. He closed his eyes and listened to the night.

Nothing but dead silence.

Probably the Greer's cat out fighting the stray tom that roams the neighbourhood. Or some delinquent assholes shooting off cap guns or lighting firecrackers in the alley. Or, like so many other nights, just a dream.

The details disappeared the second he awoke. Sometimes bits and flashes would stick or come back and grab him at odd hours of the day. But usually he was just left with a sense of eerie disquiet. The knowledge that, whatever it had been, it was horrific and terrifying. He just wasn't sure why.

He trudged to the bathroom and stood in the dark, his head lolled back, the noise of his draining bladder hitting the toilet as loud as an airplane overhead. If his mother ever heard his nocturnal pissing, she never complained. At least, not since he'd stopped wetting his bed ten years ago. Don't drink anything after dinner, she'd tell him. But did he listen? Of course not. She'd probably changed his sheets three nights a week. The crunch of the plastic mattress cover woke him up every time he rolled over, but it was always too late. He was sleeping in the wet warmth of his own urine.

Good thing you grow out of shit like that.

July was his least favourite month. Too hot in the daytime, and the air never cooled down enough at night. He yearned for mid-August when the evenings were chilly and his room, window wide open to allow any wisp of air movement inside, would become a normal temperature. Even if only for a few hours until the sun beat down on the roof shortly past dawn.

He froze mid-step, held his breath, and focused his hearing. Was that grass and leaves rustling? Just the wind in the trees? But his drapes were still. No, it wasn't Mother Nature. That was the sound of human trespass.

He tiptoed to the window and peered out. Someone emerged from the garden, a plastic garbage bag in their hand. He reached for the baseball bat that rested against the wall, never taking his eyes off the intruder. The clouds parted and the full moon bathed the yard in light and shadow.

The bat slipped from his fingers. It was his mother. What the hell was she doing out at — he looked at the clock on his nightstand — three forty-two in the morning?

He squinted. Was she naked?

He yanked the drapes shut and rubbed his eyes, the visual of his mother's bare breasts and plainly visible private parts clear in his mind. He split the drape with his fingers and peered out. Maybe he was still dreaming. Or seeing things. Nope, there she was, walking across the yard, her alabaster skin glowing under the moonlight.

She stood on the back stoop below his window and fumbled with the doorknob. Her hair fell about her shoulders, clumps of mud tangled in the mess, dark splotches marred her flesh. What the hell was in the bag?

He slipped across his room and opened the door a crack, put his ear to the slit and closed his eyes to concentrate.

The rustling of the plastic bag. The thud of a cupboard door closing and the pop of a cork. The *click-click* of a Bic lighter. Then relative silence for several minutes. At the sound of her bare footsteps on the stairs, he turned the knob and closed the door without a sound. The shadow of her legs slipped under the door as she passed by his bedroom. Her door closed with a gentle click. Then the shower started.

Gardening in the buff by the wan light of the moon. Wine and cigarettes and a shower in the middle of the night. Maybe she'd lost her freaking mind.

He flicked on the lamp, cracked the cover of a collection of Shakespeare plays, and flipped to act one of *Pericles*.

I am no viper, yet I feed

On mother's flesh which did me breed.

"Fuck me," he said under his breath. He shut the book and tossed it aside, pulled the cotton sheet over his head. A habit from his youth, as if that one thin sheet would protect him. Would keep evil at bay. What about the evil that hid beneath it? The evil in him? Who would protect him from himself?

He closed his eyes. Before tonight, he'd only imagined what his mother's breasts looked like, caught glimpses down her shirt, or sneaked a peek when her robe sometimes slipped open enough to bare part of a nipple. Now her full naked form danced behind his lids.

One hand slid into his boxers. He fumbled around in the top drawer of his nightstand with his other hand, and pulled out a sock.

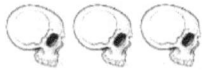

His mother flitted about the kitchen in a perfectly good mood considering it was six-thirty and she'd only had about two hours of sleep. Finnegan had sat up the rest of the night imagining their morning conversation. How would she explain her naked wanderings in the wee hours? And would he even ask her, or just stick his fingers in his ears and say "La la la la" if she tried to tell him? Oblivion was a great place to live.

She dropped a plate of crispy bacon and sunny-side-up eggs in front of him.

He looked at the plate with one raised brow. It was a far cry from her usual offering of mostly burned toast or a Pop-Tart. His gaze inched its way to her cleavage. That deep crevasse where her robe crossed over itself, held in place with a loosely tied belt. He shovelled food in his mouth and tried not to peer at the back of her knees, at the gentle rise of the arch of her foot, tried not to think of the tarsal and metatarsal bones underneath her milky flesh. His face heated and his jeans tightened over a growing erection. He blinked, pinched his thigh hard, and stared at his plate. Nothing brought reality back in focus like the sight of runny yolks.

The doorbell rang and he jumped, sending a hunk of egg onto the tablecloth.

His mother spun around, her jaw clenched, her eyes wide. She rubbed her hands down the front of her robe and took a few shallow breaths, but didn't make a move to answer the door.

He avoided eye contact. "You gonna get that?"

She took a few steps. "No." She wrung her hands. "Who would be coming by this early?"

Someone knocked on the door. "Tib? It's Dan. Are you home?"

Aidan's former partner. In the three years since the funeral, Dan hadn't been around much.

A look of relief overtook her face. She pulled the robe tighter around her body and opened the door. "Hi, Dan."

Finnegan set his fork down and strolled to the living room. He stopped at the kitchen archway and leaned against the wall. Dan stood in uniform with his newest partner next to him. He'd gone through four partners since Aidan. One got shot, one run over, and two asked for transfer. Dan was bad luck. Luckily, none of them died.

He greeted Finnegan with a jerk of his head. "Can I bother you both for a few minutes? There was an incident in the neighbourhood last night. We're just canvassing the area to see if anyone saw or heard anything."

Finnegan's breakfast sat in an uneasy lump in his gut.

His mother hesitated, then gestured for them to come in. "What kind of incident?" She tossed the comment over her shoulder, all casual and breezy.

"Did you hear anything unusual?"

She reached for her cigarette pack on the coffee table and lit one up. "Nope. I slept like the dead. Like always."

"How about you, Finn?"

He pushed off the wall with his shoulder. "Yeah, I heard some stuff."

Dan's partner pulled a notepad from his belt and slipped a pencil from a holder on the side of it. He stood, the pencil poised above the page, awaiting Finnegan's every word.

"A cat fight. Probably the Greer's damn cat. She's always getting into it with the stray tom."

His mother snorted. "Honey, they ain't fighting." She sucked hard on her cigarette.

He tilted his head and looked at her. "Then I heard a shot."

The colour drained from her cheeks.

"A shot? Like a gun?" Dan looked at him in anticipation.

"Not sure. Might have just been the brats down the street popping caps."

"The neighbourhood ne'er-do-wells in action." His mother took another long drag, her gaze on the front window.

Finnegan rolled his eyes. "I might have dreamed it all anyway, because I was asleep when I thought I heard it."

"What time was that?" Dan's partner asked.

Finnegan made a face like he was thinking hard. "Not sure. Maybe around three. Might have been earlier. Or later. I had to piss, so that's probably why I woke up." He scratched his chin and reminded himself to shave before work. "Why? What happened?"

"It's the Greers. They're dead."

His mother gasped and pulled her bathrobe closed at her collarbone. "Dead? Both of them?"

Finnegan narrowed his eyes. She was so full of shit.

"Afraid so. Looks like murder-suicide. It appears Mrs. Greer sliced her husband up and then put a gun to her head. Weirdest thing, looks like the cat got at the bodies. Poor girl was covered in blood, gnawing on Mr. Greer's arm. Must've been starving because half his left hand was missing. Even the bones."

Finnegan stared at the television. Every forkful of Salisbury steak was like cardboard in his mouth. He ate without tasting, without noticing when he'd finished the last Tater Tot. Doogie Howser chattered on the screen, but all Finnegan could see was a rerun of last night's mystery in his head. The one that played out right here is his own house, live and in Technicolor.

His mother sat beside him, smoking, drinking, not eating. Stomach ache, she said. Bullshit. It was guilt. Had to be.

He had a silent conversation with her.

"I saw you, you know."

"What? When?"

"Last night. Naked in the back yard. What was in the bag?"

"I don't know what you're talking about."

"Mother. I saw you."

"You must have been dreaming, Finny Mac. Now hush and eat your dinner."

He stabbed at the grey meat and pushed shrivelled kernels of corn around the aluminum tray. It didn't matter what she did, she was his mother and he loved her. He glanced sideways at her.

She plucked a bit of tobacco from between her teeth and flicked it into the air.

He had to keep his mouth shut for her, protect her. Like she did for him.

"Garbage day tomorrow."

He blinked. "What?"

She looked him square in the face and took a drag from her fifth cigarette in under an hour. "Garbage day," she said, smoke puffing out from between her lips with each syllable. "Tomorrow." She crossed her legs and tapped ash into the ashtray, her foot bounced up and down, her fuzzy red slipper dangling from her painted toes. "Don't forget."

1990

All love the womb that their first being bred

He could just make out the back of her head through the leaves of the ash, a small strawberry-blond dot, bobbing in the shallow end of the garden, nearest the house. A flash of leg, a hint of ass, a flailing arm. Every now and then, she'd pop out into the yard to fetch a plant from the flat on the lawn, or light up a cigarillo and blow smoke into the clear summer air.

He breathed deeply, the vanilla and tobacco of her favourite guilty pleasure wafting into his open window, along with mumbled tones of her incessant self-talk. He strained to make out the words, but only caught shifts in volume and modulation.

She ground the butt of her latest smoke against the sole of her sneaker and disappeared back into the garden, past the first ash tree, to a place his eyes couldn't find her. Finnegan laid his head on his hands, his forehead resting against the window screen, anxious for her to pop back out, to catch a glimpse of her shining hair. Ten minutes passed and she remained out of sight. He sighed and flopped onto his bed.

He pulled a bottle of bourbon out from under his mattress and took a swig right from the bottle. He shuddered and licked his lips, tipped the bottle again. He couldn't evict her from his thoughts, she was always right there, front and centre. He struggled to focus on his studies. He shouldn't have pursued his literary arts and teaching degrees at the same time. He couldn't sleep. Had no appetite.

He put on his headphones and cranked up the Walkman to drown her out, eject her with noise. It didn't work. She'd given him that tape.

He'd tried reading, but most of his books were gifts from her. Sifting through his bone collection didn't help. She'd given him that, too. In a roundabout way. Without the garden, without his mother, the collection wouldn't exist. She was everywhere he turned. He couldn't escape her even if he'd wanted to.

What he wanted was to run right into her arms.

Few love to hear the sins they love to act

Tibba stabbed her hand-spade into the ground and ripped at the earth. Sweat dripped from her brow and her nose and her chin, wetting the dirt and making tiny blobs of mud. "Should've just cut the bastard up," she rambled under her breath. Every time she came outside, saw that empty house next door and that empty rocking chair on the empty porch, she'd rant in her head. Sometimes she couldn't stop the ranting from escaping out of her mouth.

The garden, once her sanctuary, her place of peace and calm, became her confessional. Her paperless journal where she mumbled her hopes and dreams. Her wish list of ways she could have done it differently. Been better at life. At love. At murder. Destruction of evidence.

"Could've buried him right here, right next to his stinking hag of a wife." She clawed at the earth with her bare hands, the dirt digging under her nails. Her fingers wrapped around a wad of flannel tucked in the pocket of her gardening smock, its softness in stark contrast to its contents. She laid it on the ground, unfolded it with care. Between the dancing shadows of ash leaves, Greer's partial hand gleamed white. She'd stripped the flesh and muscle and tendons away with her paring knife then boiled off the remaining tendrils of goo. The bones were clean and unmarred and they didn't deserve to shine so damn brightly.

She picked up one finger bone and snapped it in half, tossed it into the trench she'd dug. She shoved the rest of them in and sprinkled some dirt on top. A flat of pasque flowers sat in the wheelbarrow to her left. She picked up one of the flimsy plastic pots, inverted it into her hand and gently pulled the entwined roots apart, careful to break as few as possible. She nestled each clump of roots into the trench, tucked dirt in beside the root balls, and gently pressed at the ground to secure the blooms in their new home. She sprinkled them with water from the green plastic watering can.

Over time they would wrap their roots around the evil of Greer's bones and bloom red and purple year after year. Turn the beast into beauty.

A shadow crossed her back, the head of an intruder looming over her, his bulbous form casting shade on her new flowers. She grabbed the spade and spun around, slicing the air with the blade of the small shovel.

Finny jumped backwards and hit his head on an ash branch. "Mom, shit! It's just me. What the hell?"

She dropped the shovel and scrabbled to her feet. "Oh, Finny." She threw her arms around his neck and sobbed onto his shirt. "I'm sorry, baby. I'm so sorry."

He pushed her away. "Seriously, Mom. What is wrong with you?" He brushed dirt from the front of his sleeveless shirt.

The sun filtered through the leaves of the ash tree and flickered across his hair. With each passing summer, the crop of coppery bronze darkened, like pennies that had seen better days. The freckles that had dotted his little-boy nose and pale cheeks joined forces and turned his complexion a swarthy tan. She drank in the sight of him, more than six feet tall, broad-chested, shoulder muscles that rippled with each movement of his strong arms. She swept her gaze over his body, pausing at the obvious bulge in his shorts.

The sun made her tipsy, like too many bourbons before dinner. She stepped toward him and touched his face, stared into his brilliant green eyes.

Adam.

She faltered and fell into his arms, her eyes never leaving his.

He held her gaze, his stare piercing, his heartbeat as heavy as her own. He licked his lips, dipped his head, and kissed her.

A rush of familiar longing shot through her. She opened her lips and welcomed his tongue into her mouth, ran her hands across his back. Her entire body ached for him. For his lust for her, his smell, his sex.

When she touched the waistband of his shorts and his erection poked at her stomach, her eyes shot open. She turned her head and pushed him away. "What are you doing?"

His eyes widened. His face reddened and a cloud crept over him. "Me? You. You." He stabbed her breastbone with one finger. "You kissed me!"

She put a hand to her mouth. "Oh, God. What have I done?" She doubled over, turned and vomited into the wheelbarrow, defiling her flowers.

He touched her back. "Mom, are you okay?"

She thrust her arm out, couldn't look him in the eye. "Leave me alone, Finnegan. Please. Just go."

"No."

She wiped her mouth on her sleeve and stood. Her body swayed and blood rushed to her head. "I said go. I need to not see you right now."

He grabbed her arm and spun her around, held her with both hands. His laboured breath was sweet with alcohol. Another wave of desire shot through her and he mutated into Adam before her eyes. She shook her head and squeezed her eyes shut. When she opened them, her son's face came into focus. "Have you been drinking?"

"So what if I have?"

"It's barely noon."

"Like you've never had a shot or two before lunch."

She squirmed to be free of him but his grip didn't falter.

"I love you," he whispered. Tears sprang to his eyes. "Why can't you love me?"

She softened. "Finny. I do love you."

"No, you don't. Not that way. Not like you loved Aidan." His eyes darted around her face. "How can you be like that with all those strangers, but not with me?"

"Finny Mac." She caressed his cheek with the back of her hand. "You're my child. My baby."

"I am not a baby!" He shook her. "I'm a man. A better man than those creeps you used to fuck for money."

Her mouth watered and her stomach cramped. "It was just the heat. The sun." She swallowed the bile that was forcing its way up. "I didn't mean it. It's just, for a second, I thought you were … that you looked like —"

"My father?"

She blinked through tears and nodded.

"You loved him like that too. But he's dead. Aidan is dead. It doesn't matter how many of them come or how long they stay, they all leave you. One way." He stamped his feet on the garden floor and eyed the dirt. "Or another." He brushed her hair from her face. "Except me. I'm right here. I've always been right here."

She shook her head. "Finnegan. No."

"I can take care of you. You don't need anyone else. I'll never leave you." He stepped closer and leaned down, one hand cradling her face.

She slapped him. "I can't. Not with you. Don't you understand? You're my blood. My son." She balled her fists. "It's not right. It's sick and wrong. For God's sake, Finny. It's abuse!"

He ran his thumb across his cheek, tears in his eyes, and took a step back.

"Finnegan." She reached for him.

He turned and walked away. At the cherry tree, he broke into a run.

1993

All Apologies ~ Nirvana

The early morning sunshine bounced off his bronze hair, illuminating his head with flecks of fire. His biceps rippled when he lifted his suitcase and backpack into his Eighty-seven Pontiac Tempest. If his looks weren't enough, he'd gone and bought that damn car with the boxy body and cracked tapioca paint job. His transformation into his father was complete. He looked so much like Adam it made her heart hurt. And he was leaving her.

Tibba inhaled smoke deep into her lungs and held it, closed her eyes, and let the music from the cassette player seep into her bones. When the trunk slammed shut, she opened her eyes. Finny bounded up the front walk.

The door hinges creaked. Tibba blew smoke straight over her head. "Did you get your books for the trip? You devour them like a praying mantis eats her lovers' heads."

He huffed. "Nice analogy, Mom. I have a few. And a couple on cassette for the ride."

"And you're sure you don't want to rent a van, take your furniture and all the rest of your stuff?" It was the last thing she wanted him to do. If he took it, it was a sign of his complete removal from their home. If he left it, then he'd be back. And he just had to come back.

"Kind of late for that. If I can make Winnipeg tonight and do twelve or more hours at a stretch, I should be there by Saturday. I start work on Monday." He pecked her on the cheek. "Mom, quit fretting. I'm going to be fine."

She touched a hand to his face and longed for the days his kisses would linger. "I know it."

But that was a lie.

She wasn't sure if he'd slept at all these past few years. Since their close call in the garden, an incident that haunted her every waking moment, he'd thrown himself into his schoolwork. Got his masters in literary arts and his teaching degree almost simultaneously.

"Is Jessica packed?"

Finny kneeled next to the fireplace and sifted through the basket of tapes. "We broke up."

Tibba sucked on her cigarette and nodded. That girl was too perfect. Too pretty. Too perky. And not too bloody bright. Her Finny needed an intellect. An equal. And he'd had trouble finding one. Not that he tried that hard.

Her rebuke changed him. He paraded a string of girls through her home. Most of them years older, all of them similar to Tibba in some way. He pushed them in her face, fucked them in his room right next to hers, didn't even try to be subtle or quiet about it. He'd turned into quite the little slut.

She sighed. At least he got laid a lot.

"You want me to leave Nirvana?" He shoved a few cassettes in his backpack and unclipped his Walkman from his belt, tucking it in alongside the tapes.

She pressed the eject button and slid the tape of the *Nevermind* album into its plastic case. "No, you take it." She handed it to him. "I'm thinking about investing in a CD player. You know," she poked his shoulder, "now that I'll save a ton on groceries."

He smirked and put the tape into his backpack.

"Finnegan?"

He stood and stepped toward her. "You're not going to get all sappy on me, are you, Mom?"

She fought back tears. "I just want to apologize for not being a better mother."

He took her hands. "To do a great thing, do a little wrong."

Her brow furrowed. "I don't understand."

"It's Shakespeare. I just mean — it's okay, Mom."

Expectation is the root of all heartache

After the stark landscape of the prairie, the horizon endless and unbroken, the craggy and picturesque beauty of Western Ontario's highways had been a treat. Until beauty became horror. At every turn, Finnegan white-knuckled the steering wheel, eyed the cliff's edge, and prepared to plunge over it when he ran headlong into a semi with no room to get out of the way. That happened often. Three long days after he left Calgary, the skyline of downtown Toronto off in the distance was as welcome as a cold beer after a hot day digging in the garden.

The Tempest eased right off the Don Valley Parkway, and merged onto Eastern Avenue. A line of smog blanketed the core, a greenish-grey strip of thick air slicing the skyscrapers in two. The skyline was dwarfed by the main pod and massive spire antenna of the CN Tower. The buildings looked unimpressive from a few kilometres away. Like Lilliput to Gulliver. But it was just an illusion. Compared to home, Toronto was New York City-big.

Finnegan cranked up the volume on his tape deck. Radiohead's *Creep* was the perfect theme song for this view. For the change of scenery. Hell, for his whole existence. It was the anthem of his life. He was a weirdo. A creep. And he didn't belong anywhere.

He could have taken a more direct route to Jane & Finch, but he wanted the full experience. The mid-sized-town-boy-meets-the-big-city shock and awe. So far, it was as disappointing as most everything was. As every day had been since Birdie died.

A wave of sorrow washed over him. Or was it melancholy? Maybe it was plain old relief. To be free from the murder house. From the lies and the secrets. From the constant presence of his mother, the rejecter. From his obsessive need to punish her.

He pulled into the parking lot of the apartment building. He'd rented it sight unseen based on an ad and a crappy one-inch square picture of a sparse living room. Twelve nondescript floors, each unit with a tiny balcony with some butt-ugly metal railings loomed overhead. Paint peeled, rugs hung over the railings to dry in the blazing heat. It was one of a few identical buildings, cheap and plentiful accommodations in the toughest part of town.

Finnegan opened the trunk, tossed his backpack over his shoulder and grabbed the handle of the suitcase, opening a slip of paper with his free hand. Twelve-fourteen. Top floor. At least he might have a decent view.

He poked the up button for the elevator. The thing groaned and rattled before opening its maw and swallowing him whole. The doors slid shut and trapped him in the tiny cage for the slow ride up. The thing stunk like piss, the walls smattered with gang tags.

He'd been desperate for a change. This definitely qualified.

He slipped the key the building manager had mailed to him into the deadbolt. It slid open, sending a hollow click echoing through the apartment. The same key unlocked the knob. He turned it and peered inside.

Dust and mildew and a hint of sour milk greeted him. He ventured in, set his luggage and backpack on the floor. Most of the tiny space was visible from his vantage point at the entry. The small living room with a grimy window and drapes that might have been white at one time, with a sliding door that led to the little balcony. "Furnished" the ad said. Which apparently meant a loveseat with worn and stained cushions, one side table, and a television sitting atop a collapsible TV table. The television looked like a prop for a Fifties sitcom, with an old-fashioned rabbit-ear antenna with tinfoil scrunched onto the ends. He snorted. His apartment was a damn time machine.

The kitchen was separated from the living room by a lunch counter. He rounded the island and ran a finger along its surface, grimaced at the grease staining his skin. The cupboard doors were smudged with fingerprints and drips of various foods. Mustard perhaps. Ketchup he guessed. Or maybe blood. A time machine and a crime scene. How perfect.

The cupboards were empty, the refrigerator warm. Inside was the origin of the sour milk smell. He turned the dial to cold and headed for the bedroom.

The twin mattress sagged in the middle, looking more like a hammock than a bed. It bore no sheets, but that was a blessing. The prospect of sleeping in someone else's skin cells and bodily fluids made his stomach lurch. Finnegan sighed. At least it was his and his alone. No mother. No old secrets hanging over his head or laid to rest outside his window.

He made another trip to the car to fetch his bones.

1994

... I taught thee

The pencils taunted him. Not the three that stood erect and at attention, their perfectly sharpened tips razor-thin and ready for writing action. No, it was the two with the rounded ends, one of them at least an inch shorter than the rest, the other lounging to one side, as if it were made of rubber instead of wood and lead.

Finnegan plucked the shorty from the cup and threw it like a javelin into the trash bin. He stuck the dull end of the rubbery one into the electric sharpener until it came to a point and aligned it in the narrow cup with the others.

Damn them all, now the three good ones had to be sharpened until they matched, stood in perfect alignment, all the same height.

He shook his head. No. No, they didn't. It was just nerves. Anxiety that jumped up and bit him occasionally. School rooms did that to him, even when he was in charge. He tugged a corner of paper from a student's essay until a small strip ripped free, held it to his tongue and closed his eyes.

The school bell squealed and he jumped. He snatched the paper out of his mouth and tossed it into the trash.

The room filled with the hum of voices and the slap of textbooks on desks. Finnegan eyed his students' ingress. The keeners up front, all eager and ready, their posture erect like perfect pencils. The first row was shared by those not so keen when it came to scholastics, but who were keen on the teacher.

The years had been kind to Finnegan, going from the scrawny, pale object of redhead insults to tall and brawny with a ruddy complexion and perfect teeth. The young ladies loved him. So did one or two of the young men.

The good students filled the middle rows, not so eager, kind of prepared, a little slouchy, but with just enough attention to muster decent grades. And then there were the ones who straggled in at the last minute or well after the bell. The ne'er do wells in the back row. He grinned at the memory of his mother using that term when she confronted teachers and principals over the constant barrage of bullying her baby boy had endured. A ne'er-do-well bitching about the ne'er-do-wells. Irony at its finest.

"Hello, everyone." He turned to the board and cleared the notes and lessons from his last class. "To Hamlet," he spun around, giddy to introduce young minds to the ultimate Shakespearean piece, and especially giddy to reach his favourite part of all, "and the graveyard scene." He wiggled his eyebrows.

He paced the front of the room, fulfilling his chosen role, the part of teacher. Back and forth he trod, making occasional eye contact with each student, sometimes choosing to put one or two on the spot. He'd pick a student who was always prepared to get the ball rolling, then point to one in the back and embarrass the hell out of them with how they'd obviously not done their homework. It was a skill his phys-ed teachers had mastered to pick on the non-athletic, the asthmatic wheezers and scrawny weaklings. Now it was his turn.

But he used that little passive-aggressive bullying tactic to make the nerds and keeners feel good about themselves for a change, and to humiliate the stupid cool kids, Finnegan's new brand of losers. The schoolyard would never be a safe place. The hallways and bathrooms would always be fraught with danger. But his classroom? The ones who were there for the right reasons, who gave a shit and tried hard and did their work and paid attention, whether they got great grades or not, he'd always make sure they were comfortable in his domain.

He gestured with his hands, read text from the curriculum-approved version of Hamlet, Shakespeare's greatest work. Not all in the literary world agreed on that. Some argued it was King Lear, Macbeth, or Othello. Or, horror of horrors, the sappy and ridiculous Romeo and Juliet.

No way. Hamlet. The drama and the linguistics and the wit. The graveyard and the bones and the skulls.

"When Hamlet held up one particular skull, he asked the gravedigger who it was. And Hamlet said ..." he pointed at a desk in the back row "… Trevor."

The boy ignored him. A friend smacked his arm and woke him up.

"What the hell, man?"

Finnegan cleared his throat. "To sleep! Perchance to dream; ay, there's the rub."

Trevor sat up. "Huh?"

The class erupted in laughter.

Finnegan walked slowly between the desks in Trevor's direction. "What was the quote, Mr. Norton? When Hamlet held up the skull. I'll give you a hint. It was a friend of his." He raised one eyebrow.

Trevor looked around. "Um. Something about a dude named," he scratched his head, "Yorick? And the Hamlet guy said he knew him well." Trevor looked downright pleased with himself.

"I'll give you one point for knowing the dude's name." Finnegan turned his back on Trevor. "Like many quotations from Shakespeare's work, this one has been mangled. Most people think it is, *Alas! Poor Yorick. I knew him well.*" At the front of the class, he spun around, revelling in the opportunity to be dramatic, and pointed at the nerdiest girl in the room, his prized student with the red hair and freckles and sharp, blue eyes. "Angelica. Do your thing."

She stood and turned to the class. She held her hand in front of her face, palm up, her fingers splayed and pointed skyward, mimicking Hamlet holding the skull. "Alas! Poor Yorick. I knew him Horatio, a fellow of infinite jest, of most excellent fancy."

Finnegan grinned and nodded. "Excelle—"

"He hath borne me on his back a thousand times, and now, how abhorred in my imagination it is!" Angelica grabbed her abdomen. "My gorge rises at it."

The class laughed, and someone tossed a crumpled up piece of paper at Angelica's head.

"All right, settle down." He couldn't believe some of the teacher shit that came out of his mouth sometimes.

"Thank you, Angelica." She had lovely zygomatic bones and a strong mandible. Oh how perfect her skull would be, stripped of its flesh. "But that last part was just showing off." He winked at her.

"Books on the floor. Pop quiz time."

He so loved to torture his students with unexpected tests of their insignificant knowledge.

1997

Let not light see my black and deep desires

The library computer took its sweet time dialling up. Finnegan tapped the eraser end of his pencil against the open page of the anatomy text. He checked his watch. Almost three damn minutes. They had to have the lowest bandwidth ever. The connection blipped and squawked, then let out a long beep, like the sound of a flat lining heart monitor announcing death. Finally, after some static, the blessed silence of connection.

A teenager slammed his books on the computer desk across from Finnegan, shuffled through papers, clicked and clacked on the keyboard.

"Hey, dude. This is a library. Think you could try for silence?" Finnegan eyeballed the boy from around the fourteen-inch monitor.

The kid could barely make eye contact. "Sorry, man." He slouched further in his chair and clicked the mouse a few times.

Finnegan fished a floppy disc out of his messenger bag and slid it in the drive. He scrolled around the folder list and double-clicked on the icon for his second-year paper on age estimation of the human skeleton.

Within a week of moving east, he'd yearned for home. Not for his mother's Swanson specials, not for the awkward silences that had grown from the guilt they shared over past indiscretions. The guilt was all they had left in common, besides DNA. No, he missed the garden and the rest of his collection. As much as he tried to forget and move on, he missed the damn bones. They lay gathering dust beneath his bed, three thousand kilometres west. He brought what he could, but it wasn't much. And without access to any new ones, studying those would have to suffice.

He found the internet icon on the desktop and double clicked it. A box popped up and he entered the user name and password the librarian had given him. All around him, voices hummed and computer keys clacked, and the incessant noise of dial-up connections irritated the hell out of him.

Maybe it was time to invest in a computer of his own. One of those portable laptop things. He could work on assignments over his lunch hour, stop wasting time trudging to and from the library on weekends. Have some privacy for all the searches he didn't have the balls to do in this public space. The old biddy librarian, with her sunken maxilla and prominent temporal process, looked like a walking skeleton. She was always looking over everyone's shoulder, policing what they surfed. Or maybe she was just a nosy old bitch, living vicariously through the library-goers, hoping to catch a glimpse of naked cock on someone's disallowed porn site.

He logged into the learning portal on the Athabasca University website and checked the class forum. The usual boring discussions were well underway. Mostly students looking for others to answer their questions, quick and easy, without the need to do their own research. A few queries about formatting papers and how to put citations in footnotes. He never shared. They had to figure that out for themselves, just like he'd had to when he got his first degree.

Sometimes he'd pose ridiculous questions just to shake up the status quo. "Does the human penis have a bone? Is that why, when you get an erection, it's called a boner?" Pretty much nobody got his sense of humour. Except for Abigail. When he tossed out the Shakespeare-inspired bone pun, "Tibia or not tibia? That is the question," she shot back without a blink: "How humerus. Especially from a guy online to study distal learning."

She was his favourite, her comments always accurate and insightful. And oftentimes a bit creepy. She was also in Toronto, according to the introductions made at the beginning of each class, and she was keenly interested in all things bone-related. They'd shared many private messages on the course materials. He yearned to confide in her, tell her about his collection, the macabre equivalent of "want to come up and see my etchings?"

She was on the forum, seeking input into her paper, preferably from someone who wasn't writing on the same topic or who wouldn't plagiarize her work. Just seeing her name pop up brought a smile to his face.

Finnegan opened a private message and offered his assistance. Perhaps they could meet for coffee and he could look it over. He did have a masters in English lit after all. She quickly accepted.

She was morbid and intense. Smart and on the ball. Who knows, maybe they'd hit it off in person and he could get a little action. Assuming she wasn't completely hideous on the outside. And even if she was, that wasn't a deal breaker.

Push ~ Matchbox 20

Tibba reached into the top drawer of her nightstand and snatched her vibrator. At full speed, it purred against her flesh. Then it rattled and shuddered. Damn thing was going to conk out on her.

Three minutes in and there was no writhing. No unrestrained "fuck yes." No hips bucking in perfect orgasm. She couldn't get past the audible gasps and groans of her aging battery-operated cock. And she couldn't concentrate and clear her head of life's daily helping of bullshit. Gone were the days when she'd get herself off three times in under ten minutes and fall asleep with the dildo still in her hand, thrumming against her thigh, so sated, so totally spent, her heartbeat pounding in her ears.

That vibrator calmed her. Eased her worries. Kept her sane. And it was a consistent lover. It never called her whore. Never got drunk, never raped or beat her. If it died, she'd just pop in new batteries. And if she did try to murder the damn thing, it wouldn't bleed all over her carpet or shit its pants as it took its last pitiful breath.

She summoned the one man she trusted. The only one she could rely on. The one she loved for real, not just loved to fuck. Aidan's face, his smile, those massive hands. But not even Aidan's memory could save her from a failing sex toy.

She pulled it from her body and threw it across the room. It clattered along the floor and landed against the wardrobe, still rattling and shuddering.

At least the furniture was getting off.

She needed some weed. Something to take the edge off, to kill the memories that haunted her. Taunted her. But she hadn't done drugs in years. Wouldn't know where to get any. She closed her eyes, took a deep breath.

In with the good air. A vision of her father infiltrated her peace, followed by Finny morphing from baby to child to teen to Adam. "Damn it." She sat up. Meditation never did do jack shit for her. She just couldn't turn off her brain. Definitely needed drugs.

She flopped back down on the bed and rubbed her eyes. Mental videos of her teen years played behind her eyelids, the pictures flickering like an old-time film reel. Faces of the boys she'd fucked, the ones whose virginity she'd taken after first showing them the proper way to roll a joint. She loved sex on pot. Except afterwards, when she'd shove potato chips in her mouth by the handful and eat cheese right off the block.

But she'd stopped doing weed many years ago when Finny walked in on her and a john. He was almost three and had started climbing out of his crib and crawling down the stairs. His innocent little eyes grew twice their size at the vision of his naked mother straddling some strange man and sucking on a fat doobie.

She installed a lock on the door the next day, and sent him out to a sitter's until he was old enough to fend for himself in the yard for an hour or so. Did he remember that night? Had she screwed him up completely? Was that what led to that kiss in the garden? It was her fault he couldn't hold onto a girlfriend. Her fault her own child had grown to hate her. Even Birdie. That was her fault too. Maybe murder is genetic.

She sat on the edge of her bed. Sunlight streamed in between the crack in her drapes. Maybe she'd stick to gardening in the afternoon. Clearly, sex with a rubber dick was no longer taking the edge off. Gardening and alcohol and cigarettes, that was her happy place.

The vibrator had stopped shimmying against the hardwood, the batteries as dead as the men in her garden. She pitched it into the garbage and pulled on her shorts.

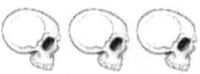

"You actually answered your phone?" Tibba checked the clock and eyed the bourbon. It was five o'clock somewhere, right?

"Well, I'm home, so yeah, I answer the phone when I'm home."

The edge in his voice stung. Like she was an intrusion. His own mother, the giver of his life, who raised him and loved him and got him to adulthood. Was she a perfect mother? Not even close. But there had to be mothers worse than her. Somewhere.

"What's new?"

He heaved a deep sigh. She imagined his eyes rolling. He had become none of her business. He'd missed every promised trip home and his phone calls became nearly non-existent. She was a stranger in her baby boy's life.

"Not much. School is great. I've got some smart students. A new crop to mold each year."

"As smart as you?"

"Smarter."

She huffed. "I find that hard to believe."

"I'm taking some online classes."

She poured two fingers of whiskey neat and took a sip. "Classes? Two degrees isn't enough?"

Another sigh. "Just something I'm interested in. And you? Anything new?"

"Yeah, tons of stuff."

There was a pause. Probably shock and disbelief. "That's great. Like what?"

"I took up yoga. Getting in great shape, like I'm thirty again." She eyed her reflection in the toaster, poked at the flabby layer around her belly, squeezed the cellulite on her thigh. He'd never know she was shitting him. He was probably never coming home again anyway. "And I'm thinking of going vegan."

He snorted into the phone. "You? You do know that vegan means nothing but vegetables, right?"

"Yes, smarty-pants. Well, maybe not totally vegan. Maybe vegetarian." She smirked.

"What about smoking, going to give that up too? And drinking?"

Was he mocking her?

"I haven't smoked in months." Lying to him was kind of fun. Maybe she'd make up a fiancé and set a fake wedding date. Would he visit her then? "But no, I'm not going to stop drinking. Girl's gotta have some fun."

"And how is the garden?"

"Oh, it's beautiful!" Her words tumbled out, her love of that garden evident every time he asked about it. She went on for ten minutes about the impatiens and the snapdragons, the colours and the aroma, gushed about how she spent all her time out there. "You know, since I've nothing else to do. No one to take care of. No one coming to visit." Her voice soured at the end.

He sighed. "Mom, I'll come home for a visit soon. I promise. Christmas for sure."

"Well, wouldn't that be lovely." She bit the edge of her thumbnail. "Finny Mac, it's been four years." She couldn't keep the desperate whine out of her voice. "Four years! I could die and you'd regret not coming home more often."

"You're not going to die. You're only fifty-two."

"Aidan was only thirty-seven."

"Mom. He was killed in the line of duty. Is there something you're not telling me? Are you ill?"

She huffed into the phone. "No. I'm fine."

"Excellent. Any new men in your life?"

She froze. "What's that supposed to mean?"

"Nothing. Just wondering if you're seeing anyone. If you've met anyone."

"You know I don't do that anymore." She fumbled with her lighter, lit a cigarette and inhaled.

"I can hear you smoking, you know. Not that I believed you'd actually quit. And I don't mean that you're hooking again. I mean, well. It's been almost twelve years since Aidan died. That's all. I thought maybe you'd find someone to love again."

She exhaled into the receiver. "Not interested."

A few more awkward exchanges and she told him she loved him, begged him once more to come home before she up and died. He assured her again that she wasn't going to die.

So why did it feel like she was already there?

Life had become a rote string of boring days and dull nights. Work, eat, drink, smoke, sleep, start again. The only thing she looked forward to was spring and her time in the garden. Getting her hands dirty, smelling the roses — literally, since there was no figurative smelling of them going on — and nurturing her plants. At least it gave her something to nurture. But the long winters nearly killed her.

She was so bored she had considered going back to hooking. What would Finny think of her then? But the idea of strange dick sickened her. Besides, who'd hire a prostitute who was pushing fifty? The mirror gave her that answer. Sagging breasts, jiggly thighs. Her wrinkles were more pronounced each month, and there were even weird discolourations on her hands and face that her doctor said were age spots.

Age spots, for fuck's sake!

She was better off working a straight job, especially since she'd worked her way up from stocking shelves, through the cashier ranks, and now supervised the day shift. No more polyester vest and pants. She chose dresses that flattered her full figure, highlighted her breasts and cleavage, her best feature. She got plenty of male attention at the grocery store. But it was attention she didn't want. Dating didn't interest her, the hooking kind or the straight kind. Even her vibrator gave up on her. If only she could get her sex drive to shut down, maybe she'd quit thinking about all this shit.

Relationships were too much damn work anyway. Too many expectations she didn't have the desire, nor the patience, to fulfill. And under no circumstances was she going to cook and clean for any man except Finnegan. Her brief stint as June Cleaver was long since over.

No matter how she tried to talk herself out of it, how she reasoned that she was better off without it, she missed sex. Good sex. Hard sex. But could she find anyone to replace Aidan in the bedroom? He, of the gentle-giant hands, of the bluest eyes that made her want to dive in and take a swim. He, who knew her truth and married her anyway. She hadn't deserved him. There was no one better. And no one better in bed. Except Adam. She sighed.

Too bad dead men don't fuck.

Though she be but little she is fierce

Finnegan picked up the paper coffee cup with both hands, warmed his fingers, and sipped through the little hole in the lid. Even his thick flannel shirt wasn't enough to take the edge off a Toronto winter day.

The double glass doors, icy with frost, welcomed a never-ending stream of humanity seeking the healing powers of a hot beverage on a Saturday afternoon. People ordered their favourite forms of caffeine, then tried to find an empty seat to perch on. He'd put his messenger bag on the chair opposite him to claim it for Abigail.

It was the heart of the Christmas season, just a couple weeks from holiday break. He still hadn't booked a flight to go visit his mother.

Must be some Freudian reason behind it. Some psychobabble that blames all his troubles on his upbringing. On spending too much time alone, on finding bones in the yard, on never meeting his father, wanting to fuck his mother. Hell, maybe it wasn't bullshit. He didn't want to go back to that house. Not yet. Maybe not ever.

He eyeballed every woman who came through the door. Too young. Somebody's grandmother. Too preppy. No way Abigail dressed in pleated plaid skirts and hair bands. The shit she said on the class forum was way too far gone for that. A woman in her mid-twenties entered, her black T-shirt emblazoned with a sparkly skull. She wore too much black eyeliner and not enough warm clothing.

He straightened in his chair, ready to flag her down.

She looked around the café and her gaze sailed right on past him. She waved to someone on the other side of the room.

He slouched back down and looked at his watch. Twenty-two minutes late. He stared out the window. Just how long would be appropriate to wait before he decided she'd changed her mind and stood him up? He tore the lid off the coffee and tossed it onto the table. He sucked on the edge of the cup until the paper softened, then crushed it between his teeth.

"Finnegan?"

Her voice was deep and gravelly, very Kathleen Turner. A tiny woman stood in front of him, bundled in an oversized parka with a faux-fur-trimmed hood. Her brown hair hung to her shoulders, with a slight curl at the end. Under the open parka, her sweater fit snugly against her thin frame, the neckline grazing her prominent clavicle. Sort of preppy. A bit mousy. Very few curves. And no makeup.

He hadn't expected her to be so, so …. Normal. Nothing about her screamed morbid bone freak. He couldn't help but be disappointed. What struck him the most was her age. He'd anticipated someone in her twenties. The fine lines across her forehead and around her eyes, which crinkled in an endearing way when she smiled, told him she was nearly forty. Maybe more.

"Abigail?" He pushed his chair back and stood, held his hand out to her.

Her cheeks pinked. "We're past that, aren't we?" She leaned into him and hugged him, reaching her down filled arms around his midsection, one ear to his chest, her oversized purse smacking him in the thigh.

The scent of strawberries and musk, a collision of drugstore shampoo and cheap perfume, swirled around her. A vision of his mother, post-coital, freshly showered, intruded on the moment.

Finnegan gave Abigail's tiny body a gentle squeeze before pulling away from the awkward embrace. "Please, sit." He snatched his messenger bag from the chair and pitched it under the table. "Can I get you a coffee?"

"Sure. Dark roast. Black."

He smiled. Perfect. He ordered the coffee and set it in front of her.

She looked away, could barely hold his gaze. Her online character was bold and brash, courageous and challenging. She hid behind the anonymity of the internet, the computer screen protecting her real persona like a shield of armour. Or maybe more like dramatic masks. Comedy and tragedy. Given the glint in her eyes, she was more Thalia than Melpomene.

He sipped his coffee and smiled at her. "So."

Her own smile seemed a permanent fixture. Her brows flickered with anticipation. Or perhaps she had a tic.

"Bones." It was all he could think of to say. The only thing they had in common. A ghoulish fascination with those ossified hunks of human tissue that prevented people from being nothing more than gelatinous blobs of organs and flesh.

Her glinting eyes lit up even more. "Did you hear that they found human remains in Spain? The oldest humans found in Western Europe. Eight-hundred-thousand years old. And they think they are ancestors of Neanderthals and modern humans." She talked as fast as she typed. And she pronounced Neanderthal correctly, with a hard T.

She pulled a notebook from her purse. "*Homo antecessor.*" She peered up at him like a dog that'd rolled over on command.

He had the urge to toss a treat in her mouth and scratch her behind the ears.

She was pretty, in a plain, no-frills way. But talking about bones made the colour rise in her cheeks and fire dance in her eyes.

She flipped her book shut. The cover was replete with doodles of skulls and femurs. Not just doodles, nothing cartoonish. Quite accomplished. She was an artist and a bone nut.

"Sorry." The light dimmed. "I get carried away."

He reached across and tugged the book from her hand. She resisted at first, and then let it go. "Don't be sorry. You're passionate. That's commendable." There he went, sounding all teachery again. He was meeting a bone-loving soul mate for fuck's sake, not one of his high school students. He glanced at her. No, she'd not been to high school for a couple decades.

He ran a fingertip over her drawings, flipped the pages to find dozens more. "Your drawings are excellent. I take it anatomy class is just a stepping stone to something more?" He handed her the book.

She nodded. "Anthropology. I'm already enrolled at U of T. Second year. Just getting a jumpstart on some other courses through distance learning. I want to dig up ancient people, discover the evolutionary links. Put other, less-scientific theories to rest."

He laughed. "That's a tall order. Those less-scientific theories are steeped in centuries of mythology and protected by the unwavering absoluteness of blind faith."

"At least you get it. My parents think I'm going to rot in hell."

"That's okay. All the fun people end up there." He upended his cup and finished his coffee. "You still worry what your parents think?"

She blushed. "I kind of have to. When I got divorced, I moved back in with them. Decided, what the hell, time to do what I've always dreamed of. They're helping me with the tuition."

They sat in silence for a minute until he remembered why they'd agreed to meet in the first place. "So, your paper."

"Right." She pulled an inch-thick slab from her bag and handed it to him.

He was beginning to regret his offer to read it.

"It looks worse than it is," she blurted out. Smart, attractive enough, and she could read his face. Though maybe that last thing wasn't a plus. "I always do my first draft quadruple-spaced with huge margins so I have a ton of room for notes."

"Cool. I'll give it a look tomorrow. Maybe you can drop by and pick it up?"

"Oh, that's a photocopy. You can just email me comments." Her eager smile dwindled and her brows furrowed. "I mean, unless you want me to pick it up."

He grinned. She wasn't adept in the art of flirtation, that was certain. "Why don't we play it by ear."

She dug into her purse and slid a piece of cloth across the table.

He picked it up, unfolded it and looked up at her in surprise. He whisked the cloth into his lap, stared at the gift it held. He ran the bone between his thumb and forefinger. His body warmed and his heartbeat hastened. "Where'd you get it?"

"Promise not to tell?"

He nodded.

She leaned in. "There's a body farm not far from North Bay. I interned there last year and stayed on as a volunteer. I sort of took a few —" her entire face turned red "— souvenirs."

"Are you joking? Can you do that?"

"Technically, no. But they just chalk it up to animal predation and move on. A few missing bones is no big deal. They're all about studying decomposition. How different environmental factors affect it. Heat, cold, moisture, flora." She flicked her fingers at him, palm up.

He relinquished the bone to her hand.

She tucked it back in her purse. "I don't care about all the goo. I just like the bones. The bones tell the story, you know?" She glanced around. "Want to get out of here?" She leaned in. "I can show you my collection."

His stomach hollowed. "You have a whole collection?"

"Hell yeah, I do." She jerked her head toward the door. "Come on. You'll love it."

1998

...nothing in his life Became him like the leaving it

Tibba flicked the tip of her cigarette into the ashtray and sipped on her merlot. The place reeked of smoke and booze, of sweat and desperation.

She hadn't been to a bar in years. Not since Aidan took her dancing, and before that, not since Finny was a preteen. There'd been no need to troll the dark corners of public houses. She'd had a full roster of long-standing customers.

But this wasn't business. It was sheer and utter loneliness. Her own son didn't want to come home to visit. What had it been now, five-and-a-half years? Almost six fucking years, and even the phone calls, which used to be weekly, then monthly, now only came on her birthday and Christmas.

How could she blame him? She'd screwed him up from the start. Killing his father. Having sex with random men in his house. He'd made a mistake — one damn mistake, a doozy though it might have been — and what does she do? She lets him know he made it. Let's him know she knows what he did. Like it absolved her of her deeds. Somehow made her cleaner. Better. Had she ever been clean? Or good?

The music, some canned top-forty crap, boomed from large speakers in every corner of the room. The seat of her barstool vibrated and pulsed with every thump of bass. It was the most action she'd had since her vibrator died.

Voices buzzed around her, like they were right in her ear, boring into her brain. A bead of sweat formed on her upper lip. The movement of bodies in the cramped space, blurred by a haze of second-hand smoke, was like a slo-mo reel in a shitty B-grade horror movie. Any minute now, some dude in a hockey mask would jump out of the shadows and start slashing people to death. And if one more person elbowed her in the back, she'd lose her shit. Should have gotten a booth instead of perching at the bar like some hot twenty-something, all on display, ready and willing. Open for business.

"You come here often?"

She cringed at the raspy whisper in her ear. The smell of vodka on his breath made her stomach clench. She turned slowly. A man in his mid-fifties, maybe pushing sixty, flashed a lopsided grin at her.

"Sorry. Lamest line on earth, am I right?" He held his hand out. "Ron. And you are?"

She shook his hand, a tad clammy, but warm. "Bored."

His open-mouthed guffaw revealed a set of perfectly aligned teeth. Too perfect. Not even his. She could see where they didn't quite meet the gums.

"I hear ya, sweetheart."

Her upper lip quivered.

He wedged himself between her and the guy on the next stool and rested the elbow of his tweed blazer on the sticky bar. "All these older guys, trying to get with the young chicks." He shook his head, the grin never leaving his face, plastered there like a rubber clown's mask. "Hey, been there, done that. Am I right?"

She took a gulp of wine and a long drag on her smoke.

"Then I saw you and thought, hey now, there's a woman I could get to know."

Translation: there's a woman he might have a shot with, a woman who's seen better days, desperate for a little human contact. A woman just like him.

He ran a finger along her bare arm.

Despite her revulsion at his appearance and demeanor, a shiver ran through her.

"A mature woman, not some overly made-up, barely dressed little girl."

She winced. Mature. Fuck you.

She finished her cigarette and stubbed out the butt. "Shouldn't you be going home to the wife? It's getting late. After your curfew and all."

He laughed. "You're feisty. I like that." He leaned in. "The wife and I haven't been on the same page for years, if you know what I mean. I need more than she's willing to give." He brushed her hair away from her face.

His advances were as awkward as a ten-year-old doing the box step. She needed the rumba. The Argentine tango. But her body defied her again. Her nipples hardened and her lips parted a sliver.

"So, what do you say? Want to get out of here?" He cocked one eyebrow.

She lit another cigarette and weighed her options. Tell this loser to fuck off and take her chances that someone worthwhile would notice her. Go home alone. Or suck it up and let baldy get her off. She hadn't had sex with a human being in twelve years.

He heaved a huge sigh. "Okay, let's cut to the chase. I want to fuck you. Hell, I'm even willing to pay for it. Because at my age, I'll take it any way I can get it, am I right?"

She took an exaggerated draw on her cigarette, sucked the smoke deep into her lungs and blew it at his face. "All right. A hundred bucks. I'll knock your socks clear across the room."

He stammered and tugged at his collar.

Chicken shit. All bravado disappears when the hunter becomes the hunted.

She was beginning to enjoy this. Like riding a bike, it all came back as soon as she was in the driver's seat.

She brushed the foggy cliché from her brain, pitched her lighter into her purse and turned to face him. "Well, you in?"

He swallowed. "Yes. There's a motel up the street."

"Why not just come to my place?"

He nodded. A trickle of sweat dripped from his temple. "I'll get a cab."

"No need, I've got my car out front."

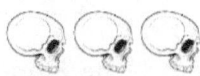

Tibba tossed her keys into the bowl on the ledge by the front door. Ron grabbed her around her waist from behind and stuck his tongue in her ear while he fumbled with his belt buckle.

"Slow down there, Speedy Gonzales." She squirmed away and headed for the kitchen. "We've got all night," she called over her shoulder, then mumbled under her breath, "and I need a real drink."

She poured two tumblers of bourbon, gunned one and filled it again. Ron had stripped off his socks and his white button-down dress shirt. He'd turned the stereo on and helped himself to the CDs. He was swaying to *Sexual Healing* in nothing but his pants and undershirt. Bugger was already lit.

She danced into the living room and handed him a drink, clinked her glass to his. "Bottoms up."

He raised the glass to his lips. "I sure hope so." He drank the entire glass and shook his head as a shiver ran through his body. He put the glass on the side table and pulled her to him, dancing around the room and singing loudly in her ear.

She laughed at first, but when the smell of his feet niggled into her nostrils, the fun began to flop.

He tripped on the coffee table and fell sideways, grabbed her arm and pulled her down with him. She landed on top of him on the chesterfield. He pawed at her ass and kissed her, stuck his tongue in her mouth and groped one breast.

He tasted like polish sausage with sauerkraut and his sweat stank of alcohol.

Her own drinks threatened to come back up. She wedged her arms against his chest and pushed him away. She sat at the end of the chesterfield and took a deep breath.

What the hell was she doing? She didn't need a measly hundred dollars. She'd budgeted Aidan's insurance money and survivor's pension, stretched what she made at the grocery store, and even managed to save enough to retire in a few years. Why was she doing this? What would Aidan think? And Finnegan? How would she look him in the eye if she started hooking again? Assuming his eyes would ever be in the same room as hers.

"I've changed my mind." She stood and grabbed her purse, pulled out the five twenties he'd given her in the car. "You can leave." She held out the cash and wiggled it at him.

He snatched the money from her fingers and huffed through his nose. "Leave? You can't crank me up, then shut me down." He threw the money on the coffee table, seized her arm and pulled her to him. He smashed his lips into hers and shoved his obnoxious tongue in her mouth.

She bit it.

He jerked his head sideways, his hand flew to his mouth. He pulled it away and looked at the palm. "You bitch. I'm bleeding." He balled his fists and took a swing at her.

She weaved, but his fist caught her chin. She stumbled backward and held the ledge by the front door for balance.

His goofy demeanor in the bar had morphed into familiar drunken rage. The faces of every man who had ever struck her, called her names, fucked her in a way she didn't want, or raped her, passed in front of her eyes. Her father was front and centre. It was as if every one of them were in the room at that moment, a parade of past mistakes taunting her, high-fiving Ron for putting her in her place. They goaded her with a fact she kept trying to bury.

You're a whore, Tibba. Nothing but a dirty slut. Only good for one thing.

Her hand touched the metal bowl with her keys in it. She clutched the edge and yanked it from its perch. Her keychain rocketed out of the bowl and hit the linoleum in the front entry. She charged at Ron.

His eyes went from anger to confusion.

The bottom of the metal bowl hit him just above the left eye. The second blow, a powerful backhand, caught him under the jaw with the edge of the bowl and sliced open his flesh.

He held up his arms to protect his face, so she kicked him between the legs. He grabbed his crotch and fell to his knees. His yells and groans barely registered through the thrum of pulse in her ears.

He lay on the carpet in the fetal position next to her mother's old trunk. Tibba kicked at his body until he stopped moving.

She cradled his head in both hands and lifted it, turned it until he looked her in the eye. "Didn't anyone ever tell you, Ron? No means no." She smirked, and slammed his head into the brass corner of the trunk.

He slumped to the floor. Blood oozed from a wound on his temple and dripped onto the rug.

She kneeled beside him, put her mouth close to his ear and sneered, "Am I right?"

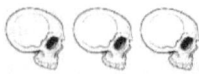

Smoke curled from the tip of her cigarette and danced around the fixture that hung from the ceiling. The light from the shitty old chandelier, half of its fake candles burned out, filtered through the haze. Tibba butted the cigarette out in the overflowing ashtray and lit another, then poured the last of the bourbon into the tumbler.

A blue tarp lay at her feet, protecting the kitchen floor. Ron wasn't that big a guy, easy to roll onto the tarp and drag from the living room. She was in no hurry. Digging up the garden by the light of the moon didn't deliver the same thrill it used to. Frost had already permeated the ground. It'd be a chore to break through the hard soil. She rubbed her lower back and cracked her aching neck. Screw him. He'd have to wait for spring.

She glanced at the clock. He'd been resting for three hours. She'd learned her lessons over the years. The longer you wait before cutting them into manageable pieces, the less spurt and spatter to deal with. His blood would be good and still, pooled where it had stopped flowing. It would just ooze out the cut ends of his dismembered parts and drip with delicious lethargy onto the blue of the tarp. Maybe she'd finger paint with it. Turn his ugly life into a masterpiece of death.

She stabbed the lit end of her cigarette into the ashen skin of Ron's cheek until it was snuffed out. Her father's old hatchet sat on the kitchen table. She'd discovered it behind some boxes in the basement a couple of years earlier. She snapped on rubber gloves to protect her skin from the slivers the wooden handle never failed to poke into her flesh. Like he was abusing her from the grave, his hatred for her never-ending. She'd considered getting a new one, with a rubber grip and a stainless blade. But the heft and balance of the decades-old hickory and weight of the forged steel with its random rust stains were satisfying.

One knee and both ankles popped as she squatted beside the body. This would have to be the last time. She was way too young to feel this old.

The hatchet blade sliced through the flesh and muscle of his left shoulder and cracked against the joint. A second blow separated the arm from the shoulder blade. She swapped out the hatchet for her best butcher knife — the one she kept hidden above the fridge because it wasn't safe for cooking — and hacked the tendons and fat and sinew away from the shoulder and collarbone until his arm came free from his body. She swaddled it in Saran wrap, tucked it into a black garbage bag, and sealed the entire thing in butcher's tape. She'd discovered the hard way that duct tape doesn't stick below zero. Had to toss out half a dozen Swanson dinners thanks to the goo that seeped from previous victims before they froze.

First time she'd done this, she could haul half a body down the basement stairs in one big garbage bag. Now it was two parts at a time, three if they were small, pausing between trips to catch her breath. She stood at the top of the stairs and took a deep inhale. This was it. The last trip to the freezer with the last body parts of the last man she'd ever let touch her like that. She should have a ceremony or something. Dance naked by the light of the moon.

She shivered. The festivities could wait for the warmth of late spring when she would haul all his parts out to the garden.

She tossed sealed packages containing a foot and a thigh onto the pile of Ron on the cement floor. The chest freezer was nearly full of leftovers and T.V. dinners. She shifted the dinners to one side and into the sliding basket. Long-forgotten and freezer-burned ground beef and chicken legs landed on the floor, destined for their final resting place in the garbage bin. She dug to the bottom of the freezer, shifting containers and pitching out food. A label — a trick she learned from her mother all those years ago, the only decent advice she'd ever given her — caught her eye. Lamb curry? When the hell had she ever made lamb curry? She peered at the label, squinted to focus her gaze on the penmanship. It was her mother's handwriting.

"Lord fucking god." She tossed the old Tupperware container

on top of the discarded meat. Thirty-year-old curry. That shit was disgusting when it was fresh. How had she not noticed that all these years?

Once Ron was nestled in his frozen coffin, Tibba yanked a Hefty bag out of a box that sat on the basement floor. She filled it with the rejected freezer meats and dragged it to the kitchen, it's weight thumping up each wooden stair. Halfway up, she paused. Pain seared across her back and the left side of her jaw ached. It was all she could do not to curl up, right there on the steps, and sleep. But a bag of frozen food would make a lousy pillow. Maybe it was time to ease off the booze and smokes. Or join a gym. Or … not.

In the kitchen, she rolled the tarp into a tight ball and wrapped it with duct tape to keep the blood and bits of flesh and splintered bone from escaping. She'd become a master of making them as little as possible. This one wasn't much bigger than a small watermelon. She shoved it into the bag of eighty-sixed food and hauled the whole thing out to the curb. Perfect timing, tomorrow was garbage day. Good thing. That lamb curry was going to stink.

I never met a girl like you before ~ Edwyn Collins

Between being a teacher during the day, a student in his spare time, and spending as much time with Abigail as possible, all Finnegan had time left for was sleeping. He'd not been in touch with his mother for months, had bailed on his promised Christmas visit again. Now that spring had sprung, thoughts of cherry blossoms, creeping thyme, and the colours of the bougainvillea left him aching for home. For the garden. For the bones.

But not so much for his mother.

She'd become shrill and jumpy and miserable most of the time. Perhaps losing the love of your life, murdering your neighbours, and having your son, who inherited your killer gene, try to sleep with you, turned you into a mumbling, more-drunk-than-usual hermit. Not even spring in the garden could make him want to go home to that.

He'd rather stay with Abigail. He was falling in love with her, no question about it. She was a conundrum, a paradox. All Jan Brady on the outside, all Wednesday Addams on the inside. The inside turned him on. The morbid fascination with death, the obsession with bones, the compulsion to dig them up, touch them, try to figure out who they were and what had happened to them. Hell, she was the female version of him.

So why couldn't he fuck her? Did he love her? Or himself? Or was it some underlying Oedipal thing, her being twelve years older and all? It's not like she was the first forty year old he'd been with. They'd kissed and made out a bit on the chesterfield. Very tenth grade, with heavy petting over their clothes. But whenever she wanted more, he pulled away. He wanted her. Needed her. But he couldn't get his body to connect with his brain. Couldn't get his pecker to pop. It made no sense. He could jack off any time he wanted to, at any hour of the day.

Regular visits to a psychologist weren't helping him figure it out. Because like hell was he actually going to share his dark twisted ruminations, even with a professional. Doctor-patient privilege be damned. What if he told them about the bone garden and they called the cops? Dug up the yard? Arrested his mother? Weren't doctors obligated to spill the beans to authorities when the safety of others was at risk?

It didn't matter how nuts his mother had become. The men in the garden must have deserved it. Had to have done something dastardly to meet their fates. And he had no plans to tell a soul. Not out of selfless love for his mother. It was self-preservation. Parts of Birdie might still be in that dirt.

His thoughts were all over the map, and the one place they weren't was on his studies. He slammed his textbook shut and hovered his mouse over the Windows button to shut down. Then a message popped up from Abigail.

"Meet me?"

"Definitely. Café?"

"Yes please."

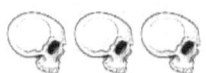

The coffee shop hummed as usual, spring bringing out the caffeine lovers in droves, along with shorts and miniskirts and tank tops. A myriad of young girls, all tarted up, pranced around the café. Finnegan looked past all the skin, waiting for his Abigail to enter the shop. It was one of the things he loved about her. She wore normal clothes that covered her body. And as hot as that body was, it was her mind that was sexy. The outside stuff, that changed, morphed from taut and pert to loose and stretch-marked, lumpy and saggy and flabby. It meant nothing, it was just the packaging. Just the vessel for the bones and the brain. And those things, for the most part, those things didn't change.

She rushed in, her cheeks pink and her eyes pinched. She sat and grasped the coffee he'd ordered for her, and drank at least half of it at once. "Thanks. I really needed that."

"What's going on?"

"They're closing it down." Her brow and forehead wrinkled.

"Shutting what down?"

"The body farm." Tears welled in her eyes, yet she managed to keep the permanent smile affixed to her face. "Funding fell through. Government didn't think the research was worth the cost, we can just use the research from the ones in the States. Like in Tennessee."

"Shit, Abby. I'm so sorry."

"Yeah. No more bones."

He could take her home. Show her the burial grounds in his mother's yard. Would she balk? Call the cops? Hate him instead of love him? His very own body farm, but where the bodies hadn't died of natural causes, nor at the hands of killers who'd already been brought to justice.

"When will it be closed?"

"Already is. They're going to appeal. But regardless, site reclamation starts in two weeks."

"Reclamation? You mean, removing the remains?"

"Yup. Probably just dump them all in an unmarked grave, or burn them up into dust."

What a waste of perfectly good bones.

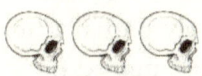

The beams of their flashlights bounced off trunks of mountain elm and white ash, catching the leaves that rustled in the breeze. Bolt cutters had clipped through the wire fence with relative ease. Abby slid right through, but Finnegan had to cut a few more links to get his height and bulk past the sharp prongs. He caught his khakis on one edge and tore his pants.

Just like old times in the garden at home. Except here, in the defunct body farm, there were no petunias, purple dead nettle, or creeping thyme. All he could see in the narrow strand of light were a few wild violets and some dandelions.

"Here, this is my favourite spot."

"Why here?" he whispered.

She smiled at him. "No need to whisper. There's no one around for miles. Part of the lack of funds to operate means no security. Just that stupid wire fence and a bunch of keep out signs." She handed him a canvas bag and shined her light back and forth along the ground. "The bodies here are the most decomposed. The oldest. All bones, none of the gruesome, rotting flesh. No guts or slimy ooze."

His stomach churned. "Please. I'd like to keep my pizza down."

"And the stench is minimal. Also, no maggots."

Another thing he loved about bones. Even if you shoved them right under your nose, they smelled like nothing. If nothing were a smell.

She took a couple of steps and scuffed the dirt with the toe of one sneaker. "Meet Red Skeleton."

He stifled a laugh. "Cute. Did you name them all?"

She pointed her light around the area. "This is Bone, James Bone. Over there is Mrs. Bonejangles, and James Bone junior."

"Junior?"

"Yeah, that one is a kid. A pre-teen boy."

At least it wasn't a twelve-year-old girl.

He squatted next to the boy. His heartbeat quickened at the sight of the boy's skull. He rubbed a thumb over the frontal bone. Hardened skin the colour of licorice, like a latex mask, fell away and landed in the dirt. "He's only partially buried." A portion of an ulna poked out of the ground. He tugged on it until the earth gave up the treasure. The part that had been exposed to the elements was white, as if bleached.

"Tests different decomp rates. Open air. Partial cover. Fully underground. Somewhere around here, there are actual graves. Well, unmarked ones with John and Jane Does in them."

He tossed the sack full of gardening implements to the ground. "How much do you want to take?"

"Let's start with the kid. If I don't hear anything in the next few days, any uproar about missing remains, we can come back." She surveyed the area. "Something tells me no one is taking inventory."

Next time, Finnegan wanted to dig up an entire grave. Go full Hamlet on this place. He tossed her a pair of gloves and handed her a small spade. He opened the bag and set it on the ground.

He plucked decayed mushrooms from beside the boy's abdomen and flicked them aside, brushed loose soil from his sternum. The child was fully skeletonized. He picked up a rib and shined his flashlight on it. "What's this marking?"

Abby looked over her shoulder. "Animal predation. There are traps and different forms of deterrent, but some animals just don't care. The skeleton is probably not all there."

He placed the rib into the bag and continued to thieve the boy's body. He exhumed the skull and turned it over in his hand. There was a small hole in the occipital. "What happened to him?"

"Shot. Found in a shallow grave out near Elk Lake. That was way back in Seventy-four or so. He was never identified."

Finnegan held the skull facing him and silently cursed Birdie for leaving him. Did the pitchfork penetrate her bones? Leave holes in her remains? Someday, someone would find her body and wonder what happened to her. Maybe by then a simple scan of her skeleton would reveal her identity in an instant. She could have a proper burial. It was the least she deserved.

He wiped his wet cheek and nestled the skull in the bag.

Abby used the spade to scrape hardened dirt away from the pelvis. She held the flashlight in her teeth, like she was giving the torch a blowjob. Between that visual, a quick mental flash of the back of his mother's head bobbing up and down, and his proximity to so many bones, his groin started to ache. He scooted up behind Abby and circled her waist with one arm, brushed her hair aside and planted tender kisses on her soft neck.

The flashlight fell from her mouth and landed next to the boy's pelvis, its beam bathing the site in shadowy light. She leaned against Finnegan and a soft moan escaped her lips.

He unbuttoned her shirt and reached inside, massaged one tiny breast. She responded by grinding her rear on his crotch before turning around and pushing him to the ground. She pulled his T-shirt up and ran her lips along his taut belly, suckled on one nipple, all the while fumbling with the buckle of his belt.

He brushed her hand away and undid the buckle, shimmied his pants down to his thighs. Abigail stood up and stripped off her jeans.

Her slight frame and white skin nearly glowed in the faint light. She straddled him and guided him inside her.

He rolled her onto her back, slid one arm under her lumbar vertebrae and the other under her cervical vertebrae, massaging her spinous processes. Months of built up tension took only a few seconds to release. Her body went limp with what he could only assume was utter disappointment at the shortest fuck of all time.

"Sorry," he whispered in her ear. "It's been a while."

She kissed his cheek. "That's okay."

Did she ever stop smiling?

She's beautiful, and therefore to be wooed

The trees had blossomed and the grass was green, trimmed low to the ground for easy walking, and clipped close to each gravestone with precise care. The stones were proof of love for those who'd been buried there. Rows of marble slabs, polished until they gleamed, the sun bouncing off their surface. Some had vases attached to them, or fresh bouquets laid to rest at the base of the stone. On some graves, paper notes were held down by pebbles and sometimes by toys — stuffed animals, wooden cars, occasionally something weird, like a plastic Darth Vader or an old Gumby with its wire bones protruding from broken rubber knees.

Finnegan preferred those to the sad and pathetic monuments. The ones with no sign that the occupant was missed. The graves memorialized with tiny markers, whose stones sat untended, dusty, forgotten.

He slipped his hand into Abby's and they strolled between the bodies, their favourite Sunday evening pastime. A group of solemn mourners gathered around a gravesite for a late funeral. Abby tugged on Finnegan's hand and led him closer to the service. They paused at a respectful distance and listened to the minister intone the same old burial rituals. Just once, it'd be nifty if someone shook up the boring funeral status quo.

The sound of sniffing and whimpering filled the air. As did the smell of reefer. Finnegan peered around and found a lone griever standing off to the side, a teenager trying his damnedest to hide his joint. An older woman seated at the side of the grave glared at him. If looks could kill, it'd be this kid's funeral, not whoever was laying in that casket. And what a casket it was. Lustrous ebony with gilded corners and golden handles.

Abby played a game she'd started the first time they'd happened upon a funeral. "Here lies Jedidiah Churchydude. He was a good man. A Christian man. On Sundays that is. Monday to Friday, he was drunk off his ass and feeling up the waitresses at Hooters before heading home for Grace. That's his wife right over there. Wave to the people, Grace!"

Finnegan struggled not to laugh out loud and piss off the minister. Thus the respectful distance.

The minister stooped and gathered a handful of dirt. Finnegan dragged Abby nearer to the grave.

"In sure and certain hope of the resurrection to eternal life through our Lord Jesus Christ, we commend to Almighty God our brother, Roger Ackroyd; and we commit his body to the ground; earth to earth; ashes to ashes, dust to dust."

The minister opened his hand and let the dirt fall onto the casket. "The Lord bless him and keep him, the Lord make his face to shine upon him and be gracious unto him and give him peace. Amen."

Each mourner paraded past the casket. Some threw dirt, a few tossed roses or other flowers. The obvious matriarch of the family pulled the pothead teen along by the ear to the graveside. Some hugging and crying, pinged with the occasional peel of inappropriate laughter, and that was that. The crowd dispersed and made their way to the line of cars parked along the gravelled access road, anxious to scarf down egg salad sandwiches and cake. A few sniffling people wandered past Finnegan and Abby.

He nodded at them, mumbled "I'm sorry for your loss." When the taillights of the last car flickered at the cemetery's exit before turning left, Finnegan grabbed Abby's hand and raced toward the grave. He dropped to his knees at the base of the dirt pile and picked up two handfuls of freshly turned earth, held it high in the air and sprinkled it on the casket. He flicked some of it at Abby. As the sun went down, they had a dirt fight and rolled around in the grass until the rumble of a backhoe and the putt-putt of the gravediggers' motorized cart echoed off the gravestones.

They scurried behind a tree and peeked out, Finnegan standing behind Abby, peering over her head.

The gravediggers released the handbrake on the casket-lowering device. The coffin silently descended into its final resting place. They disconnected the straps, rolled them up, and lifted the device from the grave, telescoping it down to a more manageable size before placing it on the back of the cart. One gravedigger grabbed a spade from the cart and the other climbed into the backhoe and fired it up. He pushed piles of dirt on top of the coffin, and the other man used the shovel to fill in the sides, all the while whistling a merry tune.

Finnegan wrapped his arms around Abby's shoulders and placed his lips near her ears. "Has this fellow no feeling of his business? He sings at grave making."

"He's not singing. He's whistling." She held his hands at her chest and leaned her head against his clavicle.

"*But age with his stealing steps,*" Finnegan sang, "*hath clawed me in his clutch, and hath shipped me into the land, as if I had never been such.*" Finnegan spun her around. "Now if only they'd toss a skull in the air, my life would be complete."

She laughed. "You are so weird." She stood on her tiptoes and kissed him, took him by the hand and ran between gravestones in the twilight. They found their favourite monument, a massive headstone that spanned three graves. The back of it was sheltered on two sides by red maples, creating a private, and, in the daylight, shaded spot. They weren't concerned about shade that night. The graveyard was nothing but shadow. Eerie, creepy, goose bump-inducing shadow.

Abby dragged Finnegan to the ground and kissed him, tugging at the fly of his khakis. They had sex in the graveyard, their favourite place to make love. Close to the bones. To the dead. To each other.

After they finished, Finnegan propped up on one elbow and traced the lines of her face with his fingers. He didn't believe in fate. Not kismet or karma or any of that superstitious bullshit. But how could he explain Abby? She was perfect for him. It couldn't be divine intervention. But it was one hell of a wonderful coincidence.

He couldn't imagine life without her. It was time. Time to do something that scared him more than any graveyard could. More than bodies decomposing in the dirt scared normal people.

It was time for Abby to meet his mother.

1999

She is a woman, and therefore to be won

Abby hated diamonds. Despised anything flashy. She was a no-bling kind of woman. Finnegan appreciated her no-frills wardrobe, makeup-free face, her matter-of-fact manner. No woman had made him feel this way before. Comfortable. Happy. Sated. Not just sexually. He was emotionally satisfied. Maybe for the first time in his life.

The nearly two years since they'd met had gone by in a blink. But despite the perceived speed of its passing, of the time-bending, space-warping whirlwind he'd been living in, it was bloody long enough.

He held the ring in his thumb and forefinger, rocked it back and forth. It didn't catch the light, didn't have cut, clarity, colour, or carat. Just a simple white-gold band with a stone made of ossified human tissue. A bone ring. She was going to die.

And so was his mother. He still hadn't taken Abby home to meet her. Still hadn't told her that Abby even existed. Once they were engaged, he'd fill her in. Maybe fly out and introduce Abby for the first time as his soon-to-be-wife. His mother would only be pissed at him for a little while, until the possibility there may be grandchildren in her future dawned on her.

Did Abby even want children? To start a family at forty-two?

He glanced at his watch. Seven-thirty-five. Where the hell was she? He dug his cell phone out of the pocket of his jeans and tapped out a text. Nine, four, four, three, three, seven, seven ... he rolled his eyes. Almost half a minute just to type the "Where" part of "Where R U?" This whole texting phenomenon was bullshit. It'd never catch on.

"Sorry, sorry, sorry."

Before he could hit send, she was at the table, out of breath, her face flushed.

"It's okay. I was just texting you." He motioned for the waiter and ordered a bottle of wine.

"Everything okay?"

She waved one hand in the air, dropped her computer bag on the floor and flopped into the chair. "Just a crazy day." She gulped most of her water. "And I'm starved. Are you ready to order? I'm having the cheeseburger."

He grinned. Cheeseburger and fries, her favourite meal. How she stayed so tiny was a mystery.

The waiter brought a basket of bread and butter and uncorked the wine. He held the bottle, label forward, toward Finnegan, and asked if he'd like to taste it.

He hated that fancy-pants crap of swirling a half-ounce of wine in a big glass, sniffing it, tasting it. It all pretty much tasted the same. "I'm sure it's fine. Please just pour it."

The waiter poured their drinks and took their dinner order.

Finnegan took a swig of wine and made a face. He swirled his glass and sniffed it. Maybe it was time to learn how to be fancy-pants. That was some lousy wine.

He made small talk with Abby, asked about school, when exams were. Anything to fill the time until he dropped to one knee. And why wouldn't that knee quit bouncing up and down? He finished the glass of wine to calm his rapid heartbeat and filled his glass.

He barely listened to her answers, just focused on the light in her eyes, how animated she became whenever she talked about her work. He caught enough to interject with appropriate questions that gave her more reason to keep talking.

He toyed with the ring in his pocket and played scenarios over in his head. He'd been planning what to say all afternoon, and at that moment, when it counted, every rehearsed word left his memory. He'd wait until after they ate. Maybe during dessert. Or perhaps when her mouth was full of cheeseburger so he could get a word in edgewise.

She was acting nervous and jumpy. Was it his imagination, or was she avoiding eye contact with him?

The waiter slid two cheeseburger platters on the table. "Enjoy your dinners."

Abby dug in, pulled the toothpick with the fringe of green cellophane glued to the tip out of the top of the bun where it speared the toppings into place, and shoved the massive sandwich in her mouth. She rolled her eyes and nodded.

About halfway through the meal, with hardly any words between them except to ask how each other's burgers were, Finnegan set his down, put his elbows on the table and intertwined his fingers.

"So, what's up?"

She was leaning over her plate, mid-bite. She raised her eyes to his, covered her full mouth with one hand. "What do you mean?" she asked through her food and dropped her gaze.

"I mean, something's wrong. You're acting weird." He reached across the small table, put one finger under her chin and lifted her face so she'd have to look him in the eye. "Spill it."

Her nose reddened, signalling that she was about to burst into tears. She pulled away from his finger, took a big gulp of her wine and wiped her mouth with the napkin. "I was going to tell you later."

His chest hollowed and he fought off his cheeseburger's attempts to come back up. "Tell me what?"

"There's a dig off the coast of Alexandria in Egypt. And my professor has secured grant funding to join it." She bounced in her seat, her face alight.

Finnegan nodded. He finished his wine and emptied the rest of the bottle into their glasses. "Okay. And?"

"And he can bring two students." She pressed her lips together and her eyes bulged.

She didn't even need to say it. He knew what was coming.

"And he asked me!" She tapped her chest with her fingertips. "Me, Finnegan! An actual anthropological dig! In addition to being the greatest single thing to ever happen to me, it will be the subject of my master's thesis. It's a dream come true."

He couldn't think of a thing to say. Just stared at her with his mouth partially open, reality smacking him upside the head. He wasn't her most important thing. He probably didn't even rank in her top five.

She took his hand, squeezed his fingers. "Isn't it exciting?"

"Yeah. Exciting." He stared at his plate, his brow furrowed. He picked up his knife and scraped melted cheese from the blue pottery. "When would you leave?"

"It's soon. In a month."

He looked up sharply. "A month? Before Christmas?"

She cocked her head and her brow creased. "Since when does Christmas mean anything to you?" She touched his arm. "Finnegan, aren't you happy for me?"

He played with the ring in his pocket. If he asked her to marry him now, she'd be forced to choose between him and her life's passion. He couldn't be the reason she ended up miserable. She'd grow to resent him, hate him even. And eventually, she'd leave him.

"Of course. It's wonderful news." He put on a smile that he couldn't quite force into his eyes. "How long would you be gone?"

She glanced at her lap. "A year."

"A year? Abby, for fuck's sake." He rested his elbows on the table and covered his face with his hands. Then he sat up. "I'll come with you." Yeah, that would work. They could get married in Africa.

"Come with me?" She snapped her head back as if he'd slapped her. "Finnegan, what would you do there? Don't you trust me?"

He slid down in his chair. "Of course I trust you. But a year? What, don't you want me to come? Abby," he swallowed the lump that had formed in his throat, "are you breaking up with me?"

Her face scrunched up. "Oh, Finnegan. Of course I'm not. The grant is only good for two students." She stood and circled the table, sat in his lap and put her arms around his shoulders. "I won't be earning a salary, just having my expenses paid. There won't be work for you, and the grant isn't enough to cover you, even if the Professor would agree to letting you come."

He sat with one hand in his pocket squeezing the ring in his fist. How easy it would be to shove it down her sweet little throat.

"I love you, Finnegan. You have to know that. Now come on. It's only a year."

He nodded. Only a year. Only an entire fucking year.

She kissed him and rested her head on his shoulder. "Unless the professor can get the grant extended. Then, maybe two."

2000

O sleep, O gentle sleep, nature's soft nurse

It had been a cool spring, like it usually was in the shadow of the Rocky Mountains. And it came with the usual May snowstorm. Tibba loved when the perennials bloomed and the buds peeked through the late snow, opening to flaunt their vibrant hues. Like an unfinished painting on a white canvas. She'd spent hours in the garden with her feet in the melting slush, cooling her hot flashes and basking in the sun that filtered through the trees, their leaves just beginning to unfold.

She'd taken her time and dug several small, deep graves. Come mid-June, she had enough holes to bury Ron, and had made her first run to the garden centre. Trays of annuals sat at the ready, waiting for the chance to escape their little pots and thrive in the earth. Until they died in the fall and she started the whole cycle over again the following spring. Didn't matter how old she got, how much her bones creaked when she kneeled in the dirt, she so loved the yearly ritual of planting the annuals. It was better than meditation. Better than any church. The dirt was her sanctuary. The plants and flowers, her saviours.

She stripped the butcher's tape from the plastic bag and peered inside. Arm and hand. She checked another. Most of his spine. It was like opening presents at Christmas where you'd already guessed what was inside. Still exciting, but a tad disappointing all the same.

When the last of Ron was buried and the annuals were planted, Tibba stood, leaned back to stretch her spine, and cracked her neck. It never used to hurt when she did that. Now most everything hurt. Her knees from years of crawling in the dirt, which beat the hell out of being on her knees in front of random men. The dirt wasn't demeaning. And it was a lot more satisfying.

She gathered up the discarded tape and bags and shoved them into another bag, squished the air out of it, and taped that into a ball.

She eyed her work. Blue lobelia, a plant she chose because it sounded like the gatekeeper to a woman's pleasure centre, accented the coleus, the bright green edge of the leaves a stark contrast to the purple centres. These were surrounded with multi-coloured nasturtiums, their tiny flowers said to be lovely in a salad.

Blech. Salad.

Tibba imagined the roots reaching deep into the earth, feeding off the flesh and twisting around the bones. These poor specimens wouldn't have to live with the evil of Ron very long. That's why she chose annuals. Poor plants wouldn't want to come back to life year after year. To exist in his putridity for an eternity.

She strolled to the end of the garden and stopped under the ornamental cherry tree. A table and chair sat just feet from the perennials that shared the earth with Adam. The plants and flowers thrived with him. Each spring, they couldn't wait to bloom and share their love for their beautiful host. She hugged her shoulders and closed her eyes, imagined Adam's perfect face, his muscular body and flat belly. Her lips parted at the image of him south of his waist. Nearly thirty years had passed and his memory never failed to make her horny. But the what-if dreams of making a perfect life with him had evanesced with time. Because it wouldn't have been perfect. Other than sex, it would have been shit.

The sun dipped toward the horizon and her stomach let out a growl. Time for dinner. And time to crack that expensive bottle of merlot she'd been saving for a special occasion. The original plan was to share it with Finny when he came to visit. But he never came.

Fuck him, off living his own damn life. No point wasting perfectly good wine on him. Before it turned to vinegar, she'd commemorate her latest kill. Her last kill. It had to be. Her back was killing her. So was her jaw.

Maybe she should see a doctor.

She shoved the garbage bag into the metal can in the alley and latched the animal-proof lid. Damn nosy cats were always getting into the old one. A wave of exhaustion hit her and she bent forward. Damn. Should have stopped for lunch. Or drank some water. She had to start taking better care of herself. Maybe she should take a cooking lesson and get off the fried steak and Finny Mac and cheese.

She snorted. Who was she kidding?

She dragged herself into the kitchen and tossed a frozen dinner in the oven. Fried chicken with mashed potatoes. She'd tried some of the new options like orange chicken on rice with veggies. Meh. Thai green curry. Gross. Ginger beef. Nasty. Who wants sweet meat? Nope, she'd stick with the old Swanson Hungry-Man meals with her favourite way to eat potatoes: Totted.

While her dinner cooked, she showered until the water ran cold, then put on her terrycloth bathrobe and slippers. No point bothering to dry her hair or make up her face. There'd be no company, no plans to go out. Not like in her younger years when she'd get dressed and made up to be alone in her house, just in case anyone dropped by. And they often did. Ah, the good old days.

In the kitchen, she uncorked the wine and poured a third of the bottle into a large glass. At the beep of the oven timer, she donned an oven mitt, retrieved her dinner, pulled the foil from the top, carried it to the living room, and set it on the coffee table. She rubbed her arm, aching from all the digging and hauling. A stab of pain seared across her abdomen. She put a hand to her stomach and pressed. A loud burp erupted from her mouth. "Wow, Tibba. Classy to the end."

She fetched her wine from the kitchen, one hand on the counter to steady herself against another onset of fatigue.

She took a sip of wine. It was rich and delicious and totally worth the thirty-five bucks she'd reluctantly forked over. Exhaustion spread to her legs and she struggled to stand. She gripped the counter's edge but her fingers couldn't get purchase on the slick lemon-yellow Formica. A sense of foreboding shot through her.

She snatched the phone from the counter, and down she went. The glass shattered, red wine spattered the linoleum and the side of the cupboard. She lay on the floor, her body frozen and unable to react, her mind sharp. She fumbled with the numbers on the phone, barely managed to press the buttons. The sunshine ceiling came into focus, half the banks of fluorescent tubes burned out. She'd always hated that damn ceiling.

Maybe next summer she'd tear it out.

In thee thy mother dies ...

"Mr. MacGillivray, can I speak to you privately?"

Finnegan set the chalk down and turned to the class. "Read chapter eight and be ready for a quiz on it when I return." He pointed at his students. "Not kidding, quietly. It will count against your final grade."

Papers shuffled, teenagers groaned, and a buzz of chatter filled the room. He figured about sixty percent of them were going to fail that quiz, no matter how easy he made it.

He clicked the door shut behind him and turned to the principal. It was never a good sign when she showed up at his door. Some kid was being expelled. Another complained about his grade. Fellow teachers didn't like his teaching style. He figured as long as a student wasn't making up stories of rape or sexual abuse, he was golden.

"What can I do for you, Ms. Fontaine?"

"Mr. MacGillivray." She pressed her lips together and glanced briefly at her feet. "Finnegan."

Uh-oh.

She touched his arm. "I'm sorry, Finnegan, but it's your mother."

His jaw went slack and his brow furrowed. "My mother? What's wrong with her, is she ill?" And why did his boss know about it before he did? He hadn't called home in a while. What had it been, two months? Six? But that was no reason to circumvent him, not to call him directly. What emergency couldn't wait until after school?

"I'm afraid she's passed."

"Passed? Passed what?" A test? A kidney stone?

She pulled her hand back. "Finnegan, she's passed away. She died."

His legs went cold. He ran his hand through his hair and

struggled to find words. "Died?" Tears sprang to his eyes and he grabbed for the wall so he wouldn't topple over. "How? Why?" He cocked his head. "Are you sure?"

Ms. Fontaine nodded slowly. "The hospital called. They tried your home phone. The school was the alternate emergency number." She leaned in and touched his arm. "You really ought to consider giving out your cell phone number."

He shook his head and laughed. "What?"

Like that mattered now.

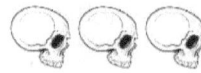

The doctor's deadpan voice recited the last hours of Finnegan's mother's life. Finnegan shivered and rubbed his free hand on his arm. Ms. Fontaine really needed to turn down the air conditioning.

She'd led him to her office and closed the door so he could be alone to find out his mother's fate. Alone. That's what he was, now and forever. All alone. Orphaned at the ripe old age of thirty.

Almost thirty-one his mother whispered in his ear. She'd always aged him prematurely as soon as the calendar hit June.

He sat with his elbows on his knees staring down at the floor between his feet. One hand found solace in rubbing the shit out of his short-cropped hair.

"Heart failure? At fifty-five?" She seemed so healthy. Had been doing yoga and some classes at the Y, she'd told him. Painting and ceramics and Aquarobics or some such shit. She'd always been a hippie, but lately she'd turned kind of New-Agey on him. Homeopathy and holistic crap, shoving her body full of herbal remedies and drinking potions that contained vibrations of healthy something or other. Or so she said.

The doctor blathered on about arteriosclerosis and the effects of all those years of smoking and too much alcohol and poor eating. She definitely wasn't big on vegetables. Nothing green, except lime Jello. Maybe they ate too much Finny Mac and cheese, and a few too many frozen Salisbury steak dinners. His mother just couldn't gag down the fish that was all the healthy rage, and never did love to cook. But fifty-five?

The last time he saw her, she'd *looked* good. Happy even. Or at the very least, not miserable. "But she looked good." His thoughts escaped from his mouth.

"Pardon me?"

"Sorry, doc. Just thinking out loud." Maybe she didn't look so good any more. He hadn't made it home since he moved away. It had been seven years since he'd seen her in person.

He fished through the principal's desk drawers. Why didn't she keep a bottle of scotch tucked away for a shitty occasion like this? He spied a pad of Post-it Notes and peeled one pale yellow square free. He ripped it in half and tucked it into his cheek, sighed and dropped into Ms. Fontaine's leather chair. "So, what now?"

Silence on the doctor's end. "I'm not sure what you mean."

Finnegan huffed. "I mean, what the hell do I do now? Come claim the body? Identify it?"

"Mr. MacGillivray, your mother wasn't a murder victim. We know her identity."

"All right. Funeral then. I guess I have to plan for that."

"That is customary."

Finnegan could imagine the doc tugging on his collar, sweating in his discomfort. His part in this conversation probably always ended at "I'm sorry for your loss."

"If you let us know what funeral home, we will transport the body there."

The body.

"Why don't you pick one and let me know where she'll be. You can leave a message on my answering machine." He could feel his face reddening. Part anger at this doctor's complete lack of phoneside manner. Part frustration at the inconvenience. Finals were about to start, for crying out loud.

His mother was gone, for good. He had to go home, if only to make arrangements. A tingle of excitement broke through the mish-mash of emotions he couldn't identify.

He'd be back with the bones.

After an awkward silence, he cleared his throat. "Thanks, doc."

"You're welcome. I'm so sorry for your loss." The line went dead.

Finnegan set the phone on the receiver as Ms. Fontaine poked her head in. "I can arrange for a substitute for the rest of the year if you need to go home."

He stood and nodded. "I guess that would be best."

She approached gingerly and gave him an awkward hug. "I am so sorry, Finnegan."

Begin again.

... he may play the fool no where but in 's own house

Finnegan stood frozen on the front stoop, the key in the lock. He rested his forehead against the door's glass and took a few deep breaths. He unlocked the deadbolt, turned the handle, and pushed the door open. The echo of creaking hinges and the thud of the door against the doorstop made the house sound as empty as it was.

Perfume and lemon Pledge greeted him, accompanied by the lingering scent of feet and cigarette smoke. Just like always. But there was something new. What was that, patchouli? He sniffed the air. Perhaps it was just death.

In the kitchen, broken glass littered the floor and red wine stained the counter and the linoleum like blood spatter after an axe murder in a low-budget horror film. She'd had a heart attack in the house. Why did he think they'd have cleaned it up? And who were "they," anyway? Just a bunch of poor paramedics. "Maid" was not in their job description. It's not like it was a crime scene. Not this time. No police required. No city-paid cleanup service included. His mother had always been the one to clean up their messes.

A half-filled bottle of merlot sat on the counter. He picked it up, put his nose to the finish. The wine still had notes of blackberry, truffles, and chocolate. He eyed the label and grinned. When had his mother begun drinking good wine? A wave of melancholy swept over him, hollowing his chest. He could have taught her what he'd learned about varietals these past few months. Could have sat in the garden with her at dusk and shared an aged Tempranillo, or popped for a decent Burgundy. It could be one other thing they had in common, outside of DNA and a guilty conscience. Assuming she'd had a conscience at all.

The handset of a new cordless phone rested near the back door.

It must have landed there after she called nine-one-one and then fell to the floor. Or maybe it got shoved out of the way by the paramedics when they tried to revive her. Did they try to do that? Or was she dead when they arrived?

He set the phone back on the charger and retrieved the broom and dustpan from the pantry. Sweeping up the glass was easy, but no matter how hard he scrubbed at the wine stain with a scouring pad, the steel wool just scraped the surface off the linoleum. The stain must have seeped right through to the glue. He'd have to replace the floor before he put the place up for sale. Or maybe toss one of his mother's old rag rugs over it and move the hell on.

In the living room, the same old furniture sat in the same place it had for all of his life. The same pictures hung on the wall, with the addition of his graduation photo, the second one when he got his master's degree, his mother standing beside him, flashing a peace sign.

At the end of the hall, just past the staircase, the so-called guestroom door was shut. That room remained what it had always been. A monument to his mother's chosen profession. A mausoleum of bodily fluids and past mistakes. Of illegal activities, shame, guilt. He shook his head, his earlier melancholy displaced by a thick layer of disgust. And a heaping dose of jealousy. Persistent, bitter hatred for a slew of men he'd never met. And one that he had.

The stairs creaked in all the same places, the banister worn down in all the same spots, and the chunk he took out of the Newel post on the bottom rung still missing. That was the summer of cold rain when he rode his skateboard down the stairs and crashed on the hardwood near the front entry. He still had the scar on his elbow. Had his mother changed anything about this house?

The door to his room was closed. He gripped the doorknob. His heart pitter-pattered and sweat beaded on his brow. The moment of truth. Time to find out if she'd discovered the rest of his bones. His hand slipped off the knob and he rubbed his belly. Not yet. What if she'd thrown it all away? She'd have probably just reburied the bones. But maybe his collection of dried plants and dead insects and buried jewellery had been shoved in the trash to make room for a treadmill.

He wasn't quite ready to find out.

He walked down the hall, the groan of floorboards a reminder that it was impossible to sneak downstairs when he should have been sleeping, should have been studying. The door to his mother's room stood wide open. From the threshold, her bedroom appeared frozen in time. The past in stasis. It was tidy. Clean and dusted where the eye could see.

He sat on the edge of the bed and bounced. The mattress still had some life in it, but he was going to toss it out anyway. Had she done her business in this room too? Had her head bounced off the mission-style headboard for anyone other than Aidan?

Finnegan let his body flop onto the old bedspread with the thousands of thread nubbins, the swirling pattern no longer discernible. Most of those threads had been pulled and the nubbins worn down, the blanket so thin in spots you could see daylight through it. He used to love that spread, would lay on it, face first, and let the lumps poke into his face. If he lay there long enough, they'd leave red indents in his cheeks and forehead, like a human golf ball. The blanket still held the faint odour of talcum powder, of liniment and strawberry shampoo. It still calmed his mind as it did when he was a small child. Perhaps he longed for a grandmother he never knew. And for a mother he knew too well.

His hands found the nubbins and he ran his fingertips along their nap, closed his eyes, and let visions of his mother race around behind his lids.

He awoke to the shrill ring of his phone. The lighted face of his watch read three-thirty. He'd fallen asleep, for two damned hours. He raced down the stairs and snatched his cell off the kitchen table, pressed the green talk button just before the sixth ring when it went to voicemail. "Hello?"

"Mr. MacGillivray? We just wanted to check in. We were expecting you a half-hour ago."

The funeral home. He'd slept through their appointment. "I'm so sorry. I can be there in ten minutes if that's not too late."

"Make it an hour. I'm free then."

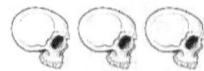

He ran his fingers over the varnished coffin. How the hell do you select an over-priced box to send to the oven and burn to ash? He may as well swaddle his mother in cash. Which would be kind of appropriate in some Freudian, kismet, sick kind of way. How fun it would be to see the reaction at the funeral, assuming anyone showed up.

Maybe some of Aidan's friends and fellow officers would come. A couple of people from the grocery. No way would Aidan's mother show up. That old bitch hated Finnegan's mother. There was only one occasion after the wedding when his mother and Mrs. Everhard were in the same room. The first Christmas. The only Christmas. The old bat wouldn't come for dinner on Christmas Day, so Finnegan's mother moved the whole thing to the twenty-third just to appease her. To build a bridge, as she put it. Apparently, that bridge led to Nowheresville, because that was it. One awkward night filled with passive-aggressive digs by Mrs. Everhard — the original one, not the newer, younger, prettier one. "It was a lovely turkey, dear. If you like, I can show you how to make it less dry next time." Mrs. Everhard said "dear" with a bitter edge. "Interesting yam casserole, dear. Your mother's recipe? Not sure I could pull off so many marshmallows without ruining it."

Good times. Maybe the old bat was dead, too.

"Mr. MacGillivray?"

Finnegan blinked and took his hand off the casket, wiped his fingerprints from the shining walnut waste of money with the edge of his sleeve. "You have anything plainer? Cheaper? It's not like she's a closet millionaire or anything." He offered a closed-lip smile.

Funeral dude, "Lance" his nametag pronounced, pinched his eyes. It could have been pity. Or possibly the realization that this particular sale wouldn't put him over his monthly commission target. "Of course. Right this way." He patted Finnegan's triceps then squeezed his elbow. He guided Finnegan to another room, much smaller, dimly lit. A lot less flashy.

Now this was more like it.

"That one." Finnegan pointed to the second-cheapest coffin. Not quite the unfinished square pine box next to it, but a step up, with curved edges, a light stain, and a matte finish. The interior had the same satin-like padded bed, but with less padding, and the fabric was obviously lower quality. Probably sateen, that slippery-slidey material cheap Eighties bedsheets were made of. The stuff that made you sweat, and any time you rolled over you slipped right out of bed and landed on your ass on the floor.

Not that any of it mattered to a corpse. His mother wasn't going to roll over. She would be the same kind of comfortable no matter what he put her in. His mother, ever the Frugal Frannie, would approve.

He followed touchy-feely Lance to a private room. Rubbed his nose against the onslaught of perfume from a million vases of cut flowers. They weren't so cloying, so sickly sweet, in the open air of the garden.

"Can I get you a coffee?" Lance brandished a blinding smile.

"Got any Irish Whiskey for that?" Finnegan reclined in the seat and threw him his best "just kidding" grin.

Lance laughed. "I wish." They sat with paperwork, discussed timing and prices and the obituary. Finnegan strained his brain to remember the names of the people who had predeceased his mother. Aidan, of course. His grandmother, Beulah. But what the hell was his grandfather's name? Had his mother ever even mentioned him? "Just say her parents, Mr. and Mrs. MacGillivray." Like it mattered to anyone now.

Lance approached his job with a stoic realism that Finnegan appreciated. No bullshit, no expressions of deep sorrow for the loss of a person he'd never met. All business, all the time. The guy looked more like a Wall Street banker than a funeral director. Finnegan had expected a stereotype — hunched back, wringing hands, pale skin, awkward interpersonal skills. Instead, here was a tall, well-built, youngish guy, maybe forty at most, with perfect hair and one hell of a tan.

"For the burial site, is there a particular cemetery you'd prefer?" Lance opened a glossy brochure, flipped it around with his fingertips, and slid it across the oak tabletop.

Finnegan admired the man's hands. The skin so smooth, the knuckles where his proximal phalanges met his metacarpals pronounced without being knobby. He closed the brochure. "Cremation. She always wanted to return to the earth." And he knew just the forest garden to scatter her in.

"Excellent. We have a preferred crematorium, reasonably priced, good turnaround time. And a lovely selection of vessels to keep her ashes in." Lance plucked another brochure from a rack on a credenza behind him. "If you want, we can keep back some of the cremains to be made into a ring or a pendant."

Finnegan's eyebrows raised. He'd only planned to throw her to the wind and toast her life. Letting her rest in peace in her beloved garden, where she could become fertilizer and nurture the soil forever. He hadn't considered keeping any of her. Until now.

"No, I don't think so. But ..."

Lance looked at Finnegan expectantly.

He glanced around and leaned forward. His hands trembled. "Could I have some of her bones?"

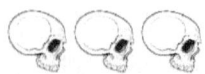

He pulled into the driveway, raced to the front door. The key rattled against the lock. It took him three tries to get the damn thing into the hole. When the door swung open, he sprinted up the stairs. The doorknob to his bedroom shimmied against his hand, like the whole house was trembling with anticipation right along with him. He eased the knob clockwise until the latch gave way, creaking hinges transported him back in time. To the first human bone his fingers ever touched.

No treadmill. No changes at all. Everything was exactly as he'd left it. He glanced around. It was like a shrine. One she'd clearly never worshipped in. It looked like it hadn't been dusted since he left.

He dropped to his knees, his khakis making tracks in the dust. He reached under his bed until his fingers found a box. "Thank you, Mother, for never cleaning under anything."

He dragged the boxes out into the light and sat on the hardwood as he'd done countless times all those years ago. He flipped the lid off the oldest box. The plants and weeds sat on top, untouched. A waft of mildew rose to greet him. He plucked creeping thyme from the top, sniffed it, looking for the smell of Christmas and turkey dinner. Nothing. The purple dead nettle wasn't so purple anymore, it had mutated into a greyish-brown, but the square stalk was still in one piece. He touched it to his lips. The flavour had died along with the scent, leaving nothing but dust.

He scrambled to his feet and flung his closet door open. The bones were right where he'd left them. His heartbeat quickened at the touch of his fingertips to the box on top of the stack. He'd been having palpitations since he'd asked Lance for his mother's bones. The guy had hesitated and tilted his head like a puppy trying to figure out what its human master was saying. Up to that point, Finnegan figured Lance had a crush on him. Something about his gait, his too-slick wardrobe, and how he smiled and touched Finnegan's arm all the time. But perhaps macabre was a deal breaker. Hesitation soon turned to disgust. Maybe even a touch of fear. As if Finnegan were a murdering psychopath. A serial killer.

Lance's answer was a resounding no. He stammered and babbled on about it being unsanitary and outside the bounds of what he was allowed to do for a client.

But the idea of adding his mother's bones to his collection was enticing. He couldn't get it out of his head. And it spurred a desperate need to reconnect with his passion.

He flicked the lid off the second box and grabbed a handful of the smallest bones. The phalanges and metatarsals. The coccyges and cervical vertebrae. A sensation he'd not felt in years rocketed through his arm. Abby's bone collection didn't make him feel this way. Even finding new bones at the body farm, exciting and addictive though it was, fell flat compared to how his own collection made him feel. He'd never pinned down what the emotion was, the sensation that turned him into a night-crawling pervert in the park, complete with hard on and heavy breathing. But oh, how he'd missed it.

And he had to have more.

JULIE FRAYN

Hell is empty and the devils are here

She looked almost lifelike, her hair coiffed, her makeup just right. She still fit into her wedding dress, though how that was possible was a mystery. She'd clearly put on weight since he'd last seen her, he'd guess thirty or forty pounds worth. It was evident in her cheeks, in the beginning of a double chin, and in the flabby arms. Either that or cardiomyopathy and death make the body swell. It was all window dressing anyway. Smoke and mirrors. The dress was probably slit up the back and tucked in around her body. All that new age bullshit hadn't done her any favours after all.

Finnegan touched her cheek like he used to do.

Cold as ice. Definitely dead.

He eyed her hands, her fingers still slender despite the weight gain. Some brown spots, uncovered by the body makeup, hinted at her age. And they'd done her nails. Or maybe she'd died that way, those shorter-than-usual talons all lacquered in blood red. How had she gardened and not ruined her manicure? How did she afford the constant manicures at all? Perhaps it was her one extravagance. Instead of saving for his education, she got her nails buffed and polished and shaped and painted. Are those damn nails why he had soul-crushing student loan debt?

It wouldn't be hard to rip one of those fingers right off. There wasn't any blood left, no ooze to stain the sateen. He could slip it in his pocket and tuck her hand under the ruffle of her bohemian dress with the red embroidered flowers. It's not like she would notice.

He raised one eyebrow and the left side of his mouth curled up.

"I'm so sorry, son."

A hairy-knuckled hand patted him on the shoulder. A familiar voice. He didn't even turn around. "Thanks, Dan."

"Far too young. Just like Aidan." His voice cracked. "I didn't even know she had any health problems."

"Me neither." Mental health, maybe.

He tried to put his disdain for her in check, just for today. He'd adored her when he was young, found her quirks endearing, her lifestyle so different than any other mother's. His adoration morphed into desire. Sick and wrong, that's what she'd called it. What she'd called him. How bloody motherly of her. He gripped the edge of the coffin.

No matter where on the Tibba rollercoaster he found himself — atop the crest and diving toward the nadir, in free fall, twisting and turning and wanting to puke, or reaching climax, only to jerk to a halt and slide uneventfully to a final stop — he couldn't make himself hate her. She was just too fascinating.

If only she were someone else's mother.

He didn't even pine for some made-up history with a fantasy normal mother anymore. Didn't ache for a regular childhood. Couldn't define "normal" and "regular" in those terms at all. Were Birdie's parents normal? The abuse and the total destruction of dreams and self-esteem, was that normal? Or was normal a myth?

His mother. Hooker and serial killer. That was his normal.

Dan patted his shoulder again. Finnegan flinched. Like most people at funerals, Dan clearly didn't know what to say or how to offer comfort without sounding like an ass. "I'll find you after the service," he whispered, and slipped away.

He'd always been a decent guy. But Finnegan would never see him again. They had nothing left to connect them except a tenuous friendship based on their mutual attachment to two dead people.

He'd acted too quickly to fulfill her cremation wishes. Should have demanded a private burial. Put his mother to rest where she loved to spend her life. Let her spend eternity under the ash tree, to feed her own garden, roots and flowers becoming one with her bones. Too late for that. The embalming fluid filling her veins wouldn't allow proper decomposition. Her skin and tissue would remain, and she'd sleep like a zombie awaiting the uprising, her nails polished to perfection.

Finnegan stepped away from the coffin and sat in the front row, his head down, hands clasped in his lap, lost in thoughts he couldn't share with anyone. Except Abby. Damn, how he missed her. Tears dripped onto the sleeve of his summer-weight tweed jacket.

The hall hummed with subdued activity, footsteps trudged past the open casket, voices mumbled overused platitudes, and he nodded without bothering to see who was speaking them.

"Sorry for your loss."

"She was a good woman."

"She'll live on in your heart."

Such garbage. They didn't know the real Tibba MacGillivray. His forehead scrunched and he raised his head, turned in his seat and surveyed the room. Maybe some of them did. Maybe some of them were clients and had been inside his house. Been inside his mother. All while he bided his time in the back yard, killing his best friend.

"I hope everything is in order, Mr. MacGillivray."

Finnegan started at the voice close to his ear. Lance the funeral dude sat a wee bit too close.

The man looked like he would burst into tears. He touched Finnegan's arm and leaned in. "Remember what you asked me? About your mother's ..." he glanced around, "... remains?"

Finnegan nodded.

"Well, please don't tell anyone about this. My mortician thinks I'm off my nut and might report me to the Funeral Service Regulatory Board." He slid an envelope from inside his suit jacket and handed it to Finnegan. "Between us." He winked and patted Finnegan on the knee, stood and straightened his jacket and tie. He bowed his head at Finnegan and sauntered away, trying his hardest not to appear suspicious. He was failing miserably, but no one else seemed to notice. Nor give a rat's ass.

The envelope was sealed, but Finnegan could feel the contents. Bones. From the size and approximate circumference, he was guessing two metatarsals and one other. Maybe cuboid. Or second cuneiform. All foot bones, from the body parts tucked deep inside the closed half of the coffin.

He slipped the envelope in the inside pocket of his jacket and smiled at the rattle the bones made. Perhaps he was smiling a little too much. He resumed his grieving son position, head down, elbows on knees, hands in pseudo-prayer, not as any plea to a mythical man in the sky to save his mother's soul, but as camouflage for the excitement he could barely keep off his face. Now to get through this ridiculous ritual, play nice with a bunch of people he'd never see again, then get home and get his hands on his mother's bones.

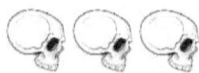

"She wasn't a conventional mother. Not a cookie-baking, craft-making, costume-sewing, nurturing type of mother." Finnegan eyeballed the woodgrain in the dais and spoke without notes. He hadn't written anything. Had no idea how to eulogize his mother at all. So when the time came to get up in front of this room full of mostly strangers, he had to wing it.

His eyes swept across mourners' faces. His rapt audience, hanging on his every word. Perhaps he'd whip out some Shakespeare and go all Hamlet on these fuckers.

Between the heads of two men he'd never seen before, a familiar face. Mrs. Schultz. She dabbed her cheek with a tissue and gifted him with a tiny wave and a pained grin.

Tears filled his eyes. She was the mother he'd always wanted. The mother his could have never been. No sign of Mr. Schultz. Maybe he'd done his wife a solid, and up and died.

Finnegan smiled at her and gripped the edge of the dais.

"No, Tibba MacGillivray was the cigarillo-smoking, profanity-spewing, TV-dinner-serving type. Rough around the edges, you might say. More like a father than a mother, except for the painted nails and hippie dresses." The audience seemed to be holding their collective breath, like he was about to say something dastardly. Perhaps they were waiting for it. To confirm their suspicions of the type of woman they all whispered behind her back that she was. To hell with them all. Only he got to think of her that way.

"That's what I loved most about her. The Carol Brady moments were few and far between. And that was okay. She never left me wanting for anything." Except a father. A backyard empty of human remains. A chance to love her like so many other men had.

He ran his finger around his shirt collar and tugged it away from his neck. Track lighting glared in his eyes.

"My favourite memory of her was her signature dish. It was the only dish she knew how to make from scratch except for the occasional fried steak or scrambled eggs. A little something she used to call Finny Mac and cheese."

A few subdued snickers rippled through the audience.

More tears welled in Finnegan's eyes. "For those that don't know, that's what she called me. Finny Mac." He wiped his cheek. "My upbringing may not have mirrored that of Beaver Cleaver, or even one of the Brady boys. Despite the red hair and freckles that I obviously inherited from my father, I was not raised like Richie Cunningham."

He scanned the faces, some with red-rimmed eyes and dripping noses, some looking bored out of their minds. Mrs. Schultz offered an understanding nod. Lance watched intently, his head cocked to one side, a knowing smile on his face.

"Despite that, she was a good mother. A kind mother. She always protected me when it mattered most." And no one had any clue just how much that meant. He glanced back at the open casket and wiped the back of his neck with an open palm. "Thanks, Mom." He knocked on the wood of the podium. "For always having my back."

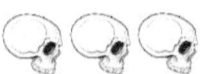

"My, how handsome you've grown." Elizabeth Schultz touched her fingertips to Finnegan's cheek.

He took her hand and kissed the back of it. Vanilla and garlic. That this never changed brought comfort. A peaceful familiarity. For a fleeting moment, he was eleven years old and Birdie was standing behind her mother rolling her eyes and tapping her foot against the carpet, impatient to get the hell out of this snoozefest of a funeral and go frog hunting.

Mrs. Schutz's eyes reddened. "When I see you, it all comes back like it was yesterday. You and Birdie, muddy and sunburned, laughing and teasing each other. Eating too many cookies and guzzling milk." She shut her eyes and squeezed his hand. "God, how I miss her." She looked up at him, her forehead pinched. "Do you ever think about her?"

His stomach hollowed. "Every day." His voice cracked and tears welled in his eyes. He slid his jacket off and rolled up his sleeve.

She gasped at the sight of his tattoo, ran her fingers over the cursive "Birdie" with the frogs behind it and the dead nettle entwined in the serif of the letters. "Is that her crucifix?" She held his forearm and brought her face closer. "Finny, it's ..." Her head snapped up. "It's identical."

He shrugged. "She wore it all the time. I couldn't get it out of my head. So I put it on my arm." That was one sorry-ass lie.

"Are you back for good? I could make you a homemade meal." Desperation flickered across her face. She needed someone to need her. But it couldn't be him. How could he bear it?

He shook his head and swallowed hard, raised his eyes to the ceiling and blinked against fresh tears. "Just long enough to clear out the house and sell it."

Her face lost what little glow remained and she looked at her feet. "I see." She tugged her large purse open. "I almost forgot." She pulled out a paper bag. Cinnamon and vanilla filled the air. "I made you cookies." She held the bag toward him.

A sob leapt from him and his knees weakened. Finnegan melted into Elizabeth Schultz's arms and wept. She cooed in his ear and stroked his head. Random people passed behind him, patted him on the back, and mumbled rote expressions of sympathy, like a procession of talking Hallmark cards.

"She's in a better place."

"It gets easier from here."

"God's got her now."

There were several rounds of "Sorry for your loss," many punctuated with terms of endearment — son, dear, sweetheart — that not one person there had any right to utter. Except Birdie's mother.

He didn't give a damn about anyone else in the room except

Mrs. Schultz. At that moment, she was his life preserver, and oatmeal raisin cookies and snickerdoodles his deliverance.

Parting is such sweet sorrow

"I'm so sorry. Wow, she must have died young."

"Fifty-five. Maybe it was all those steaks and frozen dinners. She never met a vegetable she liked. Except corn Niblets, but I'm not sure that counts." Finnegan sliced a shallot, tossed it in the pan with the hash browns and reached for the garlic. He was stunned when his call connected and Abby answered on the second ring. The sound of her voice in the morning, something he'd not heard in months, filled him with a feeling he was unaccustomed to. He guessed it was joy.

They usually only communicated by email or the occasional text, except the one night she'd called him at three in the morning. He'd had a few too many glasses of wine the night before. Could've been a couple of bottles. He woke hours later with only a vague recollection of their conversation. From then on, his limit was three drinks until she landed back in his arms. "I have to spend some more time here in Calgary, pack up all mom's shit and sell the house. But I'm dying to see you. When do you get a break?"

"Yeah. About that."

He gripped the knife handle until his knuckles whitened. "You're not coming home this summer, are you?"

"Not exactly." Puffs of her breath buffeted against the receiver. One of her quirks, when she didn't know how to tell him something, she'd just breathe heavy. "Look, there's been a development."

He squeezed his eyes shut. "What development?"

"We discovered graves. A whole group of them, looks like from the Battle of the Nile. Finnegan, from seventeen ninety-eight."

"And so these centuries-dead people can't let you have a vacation and visit your boyfriend before he loses his fucking mind?" He stabbed a clove of garlic, released it to the butcher's block and crushed it under the knife's wide blade. He peeled the paper-like skin from the clove and tucked it under his tongue.

"It's not that easy. It extends the dig, probably for a year." Her clothing rustled and she inhaled sharply.

"Are you smoking?"

A long exhale was followed by some mumbling and more rustling. She'd covered the receiver.

"It's just a hookah pipe." The sharp retort of a slap on skin was followed by an uncharacteristic giggle.

"Abby, is someone with you?" Heat rose in his cheeks and a vein in his temple throbbed. "Are you fucking around on me?"

She sighed. "Not exactly."

"What the hell does that mean?" He pitched the knife onto the counter. It skated along the Formica and clattered into the sink.

"I was going to tell you in person. But that may not be for a while." Her voice trembled.

He rubbed his forehead. "Tell me what, Abby?"

"I'm engaged."

He nearly dropped the phone. "I beg your pardon?"

"Engaged. You know, to be married."

"I know what it means Abby. You're my girlfriend. We're together." He retrieved the knife from the sink and stabbed it repeatedly into the cutting board as he spoke. "How do you just become engaged to someone else? And who? The only ones there are you and your profess —" He lifted the knife above his head, brought it down hard into the cutting board and split the wood. "Your professor? You're fucking your old fucking professor?"

"Old? Finnegan, he's forty-five. He's closer to my age than you are."

He gripped the counter's edge and gritted his teeth. "I was going to propose to you. That night you told me about the dig. We were supposed to be married, Abby. You and me."

"You were? Oh, aren't you sweet."

Sweet? Was she joking?

"I'm sorry, Finnegan, but I've fallen in love with him. We have everything in common. We're going to marry on a Nile cruise boat."

She was downright giddy.

"Is it easy for you to do that?"

"Do what?"

"Cut a man's heart out with a song in your voice and a smile on your face?"

She swallowed audibly. "I'm sorry. You know I love you, right?" Her voice caught in her throat.

He closed his eyes and pictured her body in a shallow grave in his mother's garden. "Yeah. Sure you do."

"Oh, Finnegan."

Begin again.

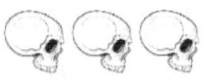

"You're certain that's what you want to do?"

He scraped the underside of his thumbnail clean with a paring knife and let the debris litter the kitchen counter. "Yes, Ms. Fontaine. I guess I'm not quite ready to give up the old homestead yet. Can I assume the sub didn't completely mess up my kids?"

"Not completely."

He could imagine her grinning.

"Excellent. I do have some personal effects in my desk." He'd already done a mental inventory of the drawers and couldn't remember anything embarrassing. "You can just toss that all away." He grimaced when he remembered one prized possession he'd left behind. "Except my annotated copy of Hamlet." The one with his notes in the margins, his comical drawings of skulls inside the front cover. "Please give that to Angelica." She's the only student who would have any use for it.

"Consider it done."

They offered each other well wishes and each promised to stay in touch, a promise neither of them would ever keep.

Next call was to his landlord. He would sell Finnegan's Tempest for scrap since it was just rust and bolts at this point, and keep any cash the salvage yard paid out. And he agreed to release Finnegan from his lease early, after he flew back east and packed up his possessions. Not that there was much that he gave a damn about.

Just his computer, his clothes, and the lock box in the closet. It hid the pieces of his new collection, some of the bones that he and Abby had found at the body farm that she hadn't kept to use in her studies. And the ring. Her ring. Even if he never got to propose, if she'd never seen the ring at all, no one else would ever wear it. He was going to bury it in his mother's garden.

A shame he couldn't bring the bones home. How to get those past the X-ray machines at the security gates? Those he would scrub clean of his fingerprints and toss in a Dumpster. A mystery for the cops that they'd never be able to solve.

He surveyed the house and made some mental notes. She'd left it all to him. Hell, she had him on the title, so it just passed without probate. No muss, no fuss. His mother was smarter than he gave her credit for. But the mish-mash of Fifties and Seventies décor? The furniture that is grandmother probably owned? That had to go.

The door to the basement stood an inch ajar. The one place he'd not inspected, or stepped foot in, since he was a teen. He hated that basement. The musty smell, the spider webs that clung to the beams and the ductwork. The furnace that fired up like a demon trapped in the bowels of hell. Maybe he'd start there. With a new, efficient furnace that didn't scare the bejesus out of him so much that even now, as a grown man, he hesitated at the top of the stairs.

His footfalls against the wooden steps sent the same hollow echoes bouncing off the concrete walls that his little-boy feet had, except louder. At the base of the stairs, the old chest freezer sat like it always had. Its orange light announced that it was plugged in and keeping whatever T.V. dinners remained, frozen. That light was a laser beam. A ray gun with the sole purpose of boring a burning hole through him whenever he went downstairs. His spine tingled with the urge to turn tail and flee upstairs and out to the safety and comfort of the garden. But his brain knew it was all juvenile crap. The furnace was just a furnace. The freezer only a freezer. And the dusty webs just the silk spun out of harmless spiders' butts. Adulthood did wonders to crush the phobias and fantasies of youth.

He opened the lid of the freezer and peered inside. As he suspected, a dozen or so frozen dinners, three bags of corn Niblets, some Tater Tots. He shoved a few Swanson boxes out of the way. Underneath, at the bottom of the freezer, lay a plastic garbage bag wrapped with butcher's tape. Probably steak.

If it wasn't too freezer burned, maybe he could salvage the steak for dinner. Niblets and Tots would round out a meal reminiscent of his younger days. The rest he would pitch in the garbage bin.

The tape peeled easily from the plastic. He unrolled the meat from its frozen shroud and pulled it from the bag. It took a full four seconds before his brain connected with what his eyes were seeing.

A hand. A disarticulated human hand.

He dropped it into the freezer and slammed the lid shut.

"Seriously, Mother?" he screamed into the rafters. Just how long had she been nestling body parts up against his dinners?

I will come home to you

The steel door slammed shut behind Finnegan and echoed down the austere hallway like the clang of iron bars on death row. Ah, high school. The prison you never escaped from, whose memories were the cellmate that shanked you in your sleep.

Every whiff of aromatic air was an assault. Dirty gym socks, the hormone-fuelled sweat of hundreds of teenagers, bleach, and the gut-wrenching stench of cafeteria food. It was a toss-up which tasted worse, gravy from a can, or toilet bowl cleaner. He'd swallowed enough of both.

He glanced back at the door — still painted some vile combination of shit brown and puke green — and eyed the panic bar. One push and he could get the hell out of this place. Walk away from the scene of so many crimes against him during his formative years.

What a stupid expression. The only thing those years formed was a fine-tuned high-functioning anxiety that dogged him to this day. He ran his sweaty palms down his pants and checked his watch. Ten minutes early.

A whistle screeched and the squeal of rubber soles on polished hardwood filled the hallway. Finnegan put his thumb on the steel latch and grasped the cold metal handle of the gym door. Inferiority crept up on him and flooded his mind with Board of Education-sanctioned abuse. Football. Volleyball. Dodgeball. Murderball. Anything ending with ball.

He opened the door and peered in. The gym floor glistened under bright lights. Taunts of "loser" filled his ears, verbal missiles launched his way for the crime of missing a spiked volleyball and letting the other team score, or lagging behind in the twelve-minute run and hitting the hardwood after Jason tripped him. It took him a minute to realize those taunts weren't ghosts of his past. They were happening at that moment, live and in person. One poor, scrawny-limbed bastard in thick glasses did his best to hold in tears, and slinked off to sit on a bench against the far wall, cradling an injured arm to his chest. Nothing ever changed. Just different actors on the same stage reciting the same old unoriginal, boring lines.

Finnegan left the loser to his own devices. He'd have to figure it out on his own, because no one was going to save him.

Finnegan ran his fingertips along the bank of lockers on one side of the long hallway and flicked each combination lock against the metal, painted alternating shades of dark and light green. What was it with all the green? The cement block walls were mint, the lockers forest and fern. Even the bathroom stalls were seafoam. Or at least they used to be. He had no intention of venturing into enemy territory to find out if they'd been updated, which was doubtful. Even the chairs in the office hadn't changed.

He checked in at the desk and squeezed his adult-sized ass into one of those chairs. The teal Naugahyde had worn down even more, had more cuts in the fake leather, some from wear and tear, some from random acts of vandalism under the ever-vigilant and watchful eye of the school secretary.

He winced at the grinding of wood and lead in the electric pencil sharpener that sat on the secretary's desk. Last time he'd heard that he was sitting in that very chair, sporting another shiner. He'd been blamed for the fight that broke out in the cafeteria because the cool kids and the jocks, well it just couldn't be their fault. Besides, the old principal would deadpan without a hint of irony, any smudge on their record and the school might not win the big game, or some such shit. Finnegan was the butt of jokes, and popular only as a punching bag. His crime? Red hair. Good grades. Social awkwardness. Oh, the horror.

He toyed with the keychain in his pocket. The one he'd made from his mother's intermediate cuneiform. Dipped in resin, it looked like a hunk of junk he'd picked up at the dollar store. His lucky charm. Like a rabbit's foot without fur or … rabbit. He closed his eyes and rubbed it. He could use all the good juju he could get.

"Mr. MacGillivray?"

Finnegan opened his eyes. The stodgy old principal had been replaced by an alluring blonde. She approached and held out her hand.

He was transfixed by her grin, lopsided like she knew a secret she was aching to tell. "Ms. Sorenson. A pleasure to meet you."

He stood and took her hand, admired the angle of her jaw, the intensity of her green-eyed gaze. She was attractive, slender, well dressed. And she wore no rings on her fingers. If he were twenty years older, he'd be hard pressed not to ask her out.

Who was he kidding? If she weren't his potential new boss, he'd have been all over that.

She led him into the office and closed the door, sat at her desk and gestured at the chair on the other side. "You don't remember me, do you Finny?"

He froze, his ass hovering above the seat. Other than his mother and Mrs. Schultz, no one had called him Finny since sixth grade. He settled into the cushion, grimaced when the leather, actual new black leather, squawked out a fart sound. "I'm sorry, I don't."

She leaned back and steepled her fingertips.

A vision of a younger Ms. Sorenson flashed through his mind. Familiar, and yet — not at all.

"I used to be Mrs. Findlay. I taught grade one. You were one of my students."

Familiar became near-complete recollection. Pretty Mrs. Findlay, she of the micro-mini skirts and sleeveless turtlenecks. Of the soft voice, the kind heart. Of green apple lip balm and Love's Baby Soft.

He swallowed hard. "I, I do remember you. You were the reason I fell in love with reading. With books. Why I got a masters in English literature. Why I teach language arts."

Her eyebrows shot up. "Wow. That's a lot to give me credit for."

But it was true. She'd nurtured his interests. Protected him from the likes of Jason. And she was his first crush. When he had to move on to another teacher in grade two, and she moved on to teach high school in another province, it nearly did him in. He refused to go to school for a week. Birdie teased him endlessly. *Finny and Findlay sitting in a tree.* And when he finally did go to school, a new girl was sitting opposite him. Raven hair. Patent leather shoes. Deborah Arbic. Mrs. Findlay was history, just like that.

"Didn't you move to Saskatchewan?"

She nodded. "Yes. I grew up there. I went back home after I got divorced. Couldn't bear to be in the same city with my ex. And there was a high school position that opened up. Then, years later, I got offered this job and figured it was hard to refuse. Sometimes physical distance is good, but after fifteen years, another kind of distance came between us. A permanent one." A satisfied grin blossomed. "He's dead. So here I am." She leaned forward and put her elbows on the desk. "I always remembered the shy little red-haired, freckle-faced boy with his nose stuck in a book. When I saw your name on the interview list, well. I was very pleased. And here you are. All grown up into an intelligent, handsome," her gaze wandered over his body, "well-built man."

His cheeks heated but he couldn't tear his gaze away from those eyes. Was Mrs. Findlay hitting on him? Yes, yes she was. And he was enjoying the hell out of it.

After a minute of staring at each other in silence, she grinned and shuffled the papers of his resume. "I see you also escaped for a few years. Why are you back?"

"My mother died."

Her face contorted and his memory of her fully formed. That concerned look came rushing back to him. The glabella, the space between her eyebrows, pinched together. The depth of her philtrum, that sensuous valley between her nose and upper lip, exaggerated by the pursing of her mouth. If he leaned across the desk and sucked on it, would she taste of apples?

He pinched his thigh for focus and crossed his legs like a girl to mask his growing erection.

"Oh, Finny. I'm so sorry. I remember your mother. She was," she angled her head, "different than most. But she never missed a parent-teacher meeting. She was so proud of you. She must have been far too young to die."

Finnegan swallowed. He hated talking about his mother's death.

Not because he got all choked up that she was gone. He hadn't seen her in so many years, some of that pain was deadened by distance. It was his morbid sense of wonder about her corpse. How he just wanted to get his hands on the rest of her bones. But other than the few Lance gave him, they were already ash.

"Can I ask how?"

"Heart attack."

She shook her head. Then a practiced professional face replaced sympathy in one blink. Probably the same face she pulled out when overprotective parents came to bail their little angels out of trouble. "Well, there's not really any need for an interview. Your resume is great. Six years of teaching experience, volunteer work with special needs students. Your educational qualifications are head and shoulders above the other candidates. In fact, I wondered why you are only teaching high school. Bachelor of Education, Masters in English Lit. And you're pursuing a degree in Anthropology?"

He blinked. A little white lie. An exaggeration. He was studying biology and anatomy with a keen interest in human skeletal structure. Anthropology wasn't too big a stretch. It sounded more prestigious. And a lot less creepy.

"You could have a professorship at a major university. U of T. Montreal. Hell, even McGill." She leaned forward. "Why here?"

"I've done the Toronto thing. Can't speak French, so Quebec is out." He shrugged. "I guess I want to make a difference before they leave high school. Besides, I'm an Alberta boy."

What a crock of shit. It was because he wanted to be close to the bones.

"That's —" she glanced away for a split second. "Admirable." She met his eyes again. "Well, Finny. Welcome back to Brisebois High."

"Do you mind not calling me that?" He tucked his hand into the pocket of his pants and rubbed a small piece of foolscap between his fingers. His mouth watered. "I go by Finnegan now."

She closed her eyes briefly. "Of course. I'm sorry. Welcome home, Finnegan."

Begin again.

Come home to me and I will wait for you

Finnegan leaned against the teacher's desk — his desk — the butt of his low-rise, skinny jeans resting on the edge, his legs crossed at the ankles. Those damn pants pinched and tugged in all the wrong places, but they made his ass look great and ensured he wouldn't been seen on day one as some lame-ass has-been. He was only fourteen years older than most of these kids, so one of his teacher plans was to try to blend in. To make sure he knew what they were into, the music they listened to, any new social trends, to fit in as much as possible. But not in an adult-trying-to-look-like-a-teenager way. Just enough to maybe earn an iota of trust.

A group of rowdy boys entered, talking and slapping shoulders. One caught sight of Finnegan. "What? Where's Old Lady Pedersen?"

"She retired." Finnegan assessed them with a sweep of his gaze. Jocks for sure. Likely bullies. Definitely the ones that nerds avoid in the halls, and they'd be heading straight for the back row.

"Who are you?" The second boy held his notebook in one hand and held that over his crotch, his other hand gripping the opposite wrist, like he was protecting his junk. Or maybe intimidated by the young, tall, hot — if Ms. Sorenson was to be believed — new male teacher with the bulging biceps strategically transected by his short-sleeved "Alas, poor Yorick" T-shirt. Finnegan's physique, which completely failed him as a child and made him the target of kids like these, now worked in his favour. He was no little old lady. No pushover. And these dudes knew it.

Ah, karma. You're not such a bitch after all, are you, baby?

Finnegan gestured to the blackboard where he'd written his name in ten-inch-high canary-yellow chalk.

The kid squinted and mouthed Finnegan's name, a blank look on his face. "MacGivilray?"

"MacGillivray." Finnegan grinned. "Just call me Mr. Mac."

The dude nodded and slid into a desk in the back row.

When the class had settled into their chosen seats, the ones they would stay in for the rest of the school year, he introduced himself, offered up his new moniker, Mr. Mac, to the entire class, and erased his name from the board.

"So. English Language Arts. That's what we're here for. What does that mean to you?" He looked at his student list. He counted four Jennifers and three Matthews, a couple of Christophers and Amandas. Damn. If he ever had kids, they'd get unusual names. Shakespearean names. Marcellus or Octavius. Rosalind or Ophelia. His eyes landed on one familiar name. "Where is Deborah?" He glanced at the pretty girl with long, black hair.

She smiled and sat straighter in her chair, but didn't say a word.

"Over here."

He scanned the room. Middle row, last desk, easy exit to the hallway, a slight girl with greasy hair who'd apparently slept in her makeup, threw him a lazy wave. "Okay, Deborah, what does it mean to you?"

Deborah yawned. "Well, as far as the English part goes, I learned how to speak that before I started school."

Finnegan braced himself for some serious anti-education debate and mentally prepared his rebuttal.

"But the language arts part, well that means learning how to use words to be better, to communicate better. It means discovering the nuance of subtle metaphor, elevating my understanding of literature by gaining some knowledge of context and concept." Her sleepy eyes came alive the more she spoke. "Learn how to express myself, my ideas and feelings on the page, how to evoke emotion and promote discourse. I mean, it's right there in the name, isn't it? Language *Arts.*"

Finnegan stared at her for a few seconds, blinked, then clapped his hands. She wasn't the pretty girl. Not the cool chick. Not the keener in the front row. But whip-smart and insightful, with an avalanche of passion disguised by her grungy exterior. Maybe the age-old high school tropes had finally been shaken up.

"That was excellent, Deborah. Yes. Arts. Words as art. Pictures painted with words, be it poetry or prose. Great works of literature, with a bias towards my personal favourite — Shakespeare."

Groans filled the air. Deborah sat straighter in her back-row chair.

"How was the first week?" A light tap on the doorjamb accompanied Ms. Sorenson's voice. She hovered just inside the classroom, spiffy in her red blazer and black pencil skirt that hugged her ass when she sashayed down the hall.

"Not too awful. Always takes a while for them to get used to a new teacher. And the teacher to get used to another round of new faces." Finnegan slipped papers into his Steampunkesque stressed-leather messenger bag.

"And you've given yourself homework for the weekend?" She gestured to the papers.

"Just a little quiz I give all my students to gauge their knowledge. I don't even mark them, just make notes."

"That's pretty dedicated. I've never had a teacher do that before." She sauntered in, ran her hand along the oak desktop.

He sidled around the back of the desk, fiddled with the pencils in an old mug, straightened some textbooks that weren't even askew. He cleared his throat. "Well, as a student, I often felt the teachers weren't fully engaged." He held one hand out. "Not you. Never you." He looked away, heat rushing to his cheeks, and other areas. "But in junior high and high school, many of them just read out of texts, didn't do anything interesting. And often made assumptions about their students based on outdated stereotypes." Just like he always did. He'd become a master at bullshitting his way through interpersonal relations.

"Well," she leaned her hip against his desk, "I hope you don't waste the entire weekend on work." She bit her top lip and scraped her bottom teeth over it, didn't bother to hide the fact that she was ogling him. "Surely you've better things to do than that." She hopped up on the desk and rested that perfect ass next to his mugful of pencils.

He did have better things to do. Dig in the garden. Expand his collection. Rip her clothes off and fuck her in the dirt just feet from where he was certain he'd find more skeletal remains. He swallowed. "I'm sure it won't take all weekend."

She tilted her head. "Are you busy tomorrow night? What if I brought over a bottle of wine? A welcome home, as it were." One eyebrow quivered as it shot up.

He sat down to mask his boner. He'd become like a puberty-infested teen with a porn mag under his bed. He hadn't had this many public erections in a decade. "Why Ms. Sorenson, is it my imagination, or are you hitting on me?"

She grinned. "That would be inappropriate, Mr. MacGillivray. Being that I'm your principal and all. We're just two old friends getting ..." she licked her lips "... reacquainted."

There's a daisy ....

He whistled along to the music, hoping *Sex and Candy* would push Birdie's taunts of "Finny and Findlay sitting in a tree. K-i-s-s-i-n-g" out of his head.

Little Finny Mac was always hot for teacher. He just didn't know what that meant back then. His fantasy at six years old was little more than wishing he could kiss her on the lips and daydreaming about marrying her.

Now, twenty-five years later, he'd blow reality out of the infantile make-believe water. Time to fuck teacher's brains out. Ms. Sorenson feigned coy, but that was in case someone popped into the classroom. She would have dropped him to the floor and balled him right on the linoleum if there wasn't any worry about getting caught. Or fired. He could see it in her eyes. Read it on her licking lips. No, there was no mistaking teacher's intent.

The house was spotless, everything dusted and in its place, the hardwood shined, the kitchen gleamed. Had to make the right impression. Show her that the little boy whose young mind she used to nurture was all grown up.

He futzed around the room, lifted the lid of one of his mother's decorative porcelain bowls. He ran a finger over the vertebrae he'd tucked inside it. He'd hidden small bits of his collection around the house. Slipped behind the cushions of the chesterfield, in the pockets of his coats that hung in the front hall closet. The small, broken bits that he couldn't identify were scattered like vermiculite atop the dirt in the one houseplant he'd managed to keep alive. No matter where he went, the bones were close by.

The doorbell rang and his heart jumped. He surveyed the room. The candles were lit, the wine uncorked and sitting next to two of his grandmother's crystal stemmed wine glasses — the ones his mother shunned in favour of cheap tumblers. A plate of cheeses and fancy crackers sat next to that. They'd agreed to order takeout, so he had three menus to offer her. He didn't give a damn what they ate.

He opened the door, took time to appreciate the sight of her. She'd shed her principal attire and stood on his doorstep in tight jeans and a snug V-neck T-shirt, her pedicured toes peeked out from gold, wedge sandals. Her blonde hair, normally tucked into a loose bun or held at bay with a black scrunchy, fell in waves around her shoulders and framed her lovely face. In the waning light of a late-summer evening, her eyes glowed like emeralds on fire. And in each hand, a bottle of wine.

Her eyes softened and she smiled. "Are you going to invite me in?"

He stepped back. "Of course. I'm sorry."

She handed him the wine bottles and touched her fingertips to his cheek. She slipped her shoes off and strolled into his home, her gaze grazing the furniture and the pictures on the walls.

Her ass was like a twenty-year-old's in those jeans. How do some women keep their shit so totally together, while others fall into, what? Disrepair? Despair? Insanity? Maybe all of the above. Once the mind's tenuous tether to reality has frayed to the point of nearly snapping, the rest quickly follows.

But enough about his mother.

"I've opened a Syrah. I hope that's okay?"

She leaned closer to the photos behind the chesterfield and smiled. "I love all wine, as long as it's good. Whatever you choose is fine." She started on the high school end of the horrific school photo parade his mother had installed over the years.

Why hadn't he taken those down? It was top of his list for the following weekend. Dump the shitty so-called family shots and find something weird and unusual to put in their place. Actual art by an actual artist.

She accepted the glass he offered and ran a fingertip along the frame of his first grade picture. "There's little Finny," she whispered. She sighed and put her glass on the coffee table. "I'm feeling very weird about this. Perhaps I should go."

He stepped in front of her, blocked her path to the door. "Ms. Sorenson, please don't." He took one of her hands in his.

She closed her eyes. "It's Daisy. Please. Call me Daisy."

He'd rather call her Mrs. Findlay. He brushed hair from her eyes and tucked it behind her ear. "Daisy." He smiled. "I'm not six years old any more. I'm not that little boy."

She opened her eyes and gazed into his. "No. Clearly."

He bent forward and placed a gentle kiss on her lips. He restrained himself from his true desire, to strip her shirt over her head and lick the crevasse between her breasts. Peel her jeans off and bury his face south of her waist. Most of all, he wanted her to stay. So he held himself in check and just kissed her.

And she responded. Timid at first, just matching the movement of his lips. Soon she had one arm around his waist and the other on the back of his neck, her chest pressed against the bottom of his rib cage, his growing erection poking her below the bellybutton. The kissing became deeper, more intense, more rushed.

She patted his sternum with one hand and pulled away. "Phew. Okay. Not seeing you as a six-year-old anymore."

He grinned. "Chinese, pizza, or Indian?"

They laid on the chesterfield, his arm under her shoulder, her hand on his naked chest, their post-coital sweat mingling on their skin. She dipped a fingertip in his clavicular notch and ran it over his manubrium, drew abstract shapes in the copper hair that decorated the skin over his sternum, then traced a line along his costal cartilage and around his fifth true rib.

He pulled away and laughed. Why did he have to be so damn ticklish?

"Well, Finnegan." She licked and kissed his nipple. "Thank you for a lovely evening, but I have to be on my way." She nuzzled the edge of his armpit and let her hand trail down his body, entwining her fingers in his pubic hair.

"Why don't you stay?" His semi-permanent erection popped

back to life. The smell of leftover squid and fried rice filled his nostrils. Flip her over and take her from behind? Or shove her off and clean up the mess of takeout containers strewn across the coffee table? He was about to opt for door number one, but she pushed herself up and off, and swung her legs onto the floor.

"I have to get some sleep. I have an early morning."

"Why early on a Sunday? Isn't that a day of rest or something?" He wrapped one arm around her waist and nibbled along her spine, starting at the C1 and counting off each vertebrae as he kissed and licked her soft skin.

She quivered at the L3. When he tucked his tongue into the valley that her ass cheeks created at her sacrum, she pulled his arm away and stood.

He reclined on the chesterfield, one arm over his head, and scrutinized her as she dressed. Her age showed in the cellulite on her ass cheeks, the stretch marks on her breasts that, though beautiful and full, were not as pert as he imagined they once were. The soft skin under her chin had started to crepe, and her triceps didn't hold the dermis taut like they did on a fit twenty-something. His erection grew stronger. "Stay the night. You can sleep here."

She pulled on her jeans. "I have to be at the airport by seven."

He sat up. "Airport? I didn't know you were going away."

"I'm not." She pulled on her shirt and tucked it into her waistband before turning around. She kneeled in front of him and kissed him.

His brows furrowed. "Then how about dinner tomorrow night? Cannery Row has a great oyster bar. Good aphrodisiac."

"Finnegan, this was amazing. And I should have told you." She sighed. "I'm picking up my fiancé. He's been in Denmark on business."

Finnegan slumped backward. "Fiancé?" He ran a hand through his hair. "What the fuck, Daisy? What was all this?"

She stood, her back to him. "I'm sorry. There's no excuse. Except that —" she shook her head. "God, I'm such a sad old lady." She turned to face him. "When you came for your interview, I was just so attracted to you. It's that simple. I wanted you." She turned away. "Selfish, right?"

He retrieved his pants from the floor and pulled them on, stood and tucked his junk in so the zipper wouldn't catch on anything tender. He took her by one arm and spun her around, gave her a long, wet, and passionate kiss. When they separated, he cupped her chin. "I understand selfish. I wanted you too. Hell, I wanted to bend you over your desk that first day." Should he tell her about his fantasies of her? How many times he'd married her in his head? He rested his forehead against hers. "Does this mean we have to stop?"

She hooked her fingers into his belt loops, her breathing heavy. "No. It just means we have to be careful."

2001

Make my seated heart knock at my ribs

It was like building a jigsaw puzzle with most of the pieces missing. Finnegan studied one of the charts tacked to his wall and slid another fragment of bone into place. He surveyed the result so far. About two-thirds of a full skeleton, with two more boxes of bones to go.

The discard pile was nearly half-full of spare parts. Like the extra bolts and screws left after building an Ikea bookshelf. Not pieces he couldn't identify because they were too small or broken. These were duplicates. One skeleton can't have seventeen proximal phalanges. Eight, max. Which meant he had bones from at least three bodies in his collection. And he hadn't finished the puzzle yet.

Hard to believe he used to think the garden was an ancient cemetery. All the evidence pointed to the contrary. Teeth with amalgam fillings. Maybe old, but not ancient. And porcelain-covered metal crowns. Those weren't used until the Fifties. At the earliest, the bodies became fertilizer when his grandparents lived here.

He crossed his arms and studied his work. Some of the bones were discoloured, some pitted in ways the others weren't. They didn't even belong to the same person. Just how many corpses had his mother buried in her garden?

A bead of sweat trickled down the side of his beer. Finnegan ripped a piece of paper towel from the roll and wiped down the bottle, set a coaster on the nightstand, took a long pull of lager, and put the bottle on the coaster. He stepped around the partial skeleton laid out on his old bedroom floor and counted ribs.

He tore off a piece of the beer-dampened napkin, tucked it in his mouth and took a deep breath, sucked the paper and counted the ribs again. Twenty-three. He was certain he'd found a complete set. Which was missing?

He dropped to his knees and examined the bones. It was the

fourth true rib on the right side. Damn, how did he miss that? He plucked the chart from the tack and examined it. Yes, fourth true rib on the right.

Back to the garden.

The empty vessel makes the loudest sound

At noon, half a block from the high school, the lineup snaked almost to the door. Did kids these days do nothing but drink coffee?

Finnegan checked his watch and scanned the café. The barista called out names and orders. Grande Americano no sugar for Clark. Venti double shot blah blah blah for Caitlin. Finnegan zoned out, played his lesson plan for next class over in his head.

"Finnegan?"

A roundish face peered up at him. Raven hair rested on her shoulders. His heart fluttered and his stomach clenched.

She smiled. "Oh, my God, it is you! Wow, Finnegan, you've grown. Like, a lot."

"Hello, Deborah. Nice to see you."

Nice to see you? Is that the best he could do? How about, holy shit Deborah, when did you get fat? And why'd you cut off your beautiful hair? Bullied any scrawny red-haired boys lately?

"I heard you'd moved away. Toronto, right?"

He nodded. "Where'd you hear that?" Because like hell did any of his former classmates give one rotten rat's ass where he was or what he was doing.

"The ten-year reunion. We sent an invitation to your old house. I assumed your mother was still living there."

We? Typical cool kids, in control of when, if, and how the students whose lives they made living hell are allowed to reconvene. "She was. She died."

Her face twisted with what could be genuine sympathy. Or she continued to excel at being fake. She put a hand on his arm. "Oh, I'm so sorry."

The line moved forward and he shuffled along with it, pulling free of her touch.

She waddled right behind him. "Do you have time to sit and chat?"

The clenching in his stomach turned into a ball of fiery pain. He took an exaggerated look at his watch. "Gee, sorry. I've got a class starting soon."

"A class? What are you studying?"

He blinked. "I'm not. I'm teaching."

"You're a teacher? That's so amazing. Where?"

He swallowed. "Good old Brisebois High. I have Mrs. Pedersen's classroom. She retired this past summer."

Her mouth curled up. "You're not serious?"

"Yes, I am." Dead serious.

She held out her mocha frappe coffechino or whatever frothy crap she was drinking.

He glanced from her face to her cup.

She shook it. "Hold this."

Ah, demanding as ever. He obliged even though he wanted to dump it over her head.

She rummaged around inside her purse and pulled out a pen and small notepad, jotted something down and tore off the paper, dropping the pen and pad back into her bag. She took the coffee back and held up the paper. "Give me a call. We could catch up. Have a drink." Her blue eyes twinkled and her smile still stunned. But there was something different. Something missing. Something … less.

He took the slip of paper. "I'll do that." But he wouldn't. Even though this was all he'd ever wanted from her. Kindness. Friendship. Simple acknowledgement of his existence. Besides, he had Daisy. Part-time. On the down low. Hidden from the rest of the world. But it was enough.

"I hope so." Deborah patted his arm, raised up on her tiptoes and brushed a kiss across his cheek. She shuffled out of the café without looking back.

He brought the paper to his nose and inhaled the scent of her fingertips, rubbed it on his cheek where her saliva still moistened his skin. He touched his tongue to the paper. His body flooded with familiar longing.

"Sir? What can I get you?"

He shoved the paper into his pocket. "Just a plain old coffee, strong, black, no crap in it. Largest you've got."

Fill all thy bones with aches

The house had lost some of its polish, but the garden thrived. Finnegan's mother had installed a flagstone footpath that started on the north end and wended its way south, meandered between the lilacs and dogwoods, around the chestnut, and past the Manitoba maple. At the end, among the bougainvillea, under the shade of an ornamental cherry tree, where there used to be nothing but untended overgrowth — the exact spot where he'd buried his best friend — there was a wooden-seated bench with a wrought iron backrest and arms and a matching table sitting among the lush and fragrant plot.

His mother's ashtray still sat there, half-filled with butts floating in rainwater. He'd considered throwing it away the first time he came across it, but couldn't bring himself to. He'd sniffed the remains of her bad habit, even dried one of the butts out in the sunshine, peeled the paper away from the strands of the filter, stained with nicotine, and nibbled on a small piece. It tasted like her, of tobacco and lipstick, and just a hint of earth.

The stones came up easily enough with the tip of the spade under one corner and the handle as a lever. He set six of them aside and dug into the soil below. It was a stinking hot June. Even filtered through the blooms of the cherry tree, the sun beat down on him, its rays heating the skin on his exposed neck. He stripped off his T-shirt, wiped sweat from his brow and chest with it, and tossed it on the bench.

Each time the shovel pinged off anything harder than dirt, he kneeled to retrieve it. A few rocks, more whole and partial phalanges, a couple of ribs, and even some vertebrae. And another ring. He eyed it under the sunlight. The thick band of a man's manly piece of jewellery, one small diamond nestled in yellow gold, flush with the band. No engraving other than the mark for fourteen karat. He pocketed it, along with a couple of fingers, and laid the larger bones on the table next to the ashtray.

He displaced two more flagstones and checked his watch. Twelve-seventeen. The rumbling in his stomach would have to wait. He wasn't quite ready to give up his archaeological pursuit. His favourite pastime. His reason for living.

Grave robbing.

He whistled a tune and stabbed at the ground, the hole deepened and widened. Almost half an hour later there were no more bones. He'd give it five more minutes, then hunger was going to defeat him. The spade pinged and revealed the top of a large rock. He dug into the earth with his hands. The deeper he excavated, the faster his heartbeat. That rock had eye sockets. And teeth.

He shimmied the skull side to side and extricated it from the packed earth, held it in front of his face and rubbed dust from its nasal passages. "For in that sleep of death what dreams may come," he whispered Hamlet's words.

He nestled the skull into a paper grocery bag, added the vertebrae, ribs, and phalanges, then wended his way out of the garden. His version of Finny Mac and cheese, with gemelli pasta smothered in a thick sauce of Gruyère, Asiago, cream and white wine, was calling his name.

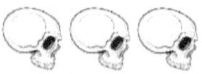

Nearly two full skeletons lay on the sixty-year-old hardwood. Each still had many missing parts — ribs and vertebrae, one femur, a tibia, and two humeri. And there was only one skull.

For so many years, his collection lay under the bed, had resided in hidden places around his room and grown large enough to spread to the closet. For normal kids, it was the stuff of nightmares filled with clacking bones and disembodied hands reaching out to grab their living limbs as they slumbered. Not for him. The actual skeletons in his actual closet were a comforting presence. And he slept like a proverbial baby, even if his dreams were bizarre and vivid and filled with death.

He took a swig from a bottle of Heineken and circled the floor, inspected his collection of partial skeletons from all angles. Given the abundance of metatarsals, the extra sacrum, and how many scapulae he'd found, he was guessing he was up to at least four bodies.

But none of them were Birdie. The pelvic girdles proved that. They were heavy and thick, with narrow inlets. So far, every one of the victims were grown men.

He toyed with the idea of joining all the disarticulated bits with wire and string. Recreating their bodies and hanging them from the front porch on Halloween night. Perhaps some red lights in the eye sockets and an audio tape of clanking chains and evil laughter. That'd scare the little bastards who steal candy and make fun of kids in pumpkin costumes. He grinned, put the bottle to his lips and finished off the beer.

He sat on the edge of the bed and it creaked under his weight. He picked up the skull and examined it more closely. Cracks emanated from the orbital socket, spread out from the temple and the cheek. Fine lines, like a spider web, darker than the rest of the bone. He dragged his laptop closer and examined the chart on the screen. He was killing his anatomy class now that he had real-life specimens to match up to the diagrams in the online textbook. Most of the damage was to the supraorbital foramen, temporal process and, zygomatic bone.

Somebody cracked this poor sucker across the face, with something hard and heavy enough to cause significant damage. Enough to kill him.

Finnegan propped the man's head on his fingertips and stared into his empty eye sockets. "Just what did you do to deserve such a fate, my man?" He rolled the skull around in his hands, rubbed the bones with his fingertips. "What the hell did you do to my mother?"

Wrapped around your finger ~ The Police

Finnegan tapped on the principal's door. "Ms. Sorenson, a word?" Daisy looked up from her computer and smiled. "Yes, please come in Mr. MacGillivray."

He clicked the door shut, turned the lock, tossed his bag on the floor and leapt over the garbage can, scooping her into his arms and shoving his tongue in her mouth. Minutes later, they released their embrace. "Damn, I missed you."

She squeezed his butt cheeks. "I'm always right here."

"How about this weekend? It's been weeks and I'm desperate for a piece of that fine ass of yours."

She put her hand flat on his chest, a gesture he'd come to know well. It meant no. Another rejection. There were more of those than invitations lately. "I can't this weekend." She shook him off her. "I'm moving."

He blinked a long blink, his stomach heavy. "Moving? Away?"

She shook her head. "No, not out of the city." She sighed. "Finnegan, I'm moving in with Carl."

His pulse pounded in his ears, his fingers twitched then curled into his palms. He envisioned Carl, her fiancé, in a deep grave in his garden. And once nature had her way with his flesh, he'd have his with the man's bones.

He pushed the visual of cracking Carl upside the head with a baseball bat out of his brain. "Moving in with him? But I thought—"

"You thought what?" she snapped, her hands on her hips. "That I'd dump him for you? That we'd get married, ride off into the sunset, live happily ever after?"

He winced. "Not exactly. But something like that." He tugged one hand off one hip and kissed her fingers. "Daisy, I love you. You have to know that."

"I do know." She touched his cheek, tears in her eyes. "But I love Carl. And I'm a realist, Finnegan."

He dropped her hand. "What does that mean?"

"It means that I'm twenty-two years older than you are. It means that there's going to come a time when you will still be a handsome, beautiful, young man. And I will be a wretched, haggard old lady. I am old enough to be your mother." She turned away. "If I walk away from Carl, give that up for you, where will I be in ten years?"

He hugged her from behind, kissed the top of her head. "You'll be with me."

"Promise?"

"Yes. I promise."

She sniffled and her shoulders quaked. "I want to believe that. But I just can't. And it's too late, anyway."

He turned her around. "Too late?"

She couldn't meet his eyes. "We set a date. We're eloping next month and marrying in Puerto Vallarta." She pulled away. "Finnegan, I have to end this. For my own sanity. And so you can find someone more appropriate."

His pulse pounded in his ears, like a freight train driving through his brain. "You're dumping me? For that older guy?"

"He's not older to me." Her tears mixed with mascara and left black streaks on her cheeks. "And love isn't about looks and age. It's about truth. About comfort."

Did she not hear the irony in her own words?

She walked behind her desk, sat in her principal's chair and donned her professional mask. "I'm sorry, Finnegan."

Begin again.

Wonderwall ~ Oasis

Deborah looked pretty in her kitten heels and snug dress, her hair pinned up on one side revealing a creamy earlobe. Since they'd met in the coffee shop, those earlobes would sneak up on him, tease him as they'd done all through high school. Even when he was sucking on Daisy's, he longed for the knob of Deborah's plump flesh to succumb to his tongue.

With Daisy's final rebuke, Deborah filled his every waking moment. Despite that, it took two weeks to get up the nerve to pick up the phone. He could stand in front of a pack of rabid high schoolers and orate for hours on the bleak futures prophesied by literary greats such as Shirley Jackson and George Orwell, yet he stammered and stuttered like an anxious seven-year-old when he asked Deborah a simple question like, can I take you to dinner? Was the rapid beating of his heart and the sudden beading of sweat on his upper lip an indication of real feelings for her? More likely some kind of Pavlovian response to the silk of her hair and the lilt of her voice. A voice that hadn't changed in all these years. A voice that filled him with intense desire one moment and hate and anger the next. The push-pull of his obsession with this woman who, since schooldays, had alternated between being Kate to his Petruchio, and Juliet to his Romeo.

His first reaction to her sudden appearance in his life was out of resentment. A long-nurtured contempt that blurred reality. Maybe she wasn't the lithe teen who used to slink around school in the tightest of Levis, but she hadn't gotten fat. She'd morphed into a real woman, curvy and voluptuous. There were vestiges of her former self — all made up, her best face forward, her personality switched to On, highest brightness, sharpest contrast, just the right volume. Yet, behind the eyes, something lackluster. Something sad. Something real.

She wasn't that vibrant girl in pigtails anymore, with the adorable gapped-tooth smile that had been corrected years ago. The braces period, he'd called it. Only someone as popular as Deborah could make teenage girls beg their parents to fill their mouths with metal. But if Deb was doing it, they all wanted to do it too. Just like crop tops and mesh gloves, crucifixes and acid wash denim.

"What are you having?" She'd been prattling on about their old high school friends and he'd let her voice fill his head while he ignored her words. They weren't his friends in high school and didn't give a flying fig what any of them were up to now.

"Finnegan?"

He blinked. "Sorry." He tugged on his collar and smiled at the waiter. "Beer. Whatever lager is on tap."

Deborah ordered white wine and continued her verbal diarrhea.

A few minutes later, the waiter slid their drinks on the table. Finnegan gulped a third of his lager down and analysed the changes in Deborah's face. The tiny crow's feet around her eyes, the obvious signs of years of smoking around her lips. Makeup helped bring back the appearance of youth, but without it, he'd bet she looked closer to forty than her actual thirty-one. Some kind of sweet karma, when the popular kids end up getting fat or losing their hair. Or in her case, aging early.

When the waiter arrived to take their dinner order, Finnegan tore his attention away from her face and scanned the rest of her. She hadn't grown an inch since high school, maybe not even since grade seven. He eyed the fake nails, the bronzed cheeks. Were the breasts real at least? Had they blossomed along with her hips and her ass, or had she enhanced all of that too? Who was the real Deborah?

An indent the width of a gold band on her ring finger broadcast that she'd been married long enough for the ring to make a near-permanent mark. Branded. Either divorced, or still married and looking for a little action on the side. Wasn't that a guy's barroom ploy? Did she think him an idiot, or maybe so desperate for her company that she could lie to him? Take advantage of him? He should be flattered that she'd want to cheat on her husband just to be with him. The least she could do was be honest about it. Once a charlatan, always a charlatan.

Not that he gave a damn. Some side-action with no obligation would be just the ticket.

He gave the waiter his order and watched him scurry away before turning back to Deborah. "So, how long have you been married?" He sipped his beer while her face contorted, her cheeks pinked, and her eyes teared up. He grinned behind his stein. Schadenfreude at its finest.

"I'm separated." Her eyes darted about the table and she cupped her hands in her lap. "It wasn't a good fit."

"Did you cheat on him?"

She gasped. "Why would you think that?"

Should he trust the wounded-puppy expression and pat her on the head? Or give her another kick? "Just wondering."

"No, I didn't. Ever." Her wine glass shook as she lifted it to her lips and gulped half the glass. "In fact, he cheated on me. Many times. And he hit me."

Finnegan's shoulders slouched. "Oh, shit. Deb, I'm so sorry." He covered her hand with his. "Really, I am."

She pulled her hand away. "Well, Jason always was rough around the edges."

Finnegan squinted. "Jason? You married Jason the jock?"

She grimaced. "Guilty as charged."

He stared at her. They'd dated through high school. Jason had publicly claimed her as his property. But he'd slept with so many other girls. How did she not know?

"We got married a couple of years after graduation. I didn't know it at the time, but he was the cheater then too. Me?" She spread her hands open. "I'm a cliché. The loser who lost my virginity to him, stayed true, and became a punching bag. Everything was my fault. Even his infidelity."

"I never did like that guy."

She smiled. "I know you didn't. Why would you? He was awful to you."

The waiter placed her food in front of her, and dropped

Finnegan's rare steak in front of him.

Finnegan tapped the side of his glass and the waiter nodded. He swirled the last of his beer then finished it off. "You weren't nice to me either." He slid the glass onto the table and eyed her face, anxious for her reaction.

She pressed her lips together into a fine line. "You're right. And I'm sorry. Not an excuse or anything, but it all seemed so different back then. You were so smart. And that red hair and those freckles."

He poked his fork into the steak and sliced off a mouthful. The meat was salty, perfectly cooked, with just a hint of garlic. Blood from the rare cut pooled onto his plate.

"And Birdie." Deborah rolled her eyes. "I mean, come on. I just went along with everyone else and made fun. We were horrible, silly children."

"Birdie" rang in his ears. Deborah's eye roll at the mention of her name made the heat rise in his cheeks. He clenched his steak knife. He stared at the slab of bloody meat, fork tines stabbing into the flesh, blood oozing. His stomach flipped.

He gave Deborah a hard stare and rolled up his sleeve, placed his forearm on the table without a word.

Her face paled and her grin twitched and flickered, then extinguished. She looked at her lap. "Oh."

That was all she had to say? He pushed his chair back. "I have to use the washroom."

He ran the cold water and splashed his sweaty face. She just went along? Was only a follower? What a load of shit. She was leader of the pack. Maybe not the meanest, but no fucking Pollyanna either. Was this some ruse to gain absolution? If he allowed her into his life, he'd end up her verbal punching bag. There were flickers of a good person in there somewhere. But he just wanted to rub her face in the past and get sweet revenge. And to gather her in his arms and taste the nectar of her full lips.

He ran his hands through his hair, yanked a few paper towels from the dispenser and rubbed them over his face. He had to get through this date. Get some distance from her and sort out his feelings. Until she bounced back into his life, he'd exorcised his

Deborah demons. Defeated his obsession. Or had he?

He had to choose. Live out his years-old fantasy, strip her naked, and have sex for days. Or cleanse her from his life, not in a kind or polite way, and never see her again. Ever.

For these dead birds sigh ....

Finnegan lit a cigarette and fouled the perfect morning air. He rested his hands atop the handle of the spade and let the smoke infiltrate the fibres of his virgin lungs. They wanted to protest, to contract and cough the tar and nicotine right out. But he resisted, held the poison in.

It was his mother's brand. The open pack he'd found in the kitchen that first day he came home. He'd almost thrown it out, along with the unopened carton in the pantry, but couldn't do it. Each sniff of the carton, each strip of rolling paper he peeled off and tucked inside his cheek, sucked on until it softened, brought her back to life. He'd always been curious what the attraction was. What magical nectar this potentially deadly stick carried. So far, it was burning pain and a desperate need to vomit.

The dirt never came out from under his fingernails anymore. Not that he tried too hard to dislodge it. He loved the grit of it, the smell of earth and musk, how the arches, loops, and whorls of his fingerprints were easily visible, the soil stamped into his flesh like tattoo ink.

He'd dug so many holes in his search for human remains, the garden looked more like an abandoned graveyard. His mother would be so pissed at him. So he'd begun reclamation. Dig up some bones. Plant something new. At first, he'd been careful with the plants he dug up, protected the roots and placed them back in the dirt when he finished digging. But those plants didn't survive the ordeal. Many trips to the garden centre followed. He navigated row upon row of annuals, perennials, what-the-fuckials. A botanist he was not.

All those years his mother forced him outside, all alone, while she tended to business in his home. The nights he'd stared at the light in the kitchen window, silently begging for it to be over, so he could be back in the warmth of the house, cuddled up next to her. The garden started out as a distraction. It became a refuge. A sanctuary. And the altar upon which he grieved for Birdie. Would she be dead if the garden didn't exist?

He closed his eyes. What would Birdie look like now? Who would she have become? He dreamed of her often but she was always stuck in that twelve-year-old's tomboy body, with those crossed eyes and that ratty short-cropped hair. Perhaps she'd have blossomed as a young woman, gotten her eyes corrected, tamed the mane and let it grow. They were destined to be best friends. Maybe destined to be more than that. And Birdie knew it. Why hadn't he listened?

In addition to killing his mother's plants, he'd upturned most of the walkway, digging until his shovel hit clay. His mother probably hadn't gotten that far. Doubtful she could have. Though he did have new respect for her. The effort she'd put into her garden, into the graves, into killing all those men. It was impressive as hell. And he had found some bones down there, near the clay level. Foot bones mostly. Could remains shift in the dirt and travel downward over time?

He shook his head and grinned. His mother, the serial killer. What he wouldn't give to talk with her now. To find out just how many had died at her hands. Were they all buried in the garden? And why were they all men? But he didn't need to ask her that question. The answer was obvious.

In the years since he'd moved away, the shrubs along the fence between the garden and the Greers' old place had become ratty and weedy. Finnegan pushed aside the limbs of a failing spirea and peered through the slats of the rotting fence. The rocking chair still sat on the porch. The patio lanterns, tattered and faded, still hung overhead.

Eleven years that house had been for sale and not one bite. The neighbourhood rumour was that the house was haunted, that blood dripped from the ceiling as it had when the cops found the bodies. The theory that Mrs. Greer had hacked her husband to pieces, then turned a gun on herself persisted. That the old bat had had enough and couldn't live with her disgusting letch of a husband one more day. But she couldn't live without him either.

On windy days, Mr. Greer's chair creaked in the wind, like it did whenever he hauled his fat ass in and out of it. That was enough to spook people into thinking they could hear Mrs. Greer yelling at him. Finnegan's mother had told him so on one of their phone calls. She took pleasure in it too, not just the crime, but the aftermath, the ghastly rumours. Shit, maybe she'd started them to keep the house vacant. To maintain the privacy of her forest graveyard.

He envisioned her walking through the yard that night, naked under the light of the full moon. She'd never admitted what she'd done, but Finnegan didn't need her confession. It was one of their little secrets. The unspoken knowledge of each other's dastardly deeds. She knew what he'd done to Birdie; he knew what she'd done to the Greers. It bonded them in lies.

Cherry blossoms lay desiccated on the bench and littered the ground at his feet. The fallen fruit stained everything it touched, leaving purplish polka dots on the wooden seat and on the flagstones. He picked up one cherry and squished it between his fingers, sniffed the fermented juice. The birds loved that tree. They got drunk on the ripened fruit and stumbled around the garden. Whenever he came out to dig, they hid in the bougainvillea and squawked at him. Alcoholics were like that. Protective of their hooch.

He tugged the bench off the remaining flagstones and dragged it out of the way. Damn thing was solid-ass wrought iron and way heavier than it looked. He pried up the stones with the spade. When light infiltrated the ground underneath, ants scurried away, sow bugs curled into balls, and newly exposed worms did a leisurely, sensual dive back into the damp soil. Not that it would matter. His spade would dismember them all and turn their home into their final resting place.

He opened the top of the old Coleman cooler and fished out a bottle of Grasshopper wheat ale, hooked the cap on the cooler's latch and popped it open. He took a long pull on the beer and emptied half of it.

With all of the stones out of the way, he began to dig. There were skeletons with missing pieces that had to be filled in. Mysteries to be solved. Time to Nancy Drew the shit out of these bones. But how would he ever identify the bodies? Match the mismatched bones to actual names, discover whatever crime against humanity they had committed to earn their place in his mother's garden?

Dusk settled in and his stomach ached for something more substantial than a barley sandwich. He grasped the shovel with both hands, lifted the spade above his head, and brought it down hard at the deep end of the hole. It ricocheted off something hard. He tossed the shovel aside and dropped to his knees. The bulbous end of a bone protruded from the earth. Too big for a femur or an arm bone. He sighed. Probably another damn rock. He slid his fingers into the dirt and loosened the object from the earth. A fat worm slithered out from the dirt packed inside a hole. His heart quickened. It was an eye socket. Another skull.

He rocked it back and forth and extracted it. The mandible remained stuck in the ground, but otherwise the skull was intact. It was small, the bone not as thick as the others he'd found, and it had no ridging of the superciliary arch.

He fell back onto his ass, the skull cradled in both hands. It was a female skull. A small female. A child.

It was Birdie.

He dropped his best friend's head in the dirt, scrabbled out of the hole and vomited into the dead nettle.

Please, please, please, let me get what I want ~ The Smiths

Finnegan ran his thumb along Birdie's jaw. The tip of his pinkie fit into the cleft in her mental protuberance, a masculine trait he'd often teased her about. More Danny Zucko than Sandy Olson, he'd say. And she'd punch him in the arm and say it was better than his gingerbread hair. It was just what friends did, tease each other about the things that bothered them the most. In retrospect, the hurt look in her eyes said it all.

He was a jerk. A bully. Just like everybody else.

He picked up her skull and poked his fingers into her orbits, caressed the coarse undersides where her brown eyes used to rest. There was a scuff mark on her parietal bone where he'd hit her with the shovel. He licked his thumb and wiped it against the injury he'd inflicted. No matter how hard he rubbed, he couldn't erase the damage.

He returned her head to its proper place at the top of her skeleton, right above her cleft-chinned mandible. He'd laid her out on his old bed, or as much of her as he could find by the spectral glow of the waxing moon and the shitty beam of an insufficient flashlight.

Through the curtain, a thin orange line crested the horizon. Another hour before sunrise, and at least three before it would be bright enough to comb through the dirt and recover Birdie's missing parts. He couldn't fill in her blanks with bones from his collection. The adult rib he nestled in between hers was too big. Too ugly. Too male.

The note she'd passed him in class the day he'd killed her — or what was left of it — rested on his nightstand. After all these years, the final remnant was still under his mattress where he'd left it. Just three square inches of paper remained after all the tiny bits he'd ripped from it, sucked and chewed on, savoured over the years. The tattered edges framed Birdie's chicken-scratch pencil marks, faded by age and from him rubbing the paper between his thumb and fingers, trying to find her in the pencil lead.

He tucked the entire piece into his mouth. Rolled it around his tongue, squished it into the flesh of one cheek like chewing tobacco. He closed his eyes and took several deep breaths.

He'd always assumed his mother had taken Birdie away. She'd just shifted her a few feet south and buried her deeper in the ground. But why? To prevent animals from digging Birdie up and gnawing on her rotting flesh? Or maybe she'd begun to stink and it threatened to expose the garden for what it was — a suburban necropolis. The MacGillivray's own potter's field.

He blinked his eyes open. Is that why his mother planted so much malodorous flora? Spread that repugnant salmon-skin fertilizer everywhere? To mask the smell of death. Overpower the scent of her crimes. She hadn't moved Birdie to protect him. It was self-preservation. Like every other choice she'd ever made.

He picked up Birdie's skull, the atlas, and the axis. "Time to make you whole again, hey, Birdie?" He smiled at her and looped a length of wire through the hole in the C1 vertebrae, then attached it to her skull through the foramen magnum. He threaded the wire through the carotid canal to secure the atlas, but still allow it to do its job. To let Birdie move her head. To nod and pivot, cock it side to side like she did when he said stupid shit and she was trying to find just the right name to call him.

The C2 connected to the atlas by threading the wire through the tiny openings, the transverse foramen and transverse process. His fingers trembled. The thin wire caught at the edge of the holes where Birdie's vertebral artery and sympathetic nerve plexus belonged. Those were dust now. Her unembalmed soft tissue had succumbed to the earth and the bugs and the worms years ago.

He continued down the cervical spine with ease, but struggled to connect the bones of the thorax. He couldn't get the kyphotic curve right. Without intervertebral discs, her spine stood in a straight line, and the bones clacked together like a cheap department store gag gift.

He sucked on the paper in his cheek, swallowed the pencil infused spit, tapped her T9 against his temple. Felt. Maybe felt would work. Or erasers.

He finished wiring Birdie's spinal column together, minus the missing coccyx. That was one itsy-bitsy little bone. Maybe the tiniest of bones were out there in the piles of dug up dirt that dotted the garden. He'd need a sifter, like archaeologists use. And some brushes.

His tongue dislodged the paper from his cheek and he spit it into his hand. His hands trembled as he tried to unfold it, spread it out, read her words one last time. But his saliva had washed away what few marks had remained, and the paper fell apart in his fingers, translucent from his slobber. He rolled it into a ball, popped it back in his mouth, and swallowed. A Birdie pill, washed down with the remains of his warm, flat beer.

He'd been savouring that paper for years, always afraid to finish it off. To suck that last bit of Birdie off of the page. And now he'd gone and done it. That was the end of her.

He ran his fingers down her spine and grinned.

Except it wasn't the end. She was back. More than paper and pencil lead. Better than a silver cross that symbolized something neither of them believed in. He had her. And he was going to make her whole again.

There's rue for you, and here's some for me

Finnegan ran his fingers through his hair to muss it up just right. He surveyed his reflection and nodded. Black T-shirt that showed off his flat abdomen and muscular arms tucked into gray dress pants that hugged his tight ass. His taupe blazer would round out an impeccable second-date outfit. Casual, but not too casual. Dressy, but not too dressy. Enough to show Deborah just how well he'd matured and just what she'd missed all the years she suffered alongside her fallen jock of a husband.

He pulled the perfect shoes out of the closet, the slip-on loafers with the monk strap, the leather polished to a near-patent sheen. He jogged up the stairs to retrieve the jacket from his bedroom closet. And to say goodnight to Birdie.

The doorbell rang. He spun at the top of the stairs and checked his watch. In the history of this house, unexpected visitors rarely brought good news. They were usually cops and someone was usually dead. He ran back down the stairs. It couldn't be a death notification. There was no one left to die on him.

Through the window of the door, the early evening sunlight illuminated a head of blonde hair. He set his jaw and pulled the door open. "Daisy. What are you doing here?"

She was disheveled, wearing yoga pants and an old college sweatshirt. She threw herself into his arms and kissed him, pulled his shirt from the waistband of his pants and fumbled with the buckle of his reversible belt.

He grabbed her by the arms and pushed her away. "Daisy, stop. What the hell?"

Tears sprung to her eyes. "I needed to see you. To kiss you." Her face contorted. "I just need you," she wailed.

"Go home, Daisy. Go be with Carl. You made your choice, and

I wasn't it, remember?" He calculated the days in his head. "Aren't you getting married next week?"

"I don't know anymore." She stepped closer. "Convince me to stay." She stood an inch from him, stared up into his face. With trembling hands, she conquered the belt buckle and unzipped his fly. "Tell me what to do, Finnegan."

He picked her up and carried her to his bedroom, dropped her on the bed, and peeled her yoga pants off. He stripped off his trousers, crawled on top of her, and pushed her legs open with his knees. The sex was frenzied and cold, he didn't even kiss her. Didn't even want to. It was over in less than three minutes. He rolled off and tossed her pants at her, reclined on the bed and glared at her.

She stood and pulled her pants on, watching him out of the corner of her eye. She bent to kiss him. "I'll be back later."

"Don't bother."

Her eyes narrowed. "Pardon me?"

He put his hands behind his head. "Go home to Carl, Daisy. Marry him. I don't want you."

"But," she gestured at the bed, "what about this?"

"Consider it a farewell fuck." He sat up and waved his hands at her. "Now scoot. I need to shower you off me. I've got a date." The look on her face morphed from wounded surprise to shame, to utter humiliation. A microscopic sample of how she'd made him feel when she chose Carl.

"Hurts, doesn't it?" he sneered. "Don't get me wrong. I love you, Daisy. But I won't be used." He stood and slipped one hand behind her back, eyed her scrawny throat. He could crush it without much force. He put his lips to her ear. "But I am going to miss fucking you," he whispered.

She drew her arm back and slapped him. She ran down the stairs and slammed the door behind her.

He dropped back onto the bed, put the heels of his palms against his eyes, and laughed. "Shit. I should probably find a new job."

My lady sweet, arise

As lord and master of the house, Finnegan had laid claim to his mother's bedroom, with the oversized closet and the full bath attached. Why shouldn't he enjoy the giant space that overlooked the neighbourhood on one side and the garden on another?

He ran his hand over the antique wardrobe she had loved so much. He'd cleansed it of her hippie clothes, dropped the whole lot off in a donation bin down the street. He attached a hook to the hanging rail and shored its old frame with cross braces. It had to be strong. Had to hold its own. For it housed his prized possession. The one part of his collection that he needed near him when he slept. When he dreamed. Appropriate since the owner of these bones was the main character in his nighttime musings.

He swung the doors of the wardrobe open. "Good morning, Birdie." He touched her temporal process and straightened her mandible. She would have loved that wardrobe, all old and fancy.

Ooh, what lovely wood. So dark. So grainy. Can we go watch some telly?

He smiled at her and chucked her under the chin. "Maybe later, my love. I've got to fix your spine."

She was almost complete. Just a few metatarsals left to unearth, the fourth true rib on her right side, and her twelfth rib on the left. The screen was a worthwhile investment. It sifted the dirt away and unearthed pieces he never would have found without it. It was like panning for gold, except a lot of the bits he washed, what he'd assumed were rocks or petrified twigs, were bone.

His knuckles clunked down along Birdie's ribcage, skipping over the missing pieces. Like an old xylophone made of the dead. "Dem bones, dem bones, dem dry bones," he sang under his breath. Damn right, Ezekiel. Dem bones gonna rise again.

He clipped intervertebral discs from the thick spongy foam sheet he'd found at the craft store. Felt was too flimsy, too slippery. The foam had the right consistency and stayed in place. That store was a boon to his Birdie building. Wire, string, foam, glue. They had everything. He'd hovered near the marbles, flicked through the bin of glass balls to find some eye-worthy orbs. But she wasn't a puppet. She wasn't a spectacle. She was his best friend. The love of his life.

He slid the discs between the vertebral bodies of each link in the backbone chain. With the last in place, he bent the spine. The thorax curved forward and Birdie took a bow.

Finnegan was replete with a sensation he didn't recognize. Lightness, as if his lungs were filled with helium and he could float away. He took one of Birdie's hands in his and closed his eyes, swayed his body to strains of the Tennessee waltz, a melody he'd tucked in a far and dusty corner of his memory. He stared into her brown eyes, noted the fine lines of her nose and the high cheekbones. He smiled and tears dripped down his cheeks. "You were the best thing in my life. And I didn't deserve you."

Her bright eyes crinkled at the corners before her smile faded and disappeared.

His throat burned and bile tingled up his esophagus.

Birdie's tears seared through her cheeks and melted her skin until her face fell away from her skull.

He opened his eyes and dropped her hand. "Why'd you leave me, Birdie? Why'd you go and leave?" His abdomen convulsed and he doubled over as sobs racked his body. He slumped to the floor at Birdie's feet and let two decades of self-hatred and anger spill out onto the antique wool rug.

This above all: to thine own self be true

"Hello, my lady." Finnegan bowed to Deborah, his hand resting on the brass doorknob.

She giggled.

He wrinkled his nose. That was an unfortunate girly titter.

He took her jacket and hung it in the closet. "Would you like a glass of wine? I have a cabernet, a Grenache, a Sauvignon blanc, some pinot gri—"

"I'll have whichever of those is white." She interrupted his recitation of wine inventory before he got to the good stuff.

He pursed his lips and turned to the kitchen. With each date, it became more obvious that Deb was less than brilliant. Should he engage her in a rousing debate about the veracity of claims by some scholars that Shakespeare didn't write his own plays? Of course he did, that theory was utter bullshit. But would Deborah have an opinion, or even give a damn? She'd probably just give him one of those doe-eyed blinking stares she donned when she was out of her depth.

Despite their uneven intellect, he did enjoy her company. For the most part. The bloom was off the childhood rose. Her reality would never live up to his fantasy. Not in the brains department. Not even the looks. It wasn't just that she'd gotten older. It was because he'd idolized her for so long, he'd turned her into the pinnacle of perfection. And she wasn't. She never had been. He'd made it all up in his head, shoved her up on a pedestal and kept her there until they met in that coffee shop. Even though he knew it was idiotic and unfair, he was perpetually disappointed.

Just another mound of evidence to pile onto the already gargantuan heap that he was a total and complete ass.

He turned to offer her the wine glass but she had disappeared.

"Deb?"

"In the living room."

She had her back turned to him, was eyeballing the family pictures lining the wall above the chesterfield of Finnegan through the school years, and the occasional picture of his mother, including one of her and Aidan on their wedding day.

Damn it. Why hadn't he taken those down? Some Freudian thing to do with his mother, perhaps. Or just more important things to do. Like bring his best friend back to life. He handed Deborah the wine.

"Is that your dad?"

"No. That's my mother's dead husband."

She squinted at him.

He sighed. "She married Aidan when I was fifteen. He was a cop. Killed in the line of duty a year-and-a-half later." He didn't expect her to remember the news reports. But he'd managed to drag out his period of mourning for a whole month. Did she not even remember that he'd missed all that school? Obviously not, since it wasn't all about her.

"Oh, that's so sad." She sipped her wine and made a face. "My, that's tart."

"It's a Muscadet."

She nodded and pressed her lips together.

He took the glass from her and drank the wine in two gulps. "I like it bone dry. I'll pour you a Riesling."

"You sure do know your wines."

He strolled back into the living room and handed her the glass. "I know what I like."

She eyeballed the pictures. "Where's your father?"

Finnegan shrugged. "No idea. I never met him."

She cocked her head and pouted. "That's sad, too."

"I suppose it could be." Especially if his father was the owner of one of the partial skeletons filling the floor in his old bedroom right above their heads.

"Didn't you ever want to meet him? To know where you came from?"

"I've often wondered. But Mom never wanted to talk about him. All she told me is that I look like him."

Deborah turned to face him, stepped closer, and lifted her chin. "Well then, we know that he was incredibly handsome." She blinked several times and ran her tongue over her lips.

"So red hair is no longer a turn off?" He took a swig of merlot.

She sighed and moved to the chesterfield. "It's not so red anymore is it? More — bronze. Like a statue."

So that was a yes. Red hair was still a deal breaker. But bronze? Not so much.

"It suits the chiselled chin and cheekbones, the deep set of your eyes." She patted the cushion beside her. "And, my oh my. What green eyes you have." She bit her bottom lip.

Well, shit. Damned if she wasn't making moves on him. How the tables have turned. Only took two damn decades. He settled into the seat beside her.

She took his wine glass and set it next to hers on the coffee table, then shimmied closer until her thigh nestled against his.

He smirked. "Why Deborah Joyce Arbic. Are you trying to seduce me?"

"Yes, damn it." She faux-slapped his arm. "Now, give in already."

Her candid smile disarmed him. Between the wine and the heat of her body, and the fact he hadn't been laid since he threw Daisy out, he did just that. He dipped his head toward hers, brought his mouth close. But not quite close enough to touch those plump, fleshy folds with the perfect, distinct, vermillion border.

She gasped.

Anticipation interrupted. It worked every time.

Her breath, warm and moist, brushed past his lips. She panted in time with her audible heartbeat.

He put his arm around her shoulder and drew her close until her breasts grazed his chest, her head tilted back, her eyes locked on his. She'd not worn a bra, the brazen hussy. He could feel her arousal through his shirt, her nipples poking into his ribcage.

How long could he draw this out before he just stripped her

naked and fucked her silly? He had her. She wanted him. A hell of a lot more than he wanted her. But what a fun game, this taming of Deborah. It was time to put her out of her misery and consummate almost two months of polite dating.

He pecked at her mouth, played cat and mouse with his tongue against her open and inviting lips, licking, flicking, retreating. Then he devoured her, his tongue deep inside her, tasting her as he'd wanted to since he was eight years old.

He'd imagined cinnamon and vanilla with just a hint of cotton candy. Instead, he got sour wine with an onion and garlic finish. Anticlimactic to say the least.

His hands traversed the soft curves of her back and hips. His fingers trailed from her knee, along her thigh, and over her soft belly until they found one ample breast. He squeezed and kneaded and rolled her nipple between his thumb and forefinger.

She moaned and shuddered.

That was the catalyst. Her match lighting his short-fused dynamite. He peeled her button-up shirt over her head and pushed her down on the chesterfield. His shirt landed on the floor next to hers. If he was worried about being too rough, her sly grin and the speed with which she shed her pants was a big fat green light.

The sex was hurried and vigorous. The look on her face waxed and waned between pleasure and — was it pain? It fed his frenzy and she responded in-kind. He held her hips, searched for her iliac crests, but couldn't find them under her bounteous flesh. He slid one hand behind her back and kneaded the knobby bits of her spinous process.

That sent them both over the edge. Mental note, when ready to finish, massage her lumbar region. Big erogenous zone for Deborah.

"Wow." She wiped sweat from her brow. "You're amazing. And you have perfect timing."

"Better three hours too soon than a minute too late."

Her right eyebrow shot up. "Huh?"

Finnegan sighed. "Never mind."

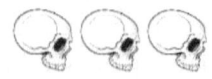

"Is it weird, doing it in her bed?"

After their first encounter on the chesterfield, Finnegan ordered Chinese and they lounged in the living room nibbling on noodles and watching a rerun of *Body Heat*. By the time it ended, she was asleep with her head in his lap. He'd carried her up to his room and they had slow, sensual sex, then fell asleep in each other's arms.

Well, *she* slept. He spent the night listening to the abrasive whistle of her breath through a deviated septum and wishing for the sun to rise. And when it did, he rolled her on her side and took her from behind. Because in case this whole Deborah thing was short-lived, he was going to make the most of it. Fulfill a lifetime of wishing and hoping and yearning in eighteen frenzied and satisfying hours.

"It's not her bed. I tossed it out and bought my own." *Bang, bang, bang.* "I always hated her headboard."

"I love all the antiques. Especially that wardrobe." Deborah pointed at it. "Eighteen-twenty Regency, mahogany panel doors with carved splay feet."

He reared back. "For real?"

She nodded. "Yeah. Worth two grand, easy. Too bad there's no drawers though. I like them with drawers."

"Serves its purpose drawer-free. More hanging space."

"Hanging space? What's in there, all your floor-length ball gowns?" She poked him in the ribs. "Come on, spill. What skeletons are lurking in your antique wardrobe?"

He swallowed hard. "That's uh, my little secret." Had he locked it yesterday? Was the key out of her reach? "Can't tell anyone what's hidden inside except those I know intimately."

She tilted her head. "Well shit, you just screwed my brains out. A lot. How much more intimate can we get?"

"Not physical intimacy. I'd have to marry you before I could tell you."

She rolled on top of him, her chin on his chest, her eyelashes batting like a pro. "Why Finnegan MacGillivray, did you just propose to me?"

Laughter snorted from his nose. "No, I most certainly did not."

Her giggle failed to mask the slight wince that skipped across her face.

He grimaced on the inside, the ambivalence of his feelings for her continuing unabated. He hated the way she chewed. But when she smiled at him, he got hard. The sounds she made during sex drove him to feats of sexual heroism. But the puerile giggle that sprang from her adult mouth made him want to choke the laughter right out of her. She was sweet and kind. Demanding and selfish. Her curvy body was a delicious sight, but the heat that emanated from her skin was intense. Their bodies stuck together, suctioned by a layer of mingled sweat. He shifted the blanket to uncover one leg and peeled her arm from his chest.

Heat not a furnace for your foe so hot that it do singe yourself.

"Well," he patted her ass, "I don't know about you, but I need a shower." He threw the covers off and rolled her onto her back, pecked her lips and headed for the bathroom.

The bed creaked and she was behind him, her breasts pressed into his ribs, arms around his waist. She kissed his back and her hands wandered south.

The woman was insatiable. At least she had that going for her.

They kissed under the spray of the shower, soaped each other's bodies. His hands counted down her ribs as he cleansed her torso. He closed his eyes and calculated the length, estimated the depth of her chest cavity. Found the fourth true rib on her right side, and her twelfth rib on the left.

When the water ran cold, he helped her out of the tub. She pushed him down onto the toilet seat and sat on his lap, her back to him. He massaged her breasts with both hands, ran his fingers along her spine and felt along her scapulae with his thumbs while she did all the work for a change. When he was about to come, he massaged her lumbar until she cried out and shuddered.

"Well, I must say." He brushed her hair away and kissed the skin that covered her cervical vertebrae. "That's the first time I've ever fucked on a toilet."

He loved how her body jiggled in his arms when she laughed.

"Me too. And the shower. And the living room."

"Are you serious?"

"Totally." She shifted side-saddle and put her arms around his neck. "Only in the bed. Once in the back seat of Jason's old Camaro. That was when I lost my virginity back in Eighty-six. And once under the bleachers after he won MVP at the city football championships. He was so excited he came all over my pants before he could even get it in." She twittered, her nose scrunched in amusement at her own anecdote.

The last visual Finnegan wanted at that moment was of her having sex with Jason the jock. He gritted his teeth and grinned. "Breakfast?"

"Oh, yes please. I'm starving."

Doubtful.

"Give me a few minutes." He shooed her up and out the door, clicking it shut behind him. He braced the countertop with both hands and stared at himself in the mirror. The face staring back at him could have belonged to any one of the bodies in the garden. Lout. Creep. User.

"Oh, my God! I remember this!" Deborah's adolescent squeal pierced the bathroom door.

He shook his head. All the clichés were true. Reality and fantasy don't mix. Be careful what you wish for. All that glitters is not gold. Absence makes the heart grow fonder. A little Birdie told me ….

"What?" He opened the door. She was bent over the dresser where he'd yet to clear off his mother's special keepsakes. His heart hardened. There was Deborah Arbic, personification of his childhood emotional tumult, of his earliest romantic rejection, holding the clay clown he'd made in fifth grade.

"This! I remember it!" She spun around and held it next to her cheek, smiled that brilliant smile. "You had to redo it because Jason smashed your first one."

Did she have to recount that particular memory with such glee in her eyes?

She turned the clown upside down and inspected its underside where he'd carved his name in the clay with a toothpick. "Aw, look. Love Finny Mac." She caressed the clown's head and pursed her lips.

Put down the damn clown. His fist clenched. Another second and he would rip it from her fingers. Then tear each finger from her hands and strip the flesh from her bones.

"Can I have it?" An after-fuck glow pinked her shiny cheeks.

He strode across the room, snatched the clown away, and placed it back on the dresser. "It was my mother's." He pulled on his sweat pants and headed for the stairs, pausing in the doorway. He couldn't leave her alone with Birdie. "You coming?" He tossed the words over his shoulder with a casual air to mask his indignation at her brash presumption. And his growing resentment of her presence in his mother's bedroom. In his home. In his life.

Her pants rustled. He turned to catch a vision of her breasts disappearing as she buttoned her top.

"I understand. You know, why you want to keep the clown. That's okay, I collect elephants anyway." She couldn't bear to look him in the eye. Chattered away while gathering her tiny handbag and the watch she'd placed on the nightstand. She stooped to snatch her purple thong from the floor and tucked it into the purse. "Started when I was a little girl. Got to ride one at the game farm once. Loved them ever since." She sidled past him and started down the stairs.

Her ass was glorious in those pants. Each step she descended, it wiggled an invitation.

He put on the coffee while she fiddled with his mother's roosters on the china cabinet. Out of the corner of his eye, he caught her touching them. Every single damn one of them. She opened the glass doors of the cabinets and fingered the crystal. Leaned in and peered at the largest ceramic fowl. She continued her word vomit, spewing on and on about her collection.

A vein throbbed in his forehead. How hard would it be to sew her lips shut? He opened the fridge, pulled eggs and bacon out and slid them on the countertop. He cocked his head. Perhaps he could peel her skin off and drape it over Birdie's skeleton.

No. He didn't want to desecrate Birdie with Deborah's flesh. Birdie deserved better.

"I have over forty now. Some are small enough to fit into a thimble. And one is so big it's actually a plant stand. I have a fig tree on it. Can't move it now because fig trees are so sensitive. They die if you just move them to the other side of the same room. Did you know that?" She peered over at him.

He nodded, opened the cupboard, lifted two mugs down.

Her question had nothing to do with fig trees and everything to do with conciliation. She'd stepped over a line and she knew it. Pushed a button she should have left unpushed. She could just apologize to him. But maybe admitting guilt wasn't in Deborah's arsenal.

"I didn't know that until I killed three of them. Thank God for Google. That's how I figured it out."

Roosters clinked together. Finnegan gritted his teeth.

"I like your mother's chickens."

"Roosters."

"Whatever. They're nice. A bit dusty." She wiped her fingers on the back of a vinyl chair. "Seems everyone collects something, you know?"

Like broken hearts. Young boys' self-esteem.

She continued her inspection of his dead mother's belongings, her back to him, bent over the cabinet, words puking out her mouth. Did she ever shut up?

He wrapped his hand around the handle of the cast iron frying pan.

She picked up another figurine, scratched at the rooster's beak with one fingernail. "What do you collect?"

He raised the pan over his head and sneered.

"Bones."

END

Thank you for taking the time to read **Pocketful of Bones**. If you enjoyed the story, please consider telling your friends or posting a review. Word of mouth is an author's best friend and is greatly appreciated.

Acknowledgements

Sometimes, it takes a village to write a book. Well, technically it's just me doing the writing. But without the support and help from so many kind folks, it wouldn't turn out as well.

Thanks to Scott Morgan, my kickass editor with the same love of profanity as his client. His brutal honesty is vital to my writing process. He has made me better. Period.

Love and thanks to my friends and beta readers, Tracy Todd, whom I've known since we were just little sprouts in 1970 something, and Claire-Edith de la Croix, the most badass nun I know. Okay, the only one.

Thanks always to Dane Low of EbookLaunch.com for yet another amazing cover.

Thanks to Regimental Sergeant Major Rob Patterson of the Calgary Police Service. Though my father and brother were both police officers, neither wore a CPS uniform. Robbie researched the 1984 dress uniform so that a couple of small details in the wedding scene would be accurate. Talk about above and beyond the call of duty!

A special thank-you to Deborah Arbic. Yes, she's a real person, but the character in the book is NOT the real Deborah. The real one bid on, and won, a charity auction item, and having a character in this book named for her was the prize. I took a small character and changed her name for Deborah. As a result, that character took on more meaning, began popping up more regularly in Finnegan's thoughts and life, became critical to his development, and ended up in the final scene. So thank you, Deborah. For the support of Heritage Park, and for helping your namesake character find a real voice.

No acknowledgement would be complete without thanking my

children, Brynn and Charlie. They are my everything and life would suck without them. Special shout-out to my Burney, fuzzy-faced, curly-furred keeper of my heart.

About the Author

Julie Frayn is a multi-award-winning Canadian author of novels and short stories that pack a punch. And a few stabs. She is fluent in three languages — English, sarcasm, and profanity. Although she didn't invent swearing, Julie wields it like the visionary vulgarian who threw the first fuck out into a crowd.

Julie writes psychological suspense filled with a lot death, a bit of sex, and sprinkled with the F-word (sometimes... not so sprinkled). Her most favourite pastime is murder night (translation: watching crime drama and drinking beer with her daughter). Her least favourite pastime is writing author bios (translation: author bios — yuck).

Long live the Oxford comma!

Other works by Julie Frayn

Mazie Baby

Winner of the 2015 Indie Reader Discovery Award for Literary Fiction
Winner of the 2015 Kindle Book Awards for Suspense
Named to three Best of 2014 lists by Suspense Magazine, IndieReader.com and
Readfree.ly

Mazie loved it when he called her baby. Until it became a taunt. What's the matter, baby? You gonna cry, baby? Multiple award-winning tale of spousal abuse.

"The characters were so real and the action so authentic my head is still reeling from its emotional impact. Excellent, and thank you to the author for pulling back the curtain on spousal abuse." ~ Veralisa Fresh

"The dialogue is raw, the character development happens at a life-like pace, and the story line — though depicting a desperate mother —

never wavers on the edge of fantasy. Though fiction, MAZIE BABY could arguably be a firsthand autobiography for someone." ~ Jessica Czarnogursky for IndieReader.

Goody One Shoe

With one leg and a pet cat, can Billie avenge her parents' murders and discover a vigilante's identity before more criminals die?

"This is what heroes look like." ~ Stacey Roberts, author
"A uniquely told story of whimsy and darkness." ~ Michele Kimbrough, author
"A well written story that isn't afraid to let the hero take a darker path." ~ Darrell E.

It Isn't Cheating if He's Dead

Winner of the BigAl's Books and Pals 2014 Readers' Choice Award for women's fiction

Jemima's schizophrenic fiancé is dead. Finn is the hot cop on the case. His love eases her pain. Befriending a homeless man allows her to heal.

"…a brilliant and insightful exploration of grief, loss and living with the mentally ill." ~ Elizabeth Ramsay, theromancereviews.com
"Jemima, struggling to understand how she lost her fiancé and trying to make sense of her life after his death, is so utterly human that she blooms off the page." ~ Laurie Boris

Romeo is Homeless

Winner of double gold medals in the Authorsdb.com 2013 cover contest
(Formerly titled *Suicide City*)

What do sixteen-year-old August, a farm girl fed up with her farm life, and seventeen-year-old Reese, a homeless boy fighting heroin addiction and the urge to cut himself, have in common? Nothing. And everything.

"Suicide City is gritty, unrelenting, tragic, desperate, sad, heart-warming, heart-breaking, and gut-wrenching." ~ Sean P. Farley

"Hands down, the best ending line of any book I've read in the thirty-one years I've been a reader. Please, do not miss this exceptional novel!" ~ Amber Jerome Norrgard

A Trilogy of Unrelated Shorts

A collection of three short-short stories
"These stories are difficult to read, powerfully written, emotionally draining and awesome. Frayn's writing is flawless. There is nothing with which I can find fault. Frayn gives us a glimpse into a world that might seem bleak but is not without heroes." ~ Rabid Readers Reviews

Two Wins and an Honourable Mention

Another collection of three short-short stories
"A roller-coaster ride of pity, punk, repulsion, and redemption."
"Unique and quirky."
"Sick, twisted, scary but with a bit of macabre humor too."

Contact

What's better than a getting a review from a reader? Hearing from them! Feel free to reach out. You can find Julie here:

Website/Blog: www.juliefrayn.com

Twitter: www.twitter.com/juliefrayn

Facebook: www.facebook.com/juliebirdfrayn

Amazon: http://www.amazon.com/Julie-Frayn/e/B00BH47C3G